A LAW

WHEN THE MAN
COMES AROUND

ALSO BY BRADLEY WRIGHT

XANDER KING

Whiskey & Roses

Vanquish

King's Ransom

King's Reign

Scourge

Vendetta (prequel novella)

LAWSON RAINES

When the Man Comes Around

Shooting Star

WHEN THE MAN COMES AROUND

Bradley Wright/King's Ransom Books
www.bradleywrightauthor.com

Cover Design by DDD, Deranged Doctor Designs
When the Man Comes Around/ Bradley Wright. -- 1st ed.
ISBN - 978-0-9973926-4-7

For Chris Lawson,
friend is not a strong enough word

Instead of a man of peace and love, I have become a man of violence and revenge.

— Hiawatha

A hero is an ordinary individual who finds the strength to persevere and endure in spite of overwhelming obstacles.

— Christopher Reeve

WHEN THE MAN
COMES AROUND

PROLOGUE

Lake Mead: Thirty miles outside of Las Vegas, Nevada

Bringing his family to Lake Mead was the first vacation that Lawson Raines had taken since becoming an FBI agent three years earlier.

It would also be his last.

The morning sun had begun its climb up the wide blue sky that hovered over the desert. Its rays felt hot on Lawson's broad shoulders as he gave the turquoise waters of the man-made lake a once-over. He could smell bacon frying back inside the small kitchen of the rental boat. He never spent any money, never really had time for it. But it was his wife's birthday, and after three years of far too much neglect, he felt it time to give her a well-deserved, full-attention vacation.

At seven thirty in the morning, the lake hadn't yet begun

to buzz. Lawson's boat rocked gently where it was anchored a few hundred yards offshore, and the water was already calling his name. Lawson hadn't missed a workout in years, and he wasn't about to let a little time off change that. When you're chasing bad guys all day, there was no room for a bourbon-and-pizza gut. He had already ripped off a couple hundred push-ups, but now it was time to get in a swim to keep his cardio strong.

"Lawson, honey. If you're gonna go for a swim, you'd better hurry. Breakfast is almost ready," his wife, Lauren, called to him from inside the cabin.

Hearing Lauren, Lawson walked back inside through the sliding doors, and then his phone began to ring.

Lauren turned from the skillet, shaking her spatula at him, a playful smirk on her face. "I know you're not going to answer that."

A golden ray of sunshine fell over her matching golden-blonde hair. He could see the sparkling blue of her eyes from where he stood some twelve feet away. They were a perfect match to the water just outside the boat. Even after all these years, he was still struck by her beauty.

"Daddy!" his two-year-old daughter, Lexi, called to him from the pack 'n play. She was the spitting image of Lauren.

As the phone rang in his hand, he walked over and gave Lexi a kiss on the forehead. Then he looked back to Lauren, her hand now resting on her hip.

Lawson smiled. "What? It's Cassie. She might need directions."

Cassie was Lawson's partner, and she and her boyfriend were his and Lauren's only real friends in Las Vegas. Since Lawson had been accepted into the FBI and moved from Lexington, Kentucky, to Vegas, they hadn't really put a lot of time into making friends. He and Lauren had been high school sweethearts, and they had grown used to only having each other to lean on. Sure, Lauren had some acquaintances at work, and so did Lawson, but the only one they had really welcomed into their world was Cassie. She was from Tennessee, so they instantly bonded over their Southern roots, including a love for bourbon, and country music.

Satisfied that it was not a work-related call, Lauren went back to tending to the bacon. She spoke with her back turned. "I'm so glad she decided to come. Today's gonna be fun!" She turned back toward him. "Well, answer the phone already!"

Lawson laughed at his wife. He also noticed just how fantastic her sun-kissed skin looked in that yellow bikini. Finally, he answered the phone. "Hey, Cass. You on your way?"

"Hell yeah I am. I got some Country Time lemonade, and enough Buffalo Trace bourbon to drown all four of us."

"I knew there was a reason I let you be my friend."

Cassie scoffed. "The only reason we're friends is because the FBI insists that we spend *every . . . single . . . day* together."

"Is Bobby with you?"

"No, he can't make it. He said he had something come up last minute. I know you are just heartbroken about that."

Lawson laughed. "This day just keeps getting better and better!"

Lawson never liked Bobby. He had always thought that Cassie was far too good for him. He seemed about as slimy as any man he'd ever met. But they say love is blind, and all he could do was let Cassie know how he felt. She was a big girl, she had to make her own decisions.

"Ha. Ha." Cassie faked a knowing laugh. "Give it a rest for one day, would you?"

Lauren walked over and snatched the phone from Lawson's hand and hit the speaker button. "Cassie, will you just hurry up and get here already. It's five o'clock somewhere, isn't it?"

Cassie laughed. "Oh lord. It's gonna be one of those kinds of days, is it?"

"Yes. Yes it is." Lauren laughed. "Now hurry up or you're gonna miss Lawson try to swim the length of the lake before breakfast."

"You just don't know how to relax, do you, Lawson?" Cassie jabbed.

Lawson picked up Lexi and tossed her in the air. "Nope. But I imagine bourbon will help!" he said as he caught Lexi. His daughter's laugh could be the only sound in the world he could hear and he would be just fine with that.

Lauren ended the call as Lawson grabbed his towel. She turned her back to him for the skillet, and he just couldn't resist. He walked up behind her, wrapped his hands around her waist, pulled her into him, and began to kiss her neck.

"And just what do you think you're doing, Mr. Raines?" she said in a singsong way as she squirmed in his hands.

"I could skip the swim. Maybe find a different sort of workout?" His smile widened, his eyes holding a mischievous look.

Lauren turned into him. "What's gotten into you? This morning wasn't enough?"

Lawson's smile lingered as he shrugged his shoulders.

Lauren gave him a long kiss on the lips. She ran her hands along his lean muscular torso but pulled away just before they made it below the waistband of his swim trunks.

"Save that for later, hotshot. Mama's gonna need a fix when the sun goes down,"

Lawson let out a frustrated breath. "Damn. I sure hope that lake water is cold."

She clawed at him like a tiger as he backed away shaking his head. He really had never seen her look better. She went back to finishing breakfast, and after a pinch of Lexi's chubby little cheek, he walked out to the deck and dove into the cool blue water.

As he swam away from the boat, his mind wandered to how great things were at that moment. It was a departure from the first two years in Vegas. It had been a tough adjustment from their lifestyle in Kentucky. Everything was different. And Lauren had taken it especially hard. Things were rocky for a while. Her being pregnant shortly after the move hadn't helped. Mostly it was the hours he was working that really pulled them apart. In Lexington, he was a detective. And while the hours were just as long and erratic, at least Lauren had her family and friends around in his absence. In Vegas, she didn't know a soul.

Getting paired with Cassie had been a godsend. She really helped Lauren cross over, and after Lexi was born, she finally had a chance to breathe. The past year, everything had slowly just fallen into place. Life was great at home, and Lawson and Cassie had become a force to be reckoned with in the bureau. "Rising stars" is how Division Director Adam Billings described them. And while that was good to hear, it caused division between them and the other agents, making it hard for them to make friends. But they had been doing a great job fighting against the influx of organized crime that had been moving back into Las Vegas lately. It had been something that Lawson knew he had become obsessed with.

Unfortunately, it was his time with Lauren and Lexi that had been sacrificed.

As he turned back toward the boat, the burn in his lungs brought him pleasure. He loved the way pushing his body made him feel. He was also eager to do nothing but hang out with the people he loved, catch some sun, and drink until he couldn't see straight. It had been a long time since he had enjoyed any of those things. Far too long. The thought of bacon and his woman in that bikini helped him reach for another gear as he stroked back toward the boat.

Twelve minutes later, his hand finally slapped the back of the boat, and as he caught his breath, he turned away from it to face the lake and the path he had just swam. It wasn't a long swim, about twenty-five minutes. He had gone at it pretty hard, so he figured it was somewhere north of a mile. That would have to do, because he could smell bacon all the way out in the water. And Lauren would kill him if he let her hard work on breakfast go cold. He turned back to grab hold of the ladder, and that was when his life changed forever.

Rolling toward him in the cracks of the teakwood deck, and dripping down over the swim platform into the water, was a long trail of a deep-red liquid.

Blood.

"Lauren!" His heart began to thump inside his chest as he pulled himself up the ladder out of the water. "Lauren! Are you—"

He slipped on the river of blood beneath his feet and fell hard onto the deck. That was when Lexi started crying. Panic set in. "Lauren! Lauren, are you all right? Lauren!"

Lawson scrambled to his feet. He noticed her feet on the floor, sticking out from behind the counter in the kitchen. They were positioned as if she were lying on her side. The trail of blood ran from around that same counter. Everything inside of him jumbled all at once, and the fear of what he was about to find paralyzed him. Lexi was now screaming.

"Lau—Lauren" rolled unconsciously from his lips. "Lauren, no!"

Emotion swelled inside him as he moved toward her, following the stream of blood. His heart breaking open with each step. In what seemed like slow motion, he rounded the corner of the kitchen counter. And there she was, the love of his life, his Lauren, lying there on the floor, her throat sliced open and her lifeless blue eyes staring up at him.

1

2018: Ten years later

High Desert State Prison: Thirty miles north of Las Vegas

Lawson Raines counted down in his head as he fired off the last of his daily routine of four hundred push-ups. He had already finished his five-mile run in the prison yard. Just the same as he had every other day for the last ten years, or 3,650 days, or 87,600 hours, or 5,256,000 minutes. He could tell you all those numbers down to the minute, not because it was the amount of time since the last day he had tasted freedom but because it was the last day he had seen his daughter, Lexi. She would be twelve now, but he only knew her face from when she was two. Ever since that day, when the very justice system he had vowed to serve wrongfully sentenced him to life in prison for the murder of his wife, he'd been counting the days, hoping he would get the chance to right what someone else got wrong.

"Today's the day, Lawson. You excited?" John Simpson said through the bars.

Lawson had always liked John. In a sea of terrible human beings, he was the one man Lawson respected. He always found it comical that such a skinny little man was a prison guard. He was one of the few guards who didn't use every moment to try to make all the inmates feel inferior to his almighty, key-holding power.

Lawson popped up from the floor of his cell after his last push-up. "Only excited about the fact that I'll never have to see your ugly face again."

John laughed. "I don't know how you did it. I really don't. But promise me you'll make the most of it?"

Lawson pulled his white V-neck T-shirt over his swollen muscles. Every inch of him was a rippled fury. When all there is to do is read and work out, that's what happens. And Lawson always took advantage of both.

"Don't you worry about that."

"You know, a lot of your fellow inmates are going to be upset to see you go. Don't know what they'll do without you to protect them."

"They'll manage."

Lawson had looked after the little guy in prison for years. It wasn't always that way, however. When an FBI agent gets thrown in with general population, there are many a man who want revenge. Not because Lawson had been the one to personally put them behind bars, but because he represented the people who did. The law. The first two years had been brutal, absolute hell. Too many savage beatings to count. But little by little, he trained, and worked his way to where there wasn't a man in any of the prison's 2,671 beds that could take him.

John said, "I'm not sure they *will* manage. So are you going to tell me how you did it, or not?"

"Did what?"

"Come on, Lawson. You were convicted of first-degree murder and sentenced to life in prison ten years ago. And for ten years nothing changed for you. Then all of a sudden the governor of Nevada decides to pardon you, and boom, you're free? That doesn't just happen. What gives?"

"No clue. I guess my luck has turned."

Lawson played dumb, but the reason he had been pardoned had absolutely nothing to do with luck. It had everything to do with the reputation that he had developed on the inside for being a man who knew how to get things done. The governor was just one man in a long line who had acquired his services. See, criminals know a lot of things about a lot of people. And a lot of people on the outside with a lot of money have a lot to lose if those criminals talk. Lawson had done a good deal of *favors* for many powerful people over the years. The first favor he called in was to the governor, and he was more than grateful that Lawson had been able to keep certain things from being leaked to the public. You could say he was "pardon Lawson from life in prison" grateful.

"BS," John huffed. "Luck, my ass. People talk. We all know you have been running things in here for a long time. But I know you're not like the rest of these animals. I'm glad to see you're getting out of here. You never should have been in here in the first place, as far as I see it. Any idea what you're going to do on the outside?"

"No." Lawson kept it short as he started the first of his four hundred squats.

"You've always been a man of many words," John said, sarcastic. Then a comically serious look washed over his face. "You're only thirty-seven, maybe you should try the UFC or something? I've seen you fight. You could be the champ."

"Not sure they let convicted murderers on the UFC roster, but I'll write Dana White a letter and let him know your opinion."

"Fine. Don't listen." John smiled. "Just try to stay out of trouble. I'll be back in an hour to walk you out."

Lawson continued his squats. It had yet to sink in that in an hour he would be a free man. He had little memory of what that felt like. The last ten years of his life had been hell. Not because life in prison was so difficult for him. It wasn't that at all. It was the fact that Lauren's sister had taken Lexi back to Kentucky and never let him see or speak with his daughter again. It was the fact that Lauren was dead. And as much as anything, it was the fact that her killer had been able to run free all those years.

Lawson didn't know much about what his life would look like once he walked outside those prison walls, a free man for the first time in ten years. But he did know one thing for certain: whoever murdered his wife out on that boat all those years ago, and stole his beautiful life right out from under him, was going to wish that the governor had never let the lion out of his cage.

2

LAWSON GATHERED THE FEW THINGS IN HIS CELL AS HE awaited John to walk him to freedom. It didn't take long. All he had was a notebook and a couple of pictures of Lauren and two-year-old Lexi. But he made sure not to forget that notebook. He changed into the black jogger pants he was given, then walked over to the small sink on the back wall. He put his hands on both sides and leaned over it as he stared at his reflection in the cage-covered mirror. He didn't recognize the man who stared back at him. He looked, and felt, nothing like the man who was thrown in that prison cell ten years ago. Aside from the obvious—his much more muscular frame and buzzed haircut—through his eyes he could see that the man inside was much different. Hardened. The man with his family on that boat on the lake had been a man with a clear vision of how the world worked. The man in the mirror was a man who had seen all those lines blurred—smeared.

A man spoke up from outside his cell. "Lawson Raines."

He recognized the voice immediately. Vincent Ricci. A real scumbag, and an infamous enforcer for Nero De Luca, the head of the De Luca family and the biggest crime boss in Las Vegas. When he first came to Vegas, Lawson investigated Nero's father, Tony. Nero had moved into power when his father died several years back. Just like the governor, Lawson had done a few favors for Nero over the years as well. Lawson never knew if he would get the chance to make use of the contacts he was making in prison, but he knew having friends in *all* places would be a pretty good strategy if he ever tasted freedom again. It didn't matter if they were good guys or bad guys, because there was no difference to Lawson anymore.

Lawson turned from the mirror. "Vince."

"Heard you got a pardon. Too bad, I haven't had the chance to embarrass you in front of the guys."

Lawson walked over to the bars, his chiseled jaw set, his face null of emotion. "That is a shame. Lucky me, I guess."

"Yeah, smart-ass, lucky you."

"There a point to this visit, Vince? Or are you just taking a mental picture of me for your shower fantasy later?"

Vince grabbed the bars of the cell and shook them in anger. His muscles bulged around his tank top, and it reminded Lawson of a silverback gorilla beating on his chest to show his dominance. Lawson had heard many stories over the years about Vince. Every man on the street feared him. Lawson couldn't care less.

Vince's voice was strained, and his face was red as he pointed at Lawson. "You'll get yours, Lawson. You hear me? You'll get yours."

Lawson smirked. "That your speech? Riveting. I'm sure I will get mine, Vince. But unfortunately you won't be there to see it."

Vince backed away from Lawson's cell. "Whatever. Boss

is sending a car for you. Says he wants to thank you. I don't know what you did, but don't bring that smart-ass attitude in there with him."

"Thanks for the advice. And, Vince? Don't drop the soap."

Vince shook his head and held up his middle finger as he walked away. "I'll be out of here in no time, Lawson. So don't worry, I'll see you soon."

"Can't wait."

John walked up and called for Lawson's cell to be opened. "What was that all about?"

Lawson grabbed his notebook and pictures. "He's just jealous."

A buzzer sounded and the cell door slid open.

John said, "All right, big man, this is it. Follow me."

As Lawson followed John down the hall past all the inmates, memories flooded back to him. Memories he hoped would fade away fast. He remembered his first meal on the inside. He could barely chew, his jaw hurt so bad from an initiation beating. He remembered his first shower, he never even made it to the water. He remembered his first altercation in the yard, three men took turns on him, nearly beating him to death. He spent a week in the infirmary after that. And then he remembered when everything changed. When the old Lawson Raines turned off and a new switch flipped on. The survivor emerged. After he tuned up two big guys in the laundry room by himself, everything began to shift. He became someone—*something*—else.

"What's the first thing you're going to do? Get a pizza?" John smiled as he opened the door. The door to freedom.

"Rob a bank."

John smiled and gave him a pat on the back as he walked

out the door. Lawson had heard along the way that the sunshine on the freedom side of the prison felt different than back in the yard. It wasn't. The sun was the sun. He didn't know how he would feel when he walked out into his new life, but he quickly found that it wasn't much different. Sure, he was no longer physically trapped behind bars, but without his daughter, and his wife, he might as well be.

In front of him was a black Mercedes sedan. Beyond that, nothing but desert sand. He thought he might see his old partner, Cassie, there waiting for him. But she wasn't. Only the fancy car of a crime boss and an Italian meathead in a dark-purple silk suit holding the door open for him. Lawson knew if he got in that car that his life on the outside would be taking on the exact opposite of the one he'd left ten years ago. Every day he would be doing things for people who didn't give a damn about him or anyone else. People who didn't give a damn about the law. Lawson had already decided that he was just fine with that. He would be making money, and he would be able to move in circles of people who were on the pulse of what was really going on. People who would know exactly who was responsible for Lauren's death.

And that was all that mattered.

Lawson walked toward the car. With a nod toward the gold-chain-clad meathead, he entered willingly into the Mercedes. Entered willingly into the next chapter of his life.

Come what may.

3

———

THE BLACK MERCEDES SEDAN ROLLED DOWN US 95 TOWARD the Las Vegas Strip. The afternoon sun beamed through the tinted windows, and the already hundred-degree July heat worked its way in with it. Lawson reached down and lowered the air conditioning in front of him. The cold air blew into his face, a sensation he hadn't felt in years. It reminded him of when he used to get in the car to help Lexi fall asleep. He would drive around for hours, AC on full blast, giving Lauren a much-needed break back at the house. Lawson imagined that being on the outside was going to be full of painful memories. He knew that everything he would come into contact with would trigger something. That had been the only saving grace of being trapped in that cell. At least there was nothing familiar. Nothing to trigger the pain of losing his family, which he was now already experiencing, and he'd only been out for ten minutes.

This was going to be harder than he thought.

Meathead spoke from the driver's seat. "Mr. De Luca said to tell you he was going to take good care of you. He's got you all set up in a suite at Caesar's Palace. You're a lucky man to have the boss man on your side. Some advice?"

Lawson looked up and found the man's eyes in the rearview mirror. "No thanks."

The driver shook his head. "No thanks? Ha. A hard-ass, are you? Well, I'm gonna give it to you anyway."

The driver paused for a reaction. When Lawson gave none, he continued. "Don't screw this up. You only get one chance. Not sure how you managed to get on his good side already, but you're gonna want to stay there."

"Sage advice."

Lawson could tell by the man's silence and his blank stare in the rearview mirror that he hadn't a clue as to what that meant. A large SUV pulled up beside their Mercedes, and before Lawson had time to notice anything out of the ordinary, the SUV swerved and crashed into the side of their car, sending them momentarily off the road. Lawson's driver recovered by pulling back onto the pavement. Rocks and dusty sand clouded all around them.

"What the hell? You already have enemies?" Meathead shouted.

Lawson looked into the passenger window of the SUV. He didn't recognize the man staring down at him right before the SUV once again swerved and crashed into the side of their car, shaking it wildly and running them off the road. Lawson knew that he indeed did already have enemies. When you do favors for people on the inside, there is going to be some retaliation from those on the other end. They had tried to get revenge inside the prison, but Lawson had always managed to handle those attempts. It didn't take long for them to take aim as soon as he made it to the outside. This time, his driver lost control of the Mercedes and the front end whipped around to the right. Two hard spins later, the SUV tapped the Mercedes again and the car flipped over, rolled twice, and came to a stop on its head.

Lawson, momentarily disoriented, recovered quickly and noticed that his driver was unconscious in front of him. As the SUV came to a stop just outside the upside-down car, he quickly unclipped his seatbelt and fell onto his side to the roof below him. The door beside Lawson opened, and just as a man's arm reached in, he moved to the opposite side of the car, opened the door, and crawled out. As he got to his feet, a large man in a dress shirt and slacks rounded the back of the overturned car. His sleeves were rolled up like he was ready to do work. But he wasn't prepared for the man he was approaching.

Without saying a word, the big man reached back and threw a powerful right hand in the direction of Lawson's face. Lawson swatted the man's arm, stepped in with force, and busted the man's mouth with the crown of his head. The big man dropped, and as he did, Lawson heard footsteps coming up behind him. Lawson turned and brought his right hand around like a hammer, bludgeoning the dark-haired man in the forehead. The man dropped to his knees, and Lawson hurled a right hook around so fast that when he hit the man in the temple, he was already unconscious by the time his head bounced off the Mercedes door beside him.

The last man walked around the car but pulled up short. Lawson could see when he turned around that the man was contemplating whether it was worth it or not.

The man said with arrogance, "Look, I don't know who you think you are, but you are making a big mistake here."

Lawson looked down at the big man that he'd head-butted, now lying on the ground, then glanced back over his own shoulder at the other man on the ground he'd just knocked out.

"You sure about that?"

The man smirked, ran a hand through his thick black hair, and popped his knuckles in preparation for a fight. "Don't be too proud of what you did to those two. They learned how to fight in Girl Scouts. I assure you, I'm not like them. I don't care how strong you are, that has nothing to do with fighting."

Lawson nodded, his deep voice more of a growl. "I agree."

Lawson took two steps toward the man, and the man took two steps toward him. The man led with a right hook. Lawson caught his wrist with his left hand, grabbed the man's throat with his right hand, and spun him around, slamming him against the Mercedes. The entire vehicle shook under the force. When the man looked down, his eyes widened when he saw his feet were dangling about three inches off the ground, his back pinned against the car.

"You want another chance?" Lawson asked as he held him in the air.

The man nodded, his face turning maroon from Lawson's grip on his throat.

"Who sent you?"

The man clawed at Lawson's hand, desperately trying to free his neck for a much-needed breath. Lawson only tightened his grip, and the man's eyes rolled back into his head.

"Who sent you?"

The man couldn't speak, but he managed to convey his thoughts through raising his middle finger. Lawson didn't find the gesture funny. He released the man's neck, grabbed two fistfuls of his shirt, then turned him from the car and tossed him several feet away onto the rocky desert floor.

Sweat dripped off Lawson's forehead. So far, life on the outside was no different from his time behind bars.

"Tell me who sent you, and that will be the end of this."

The man staggered to his feet as he gasped for air. He took a moment to slap away some of the dust that had gathered on his pants, then stood up straight.

Lawson turned to face him. "Last chance. Who sent you?"

The man didn't answer. Instead, he stalked toward Lawson, his fists in front of his face, ready to fight. Lawson stepped toward him and front-kicked his kneecap, popping it out the back side of his leg. The man crumpled to the ground like a smashed soda can. Lawson stood over him, placing his foot on the knee that was now turned in the wrong direction. The man let out an agony-filled scream. Then, before Lawson had the chance to ask again, the man answered his question.

"Serge Sokolov! Please, get off my leg!" he begged.

Lawson obliged, stepping to the side. The man wasted no time, offering threats to try to scare Lawson, desperately trying to save his own life.

"You are a dead man, Raines. When Sokolov hears about this, he's going to kill you!"

"Wasn't that your job?"

Allowing no time for an answer, Lawson stomped down on the man's forehead, knocking him unconscious. Lawson knew of Sokolov. He had a lot of men inside the prison. He ran the second largest crime outfit in Vegas. Sokolov and only one other organization in Vegas were a potential threat to De Luca's stronghold. On the inside, Sokolov controlled the Aryan brothers. The only other threat in Vegas was a man they called Darkness. Lawson always thought the name was ridiculous, but it did make sense, seeing as how he was black and controlled the black population at the prison. He had done a few favors for Darkness as well, probably why Sokolov sent men for him. It wasn't really a conscious decision not to help Sokolov. But he always considered that on some level he chose Darkness because he could never stand to listen to that nails-on-a-chalkboard Russian accent.

Lawson searched the pocket of the man's shattered leg, found the keys to the SUV, and went over and started it up. He went back to the Mercedes for his notebook, then back to the SUV. The air conditioning felt like a transcendent experience. He glanced out the window at the carnage he was leaving behind. He knew it was going to catch up with him sooner or later. He put the SUV in drive and pulled back onto the highway. Without anywhere else to go, he figured the suite waiting for him at Caesar's Palace sounded like as good a place to start as any.

4

TEN MINUTES LATER, LAWSON CONTINUED DRIVING TOWARD the Las Vegas Strip. De Luca was going to love the fact that he had just taken out three of Sokolov's men. But Lawson didn't really care. He was focused on the private shower waiting for him in his hotel suite. It's an event you take for granted until you have experienced ten years of having a horde of woman-deprived meatheads circling you like sharks as you washed yourself. Lawson physically shuddered at the thought. Then the picture formed in his mind of a king bed, all to himself, and a minifridge full of bourbon. He could almost taste the oak-filled, caramel-colored liquor on his lips. For the first time in a long time, he was looking forward to something.

That was before he glanced in his rearview mirror.

About a half mile behind him, down the long and straight desert highway, cresting the only hill on the entire road, he could just make out flashing red and blue lights. Then another set appeared behind those, and then another.

Damn.

For a fleeting moment, he had the urge to stomp on the accelerator and make a run for it. Once upon a time, he had been a damn good FBI agent. That knowledge of the system was stored deep inside his lizard brain somewhere, and for a second he considered using it to get away. But as much as he hated that jail cell he had just come from, he didn't want to live on the run either.

Before the police cars were on him, he applied the brakes and pulled over to the side of the road. He had a lifetime of fight inside him, but he wasn't going to waste it on some guys who were just doing their jobs. He tucked the notebook down in the back of his joggers and placed his hands at ten and two.

THE POLICE CRUISER veered off the road and into the parking lot of an old, dilapidated motel, just on the outskirts of Las Vegas. For the last ten minutes, Lawson had been trying to figure out why the cops hadn't turned around and taken him back to High Desert State Prison. The officer driving was clearly instructed not to say a word, and he was certainly good at following orders. He also sent the other two patrol cars away before he began to drive. Whatever was going on, someone didn't want people to know where he was taking Lawson. Or who he was being taken to meet.

As the officer stopped the car in front of the bright red door of room number seven, Lawson couldn't help but feel like that number was going to be anything but lucky for him. No good could come from a diversion like this. No, he wasn't heading into a cell, but he figured whatever he was going to find behind that door would more than likely be worse.

The officer nudged him into the empty motel room. Two full beds, one TV, and, Lawson figured, hundreds of diseases filled the stained and dirt-covered room.

"Have a seat on the bed. Someone will be with you in a minute," the officer told him.

"Oh, *now* you want to talk."

The officer didn't react as he turned and walked out the door. Lawson did his best not to touch the bedspread he was sitting on. This certainly was no suite at Caesar's. Lawson's mind was running. He'd just been released from prison, and the only person there to greet him had been a mob boss's lackey. Then a few minutes later, he was ambushed by three men from a different crime boss. And they were going to kill him or at least take him somewhere to torture him. As if all that wasn't enough, he was picked up by a police officer and discreetly escorted to a dump of a motel, smack-dab in the middle of nowhere.

He glanced over at the clock. One o'clock. He had only been out an hour and it was already turning out to be quite the eventful day. As he sat in silence, he couldn't help but wonder why Cassie hadn't been there to pick him up from prison. Sure, he'd all but stopped communicating with her, but only because he didn't want to burden her. She had been going through a divorce, and he wasn't a whole hell of a lot of fun to visit in prison. Maybe she took it personally. Having no friends was a tough way to go through life.

The hotel door opened and bright yellow light poured into the room.

Lawson rose to his feet and said the first thing that came to mind. "Think of the devil and she shall appear."

It was Cassie. However, she looked much different than the last time he'd seen her over a year ago. She had really thinned out and let her blonde hair grow below her shoulder blades. Her pale skin was as smooth as ever, seemingly unfazed by the decade that had passed. Cassie stood silent in the doorway.

"Divorce looks good on you, Cass."

She couldn't help but smile. "Still an asshole, I see? Well, whatever weight I lost, looks like you added in muscle. Good God, Lawson."

Lawson shrugged his shoulders, and Cassie let the door shut behind her as she rushed over to him, arms stretched out for a hug. Lawson involuntarily recoiled from her reach. It had been a long time since he had been embraced.

Cassie took a step back, and a sympathetic look formed on her face. "Been a while since you've had a hug? Come here. It will only hurt for a second."

She rushed back in, and this time Lawson stood his ground. For a moment, the feel of her arms around him and the smell of her perfume froze him. Cassie took one arm at a time and placed his arms around her.

"There ya go, big guy. Don't worry, it'll all come back to you," she joked.

Lawson gave her a halfhearted squeeze. The feeling almost overwhelmed him, and it was something that he was completely unprepared for. It was almost like the feeling of a first kiss. He had only ever had platonic feelings for Cassie, and still did, but what a sensation it was to have another human show you love. He hadn't realized just how much had changed for him until that moment. He was an entirely different person now.

Cassie let go and backed away. "Well, that was awkward. Thanks."

"Sorry, I . . . why all the theatrics to bring me here? Why not just pick me up outside the prison yourself?"

"Well, hello, Lawson. No, no, things are great. But enough about me . . ."

Lawson smiled. "Same old smart-ass Cass." He pointed to his head. "There's a lot going on up here right now. Just trying to process."

Cassie took his hand, but he pulled away. She took it again with force and made him take a seat beside her on the bed. "I get it. Nice work on the bozos back there on the side of the road, by the way. Looks like you made some friends while you were away."

"Yeah, something like that. You here to take me back?"

"Take you back? To prison? For smashing a couple of mob losers? No, you aren't going back to prison. Not today anyway."

"Then what's with bringing me here?"

"Well, I missed you, first of all." She patted him on the knee. "And since we're skipping the small talk, I've come to collect on the provision of your pardon."

"Provision?"

Cassie raised an eyebrow. "Well, yeah. You didn't think I could get the governor to give you a pardon without there being some sort of consequence, did you?"

Now it was Lawson who raised an eyebrow. "*You* got the governor to give me a pardon? No offense, but I already paid off the provision of my pardon."

"What? You mean, making sure Ronnie Freeman got what he deserved in prison? Keeping him from telling the world about the governor's pregnant mistress? Really?"

Lawson was confused, and it showed. "How did you . . ."

"Come on, Lawson. I've been trying to get you out of jail

27

since the day they wrongfully put you away. And I've been trying to find out who killed Lauren every single day too. What, you think I just didn't care? Thought I gave up on my best friends?"

Lawson didn't respond. Hearing Lauren's name with the word killed in the same sentence still stung. He would never be able to move past it.

Cassie patted his hand. "Sorry. I didn't mean to bring it up. You just need to know that I have been fighting for both of you. But getting you out of prison came with a price."

Lawson looked up at her. "I didn't mean to imply that—"

"Don't. You don't have to apologize to me. I'm sorry you've lost so much of your life, Lawson." Cassie took her hand from his knee and reached for her back pocket. "Here. I thought you would want to see this."

Cassie handed him a photo. A photo of a girl who was about twelve years old with long blonde hair, the spitting image of Lauren Raines. Lawson shot a look at Cassie. Cassie nodded, letting him know that it was in fact a picture of his daughter, Lexi.

Cassie said, "She looks so much like her, doesn't she?"

Lawson didn't answer. He couldn't take his eyes off his beautiful daughter. He rubbed his thumb across her face. Across Lauren's face. The resemblance was uncanny. Emotions that he had long suppressed rose up inside him like a tidal wave. He was overwhelmed.

Cassie continued to talk while Lawson admired the photo. "I had an old private investigator friend of mine catch this shot of her outside her middle school. I've tried to contact Lauren's sister about a million times, Lawson, but she just won't talk to me."

Lawson didn't look away from the photo. It didn't

surprise him at all that Lauren's sister, Erin, wouldn't speak to Cassie. Lauren and she had had a falling-out. As long as Lawson had known Lauren, they had never so much as spoken a word. Lauren said it was a lot of reasons, but mostly it happened when Erin started dating her husband, Dan. According to Lauren, Dan was a real pretentious prick. It was ambiguous at best how he made his money, but he had a lot of it. And Lauren said that all she ever heard that he did with it was gamble and play poker. Ironically, Lauren's sister had met Dan in Vegas. He was always there playing big cash games and rubbing elbows with plenty of well-known lowlifes. That was what hurt the most when Lawson learned that Lexi would be raised by them. He didn't want his daughter growing up around those terrible influences.

Lawson was still staring at Lexi's angelic face. "Did the investigator find out anything else about Lexi? Anything at all?"

"Well, she is one of the few twelve-year-olds on the planet without any sort of social media accounts."

Lawson looked up at her, confused.

Cassie smiled. "Don't worry about it. It's a different world out here now on the internet. Anyway, I'm sure it's by design that she isn't on social media. Lauren's sister probably makes sure it's that way. But he did find a flyer on the fence at the school. Apparently Lexi likes to sing. She performed an Adele song at the school's talent show. Not sure how that went, but just so you know, if you're going to sing an Adele song, you gotta be damn good to pull it off."

In that moment Lawson felt more lost than he ever had. He knew his little girl was growing up, but to hear even a little bit of news about her real life, what she likes to do, was like getting kicked in the gut by a mule. Lauren had always loved to sing too. Never a day went by that she wasn't milling about the house humming a tune. The pit in his stomach only widened. And after the initial longing for Lexi that seeing her picture brought on, that familiar sting immediately followed.

The sting of rage that had been burning inside him since that day someone took everything from him.

5

LAWSON DECIDED TO BRING THE CONVERSATION BACK TO business.

"So you're trying to tell me that I owe the governor for a debt I already paid?"

Cassie stood and started to pace the motel room.

"No, I'm sure the governor believes you are all square. He's not the one who mandated the provision."

"Are we speaking in code here, Cass?"

Lawson grew tired of the long route Cassie was taking to get to the point.

"No. What I'm trying to tell you is that the governor wasn't responsible for your pardon, it was the FBI that pulled strings."

"FBI?" Lawson was dumbfounded. "What the hell is going on? Why would the FBI care if I rotted in a cell or not? They certainly didn't care ten years ago."

"Because I convinced them that you could be trusted, and that there were far better ways to make use of you than three square meals and a community shower."

"So you're a special agent now?" Lawson said.

"A lot can happen in ten years, buddy."

"I have zero interest in working with the FBI. Zero interest in helping any government agency, for that matter. In case you forgot, the 'system' didn't exactly do me any favors."

Cassie stopped pacing.

"Look, I get it. I really do. The system failed me too. I lost two best friends that day, in case you forgot. And I know that doesn't compare to what you've been through, Lawson, but it changed my life too. And anyway, what choice do we have? If we don't work to get rid of problems, aren't we just a part of them?"

Now it was Lawson who stood. His hulking frame towered over the short and thin Cassie.

"No, Cassie, the system *is* the problem. At least for me."

"It's not. And it wasn't. Someone set you up, and I'm offering you a chance to find out who."

"You are? I must have missed that part of your pitch."

"Lawson, you know how this works. This isn't a pitch. They will make me put you right back in that jail cell if—"

"If what? If I don't do what you want? How is being a prisoner out here any better than being a prisoner in jail?"

"Whiskey, for one."

Lawson wasn't amused.

"Are you taking me back to the prison, or am I free to go?"

"You always were hardheaded. Lawson, I am offering you a way to live out here, doing what you are good at, while you try to find out what really happened that day on the lake."

"I hope you're better at being a special agent than you are

at motivational speeches. Stop beating around the bush and give it to me straight. I'll shut my mouth until you're completely finished. Then I'll tell you to shove it up your ass."

Cassie put both hands on her hips. It had been a long time, but Lawson had seen this move a hundred times. They were falling right back into their old partner routine of getting on each other's last nerve. What usually came next was a solution to the problem they were trying to solve. Lawson could only hope that would be the case today.

"You want it straight? Fine. No more sugarcoating. You work for the FBI now. We got you out of prison, but if you want, we can put you right back in. But then you wouldn't have a chance to solve Lauren's murder, and you wouldn't have a chance of seeing your daughter. Not ever again. Instead, the first thing the FBI needs is to be able to trust you. Once you show them that, then we can really put you to work, the FBI could really use someone with your skills. Best part is, all we want you to do is use the contacts you've made and the reputation you've already built in prison with organized crime here in Vegas."

"How the hell is taking down an organized crime boss of any worth to the FBI? If they haven't done it in the ten years I've been gone, what makes you think I can have any effect?"

"I thought you were going to tell me to shove it up my ass?" Cassie taunted.

Lawson folded his arms across his chest.

"I'm getting there."

"Well, for one," Cassie continued, "it will show the FBI you can be trusted, and that you are who I am telling them you are."

"I'm not that guy—"

"*Second* of all . . ." Cassie paused for effect.

Lawson could tell this was the point where his old partner had lost patience with him. For a moment, it almost made him miss working with her.

"Second of all, we believe that Sokolov is harboring Russian spies for his government."

"You *believe* he is?"

"We know he is. So obviously you can help with that. The CIA is putting pressure on us to make something happen."

It was Lawson's turn to put his hands on his hips.

"Did I go to prison in 2008 only to come out and it's 1984 out here? Isn't this whole Russian spy thing played out?"

"Like I said, a lot has happened since you went away. Russia is back to its old tricks. Interfering with our latest election, funding programmers and hackers to infiltrate our data systems, we don't know how deep this goes. Even one of our generals may have been involved with them. It's getting out of hand."

Lawson was trying to take it all in. He had kept up with the headlines while behind bars, but he also knew that no matter your political views you couldn't trust a damn thing the newspapers and television news media were reporting. And frankly, he didn't give a damn about any of it. But what Cassie said about him not being able to right the wrongs that happened to him ten years ago if he were to remain behind bars was 100 percent true. He didn't like when Cassie was right, but she was; he didn't really have a choice. That didn't mean he had to be of much help. He could string the FBI along while he worked on what really mattered.

Revenge.

Cassie broke his train of thought.

"That brain actually processing this, or have you gone full meathead on me?"

She looked at him as if she was waiting for a smile. She was going to have to keep waiting.

Lawson finally gave in. "So what's the play?"

Cassie took her hands from her hips and folded her arms across her chest. A wry smile on her face. At least someone was enjoying this.

"You play it just as though we never had this conversation. The world believes the governor pardoned you, so let them. You go to your suite that Nero De Luca has waiting for you at Caesar's Palace."

Lawson raised an inquisitive eyebrow.

Cassie returned it with a knowing raise of her own.

"Go to your suite and let De Luca take you into his fold. Be his enforcer, or whatever he wants you to be. Use the fact that Sokolov already sent men for you, and convince De Luca to let you use your old FBI skills to set Sokolov up and take him down. I'll be here to help you with that side of things."

"And with who killed Lauren." Lawson wasn't asking.

"And with who killed Lauren," Cassie agreed. "We have someone in Caesar's already. A maid. She'll be leaving correspondence and info in your safe. She'll also supply you with money and a secure phone that you will only use to talk to me. Understand?"

Lawson nodded.

"I'm sure De Luca will supply you with all the weaponry you'll need, and probably money too. Use it to buy yourself a nice suit or something, will you? Maybe some extra-strength deodorant?"

Lawson could tell she was trying to lighten the mood. This was a trick she had used many times before while they were partners. When Lawson's mind was working, he knew he could become a very serious man. This had always made Cassie uncomfortable, and jokes were her way of telling him so. But she wasn't his partner anymore, and feelings of empathy and compassion hadn't been around Lawson's system in a very long time. And he wasn't sure they would ever make their way back to him again.

"So how am I supposed to get back to Caesar's?" Lawson said.

He could tell by the look on Cassie's face that she was disappointed that they weren't just going to fall right back into the way things used to be. So she took things serious herself.

"You figure that out, Lawson. It's time you started using that detective brain of yours again. If it's still in there at all. I hope all the push-ups and fistfights while you were locked up didn't completely dumb you down. If so, my boss is sure going to be upset with me."

Lawson gave Cassie a stern look. "I'll try not to make life hard for *you.*"

It was a low blow. He could tell by the look on Cassie's face.

"Right. Good to see you too, Lawson. I'll be in touch."

Cassie threw a hundred-dollar bill on the dresser, then turned and left the room. Cab fare, he assumed. The old Lawson Raines, the one with a sense of humor, would have made a joke about feeling like a cheap hooker. But that man was dead. And it seemed he had already managed to push away the only person he knew in the entire free world.

So far, things couldn't be going worse.

6

LAWSON PAID THE DRIVER, THEN STEPPED OUT OF THE CAB, right into the Las Vegas oven. He shielded his eyes from the afternoon sun and took in the monstrosity that was Caesar's Palace. He didn't linger long, though, because he knew the inside of that casino would be pumping the AC. He walked into the lobby and was greeted by marble floors, Roman statues, a fountain, and sixty-eight degrees of pure bliss. Oh, and hundreds of people roaming free, without a care in the world.

The difference between where he had just spent the last ten years of his life and where he currently stood very quickly began to overwhelm him. He realized that he didn't know how to act amongst all this free will. And oddly, as he took in the thousands of square feet of open space, he actually began to feel claustrophobic. He needed to get to his room, back to a space that he could control, and he needed to do it now.

Lawson walked around the fountain, and the line at the check-in counter looked like the serpentine body of a never-ending snake. There was no way he could wait in that line.

There was no way he could stay in this space, people rushing all around him, bumping into him, shouting, laughing, bells ringing from the casino, forks and knives hitting plates at the adjacent restaurant, the water rushing in the fountain, the—

"Mr. Raines?"

Hearing someone say his name jarred him from his growing state of panic. When he turned around to find a young man in a suit extending his hand, he realized that his breathing was labored, and though it was very cool inside, he was sweating through his T-shirt.

"Lawson Raines? I'm Johnny De Luca. My father sent me to welcome you. Are you all right?"

The young man's deep brown eyes seemed genuinely concerned. He had all the markings of an Italian mobster's son. The nice suit, the gaudy watch, the expensive shoes. Even though Lawson was in an altered mind state, his old FBI-detective profiling skills kicked in as instinctively as taking a breath. What didn't add up was the soft demeanor Johnny displayed, and thankfully he didn't have a pound of grease in his hair.

Lawson took a deep breath, swallowing the feeling of being overwhelmed, as he shook his hand.

"Yeah, I'm Lawson. Get me out of this jungle, would you?"

Johnny winced a bit when Lawson shook his hand.

"No problem. Wow, that's quite a grip you've got."

Lawson nodded. Had he really digressed so much that he forgot how to shake a man's hand?

"Follow me, you're going to love the suite. Dad spared no expense for you."

Again, Lawson nodded and followed the young man to the elevators. He couldn't wait to get himself inside that confined and mostly private space. He realized in that moment that nearly everything about him was different than his old self. Different than nearly everyone on the planet.

A few minutes and a calming elevator ride later, Johnny was opening the door to Lawson's new temporary home. He could instantly see that Johnny was right. Nero De Luca had indeed spared no expense. The suite was opulent, and sprawling. As big as an entire row of jail cells. Lawson couldn't help but feel as if he were being wooed. Though all of this would be free of charge to him, he knew it was going to have a large price tag when it was all said and done.

"Can I show you around?" Johnny asked.

Lawson could tell he was proud of the room.

Lawson walked into the large formal reception room. It was all open and included a step-up bar on one end, an over-sized dining room table on the other, and couches and other seating in the middle, enough for a lot more people than Lawson would ever have inside.

"Actually no. I'm good."

Johnny looked disappointed. Then he pointed to a door past the dining room table.

"No problem. Your bedroom is right through there. In the closet you will find plenty of clothes and there's some money in the envelope on the nightstand to get you started."

"Great. So what's the catch?"

Johnny looked confused.

"Catch?"

"What does your dad want? Though I'm sure he is a splendid human being, he isn't doing this out of the kindness of his heart."

"That will have to be between you and him. You have a

dinner meeting with him tonight at STK in the Cosmopolitan Hotel."

"STK?"

"As in steak. The place is dope, Mr. Raines. And the food is fantastic. You're going to love it."

The thought of a crowded dinner at a swanky steak house made his skin crawl. But the thought of a big, fat, buttery steak was enough to push that other feeling right out of the way.

"There is a cell phone on the nightstand as well. Anyone you will need to contact is in that phone. But if you need anything, just tap Johnny in the contact list. I can arrange anything you will need . . . or want."

Johnny followed that last bit with a wink. Lawson knew he meant women. Lawson gave no response, he just looked back toward the door. Johnny got the hint.

"Right. Okay, enjoy the suite. I have a masseuse coming to set up for you in about an hour. I'll text you dinner information in just a bit."

"Cancel the masseuse. And anything else you might be planning."

Johnny looked for a minute like he might protest, then decided against it.

"Not a problem. Enjoy your day, Mr. Raines."

Johnny left the room, and finally Lawson could relax.

7

LAWSON WOKE UP TO A DINGING SOUND. HE COULDN'T PLACE the noise in his mind, and before he opened his eyes, he expected one of the prison guards to be playing some sort of trick on him. But something was off. The smell around him wasn't . . . dank. There were no scents of body odor wafting his way. What he did smell was, well, clean.

Lawson shot straight up and opened his eyes, searching for the bars that had greeted him every morning for the last ten years. Instead, he was on a carpeted floor, surrounded by men's clothes. The odd dinging sound that woke him was lit up next to him. A cell phone. Lawson vaguely remembered being uncomfortable on the ultrasoft bed. And he could just barely piece together the memory of feeling like there had been way too much space around him and how it had made him uncomfortable. So he had shut himself inside the small walk-in closet and finished his nap on the floor. The small confines made him feel at home. His first day out was getting awfully strange.

The text message that had awoken him had been from

Johnny. He was instructing Lawson to be out front at Caesar's for the Mercedes that would drop him off down the street at STK. For a moment Lawson thought if it was down the street he would just walk. Then he remembered that in Las Vegas, across the street could be as far as a mile.

He walked out of the closet, and though he knew that night had fallen, he could hardly tell with all the light coming in from the massive window at the end of the bedroom. He walked over and admired all the flashing lights of the Strip. Just below him on the street, thousands of people were enjoying a vacation—laughing, drinking, gambling, taking in all the fun that Las Vegas could be. But Lawson only felt pain as he looked over the grandeur. The only thing he saw were memories with Lauren. And that only brought sadness. He took a deep breath as he stared at his own shadowy reflection in the window. He thought it to be a fitting metaphor.

He walked away from the window and directly toward the minibar. He took out a miniature bottle of Buffalo Trace bourbon, twisted the hunter-green cap, and downed the entire thing. The familiar burn flowed down his throat and flamed all the way to his stomach. He let out a hot exhale, enjoying the fond spirit. Since he had never had a problem with alcohol, it had always been used for fun and celebration in the past. The bourbon reminded him of home since it was made just a few miles down I-75 from where he grew up in Lexington, Kentucky. But now, thoughts of home, just like all other thoughts, it seemed, only caused heartache. Lexington was where he met Lauren, and according to Cassie, that is where his daughter was right now.

Without him.

Lawson turned and fired the small glass bottle against the

wall. It shattered. Another metaphor. This time for his broken heart. Time hadn't healed any of his wounds. They were still as open as the day he climbed back up on that boat and walked through that river of blood to find Lauren. Anger pulsed through his veins. Heartbreak poured gasoline on the fire. His chest was heaving, and his eyes were wet with tears. There were a lot of question marks in his life. He was walking back into a world that he could hardly remember how to live in. People, bad people, wanting him for the work he had done to survive in prison. Some of them wanted him dead, some of them needed his strangely acquired set of skills, but either way, none of it was anything Lawson cared about. The biggest question hanging in his mind was revenge. Who killed his wife? Who framed him for the murder, and why?

Who destroyed his life?

The why in the equation, as far as feelings, was inconsequential to Lawson. The only reason the why mattered was because it might lead him to who. And all he knew was when he did find out who was responsible, he would be bringing the wrath of God with him to their doorstep. They took everything from him. And they were going to pay. Somewhere, right then, his daughter was living her life without her mother, or her father. There would be no barrier high enough to keep him from righting that wrong.

There was nothing he could do for his daughter right then. And that further split his already broken heart. He couldn't go to her until he figured out who he was going to be. They wouldn't let him near her even if he tried. He had been around law enforcement long enough to know that until he had his life together, no one was going to let him in hers. Because for all they still believed, he was a murderer. No pardon, whether it be from a governor or the FBI, was ever going to change that.

The FBI.

Now there was a curveball he hadn't seen coming. Especially with Cassie leading the way. They must have been pretty hard up for good help if they were trying to pluck has-beens from the prison slush pile. Sure, before going to jail he was doing a great job for the FBI. It had always been one of his goals to become a special agent and then maybe one day move over to the CIA. And ironically, spending so much time in prison had only made him more qualified. Now he knew life from the other perspective. The criminal mind. If he was good at reading people before prison, he was a certifiable expert at it now. Couple that with the fighting skills he had acquired on the inside, and there may not be a better person for the job. But he didn't see how that figured into his life either.

The next steps he knew he was about to take would only throw him further into that criminal mindset. He was going to have to break every law in the book to make things right. And there wasn't a trickle of hesitation in his body when he thought about it.

Maybe that is the sort of man the FBI or the CIA would want.

Maybe Cassie springing this on him really was a blessing. An entire world of backup would be there for him if he needed information. If he worked it right, he might get everything he wanted out of this situation.

That, or the FBI would have a front-row seat to one of the most devastating personal wars ever waged. At the end of the day, Lawson didn't really care.

With or without the FBI, someone was going to pay.

Probably a lot more than one. And after he was finished bringing the house down on the parties responsible for Lauren's death, he didn't care whether they gave him a medal or locked him up for good.

The phone dinged again, his car was waiting downstairs. He quickly checked the safe to make sure his notebook was secure.

Step one had to be taken: infiltrate the underworld of crime to find out who knows what. Nero De Luca was the perfect place to start.

Lawson tossed his phone on the bed and walked back into the closet. He sifted through the gaudy-colored clothing until he found a black suit at the end of the rack. He plucked a black button-up shirt, a black belt, and some black dress shoes, and put on his new life.

He stared at himself in the full-length mirror attached to the back of the closet door. De Luca's tailor had nailed the fit. And though Lawson didn't recognize the man staring back at him, at least he was dressed the part.

The funeral attire would be fitting seeing as how he was prepared to send any man who stood in his way to their grave.

8

THE HOSTESS LED LAWSON THROUGH A MAZE OF TABLES. STK was an odd steak house to him. Most of the steak houses he'd been in, with stuffy white tablecloths, were geared for the old-white-man-with-money demographic in mind. This restaurant couldn't be more opposite. The lights were low, and there was a DJ in the back corner—yes, a DJ in a steak house—and more beautiful young people along the bar than Lawson had ever seen in a place like that. Something must be going okay in America if all these young people have this much disposable income.

The hostess walked him past a wall of white horns and into a room adjacent to the main dining area. Where you could still be in the mix but also enjoy some privacy. When she walked him in, the cast of *Goodfellas*, *The Godfather*, and *Casino* were all waiting there for him. Everyone stood except for the man in the middle of the table, which was against the back wall at the middle of the room.

"Lawson Raines." The man set down his glass of red wine and spread his arms wide.

"Don Corleone," Lawson quipped.

All the men standing on either side of De Luca turned their attention to Nero, apparently waiting to see how their boss was going to take this strange man making a joke at their intimidating boss's expense.

De Luca smiled. "The big, bad Lawson Raines has a sense of humor." He gave a sweeping glance to all his merry men. "Don Corleone." He laughed. They all broke their trance and began to laugh with him. "I like it. I only hope I don't look like him too."

He didn't. Nero De Luca more closely favored Al Pacino from the movie *Any Given Sunday*. Not very tall, fit for a man in his late fifties, short salt-and-pepper hair, and an arrogant scowl permanently etched in the lines of his leathered face. Lawson didn't answer. He just stood in front of De Luca and waited.

"Have a seat. How do you take your steak?"

"Rare."

"Ah, see, boys, I told you this was a *real* man."

Lawson took a seat opposite De Luca. A woman in what was hardly enough material to be called a dress poured a glass of red wine, and his men finally returned to their seats.

"That was a real bang-up job you did on Sokolov's men. I must apologize for not being better prepared. I believe I underestimated the amount of people you pissed off when you did favors for their enemies." De Luca gestured to himself.

"It was nothing."

"Nothing?" De Luca's smile widened. "You see, fellas, that's how it's done. You handle things like it was all part of the job." He glared back at Lawson. "But those weren't any

47

ordinary men, from what I'm told. Some of the meanest of Sokolov's bunch."

"If that's true, you don't have much to worry about."

De Luca laughed.

"You say that, Mr. Raines, but they have been giving my men plenty to worry about over the last few months."

"Sounds like you need some new men."

Lawson didn't mince words.

Another scantily clad woman set a New York strip down in front of Lawson. A dab of garlic butter was melting on top of it, the juices from the steak still sizzling on the heated white plate. His stomach growled at the sight of it. His mouth watered for a bite of it.

"That is why I brought you here, Lawson. Because I can't say that I disagree with you."

That brought some unrest amongst the men. De Luca wasn't doing Lawson any favors by speaking about them like that in front of him.

"I need more men like you. Men who can take care of business and then go about their day. Smart men like you who can help me figure out who is stealing from me. Keep my assets safe my investments making money."

Lawson didn't touch his food.

"What makes you think I want to work for you?"

De Luca's charming tone changed at Lawson's insubordination.

"What makes you think you have a choice?"

Lawson stood from the table. Several of the men stood and drew their weapons.

"Every man has a choice, De Luca."

De Luca didn't wave his men off.

"That is true, Mr. Raines. And it is also true that every

choice has consequences. The question is, are you willing to live with them?"

Lawson eyed the table in front of him. He would be able to get the steak knife to De Luca's throat before the men could shoot him. He was faster than he looked. But that wouldn't do him any good. He'd be dead. And now if he didn't indulge his urge to kill him, it really wouldn't do him any good going forward to be on the bad side of De Luca, even though every fiber of his being wanted to tell this sleazeball to blow him. So Lawson took a deep breath . . . and waited.

After a few more contentious seconds, De Luca waved his hand for the men to put away their guns.

"I can't help but feel disrespected, Mr. Raines. I put you up in a nice hotel, I put some cash in your pocket, I treat you to a wonderful dinner and offer you a high-paying job to do what you are good at. I'm going to do you yet another favor and chalk this up to you not being used to how things work out here in the real world."

De Luca took a sip of his wine, then rose to his feet.

"You see, out here you aren't the man anymore. I am. And when *the man* offers you a job, it isn't an *offer* at all. Do we understand each other?"

Lawson didn't look away from De Luca, but he didn't offer an answer either.

"Let me make this easier for you, Lawson. You help me out, and I'll help you out. I am generous enough to make this more of a partnership."

Lawson broke his silence.

"I know what I bring to the table, De Luca. But what can you offer me? I can make money in other ways."

De Luca raised his eyebrow.

"Well, I'm not sure you can, Lawson, but okay, how about we start with me letting you live?"

Lawson went quiet again. From the sound of it, De Luca needed him. So Lawson wasn't going to make it easy for him.

De Luca picked up a cigar, lit it, and blew a puff of smoke into the room as he comfortably waited through Lawson's silence. Then he smiled. A dark and sinister smile.

"Oh, and there is this business of your wife."

Lawson's temperature rose. His muscles tightened, coiled inside like a cobra ready to strike.

Careful, De Luca.

"I can help you find who did this to you. That should be something we both can agree would interest you, can't we, Mr. Raines?"

"If you know something about what happened to my— about what happened, tell me now, De Luca."

"Or what, Lawson? Or . . . what?"

Lawson took a breath. He knew a situation like this would arise once he started digging, he just didn't think it would be this soon. The time for talk was over. De Luca had pulled the trump card.

Lawson shifted his weight as he shifted his demeanor. A deep breath calmed him.

"What do you need me to do?"

De Luca puffed his cigar once more, then took a sip of wine. His smile was now one of pride.

"Welcome to the De Luca Corporation, Lawson Raines."

9

——————

Lawson walked back into his hotel suite at Caesar's Palace. He hadn't planned on coming back to the room after the meeting with De Luca. He knew that indulging in De Luca's hospitality would only obligate him to Nero. But now, none of that really mattered. On the walk back to Caesar's, it once again occurred to him that working with De Luca could actually be a good thing. It gave him a way to move freely amongst the people who really knew what was going on in Las Vegas: the criminals.

Lawson made it back to his suite. As he removed his blazer and began to unbutton his shirt, from somewhere in the room he could hear the muffled sound of a cell phone ringing. He walked toward the bedroom, and the sound grew louder. Inside the closet, he could tell the ringing was coming from somewhere near the safe. Cassie must have had the FBI phone planted there while he was at dinner. The phone had stopped ringing, but a single chirp followed as he picked it up from the top of the safe.

A text message from Cassie. Just like the phone that

Johnny left him, it wasn't the first time he had seen an iPhone, they had just been released before he went to prison. However, these were his first couple of times working one, and it still felt like a device from another planet. After a few seconds of fumbling with the new-to-him technology, he finally managed to click on the messages app.

Cassie: *You passed the test. Glad you didn't answer. But just so you know, from now on you can. We swept the room, there were no cameras. Only two bugs. You can speak freely. All those bugs will ever hear is music and random television shows. See that virtual keyboard below this message? That's where you type back to me. Don't worry, you'll get the hang of 2018 soon.*

Though many years had passed, Cassie still felt like his sister. Another text came in.

Cassie: *Hello?*

She was still as impatient as ever too. Then another text.

Cassie: *Forget it. I'm sure you could use a drink. Come buy me one. I'll be across the street at O'Sheas. There's a band.*

The last thing Lawson felt like doing was being around another crowd. But if he wanted to get to the bottom of what happened out on that boat ten years ago, he had to get started. And Cassie was the only source of information he had at the moment.

Cassie: *Just get over here. I'll show you how to use the phone when you get here.*

Lawson put the phone in his pocket, grabbed his blazer, and headed for the door.

LAWSON WALKED into O'Sheas and immediately felt every

last one of the ten years older that he was since the last time he'd been to a bar. The music was louder, the people were younger, and instead of wanting a drink, he wanted a pistol. He scanned the bar from the doorway. It was an Irish bar inside the LINQ Hotel. Last time he was on the Strip, the hotel was called Imperial Palace. And the entire walkway full of shops and restaurants he walked through to get there, now known as the LINQ Promenade, didn't even exist. The bar was full of beer pong tables on the left, gaming tables in the middle, a band at the back, and a bar down the right wall.

Four seats down on the bar sat a blonde, and it took a double take to realize it was Cassie. She was in a sequined blue dress, the back plunged to reveal her muscular back. She looked a lot different than at the motel earlier. Different than she had ever looked. But there is a certain mind melding that good partners have, and he couldn't believe that theirs was still going strong. He knew she was in character, and the fact that there was an empty seat beside her was no coincidence at all. Not in that crowded place.

Lawson weaved his way through the crowd of twentysomethings and sidled up to Cassie. She looked up, placed a hand on his arm, and gave it a squeeze.

"Have a seat, handsome. Buy me a drink?"

"No thanks."

Lawson wanted to make her work for it. He nodded to the bartender.

"Buffalo Trace. Neat."

Cassie didn't skip a beat. She leaned in, draping herself on him, practically forcing him to take a seat.

"You wouldn't leave a lady thirsty, would you?"

Lawson glanced at her. He barely recognized her behind the pound of hooker makeup she had piled on for the occasion. He had to fight the urge to recoil from her touch. He still wasn't used to someone being so close.

"Seriously? Teal eye shadow?"

He felt her pinch down hard on his leg.

"Just play along already, would you?"

Lawson gestured to the bartender to get her another of what she was drinking. It was gin, he could smell it on her breath.

"What happened to the whiskey-drinking Tennessee girl I used to know?"

Cassie traced the outline of the back of his collar with her finger. "Escorts don't drink whiskey."

"Get to it already. I'm already tired of shouting over this obnoxious band. You couldn't invite me to a lounge? 'Escorts' work there too, you know. You really think someone is watching that closely?"

Cassie leaned in. "Second roulette table, closest to the back."

Lawson didn't turn around. Instead, he used the mirror above the bar to find who she was alluding to. Johnny De Luca. Not only was the kid his concierge, but Nero had clearly designated him to be his shadow as well. He was wearing a black ball cap pulled down low to help him stay hidden. He forgot he was wearing a flashy thirty-thousand-dollar Rolex. It was the first thing Lawson noticed.

"He walked in pretty much right behind you. I see your detective skills haven't yet found their way back to you."

Lawson didn't acknowledge the jab.

"Anyway, let's make this quick," Cassie said. "What did De Luca have to say at STK earlier?"

Lawson took a slow sip of his bourbon. It was delicious. Every sense seemed heightened after being locked in that cage. Especially his taste buds. He didn't know how he wanted to answer Cassie's question. Because he didn't know if he wanted her involved. The things he was going to have to do to get to the bottom of what happened to his wife most likely weren't going to be sanctioned by the federal government.

"Who set me up?" he answered with a question.

Cassie gave him that old Cassie look. The one letting him know she wasn't playing.

"Lawson, I can't help you if you don't help me. I told you, if I knew and could prove who was responsible, they would be dead or in jail."

Lawson took another drink and watched in the mirror as Johnny placed another bet behind him.

"Lawson, I'm not playing around here. You need to tell me what De Luca is up to."

That was all he needed to hear. He had already had enough of people trying to tell him what to do. He was supposed to be a free man, but the way people were treating him, it was like he belonged to them. He'd had enough of feeling like a prisoner. Lawson reached into his pocket, pulled out a hundred-dollar bill, and left it for the bartender. He stood up, kissed Cassie on the cheek, and walked toward the restroom. He knew she couldn't break character with Johnny watching, so if he just left, she couldn't try to stop him. He felt her tug at his blazer, but he was already gone.

10

———————

LAWSON FELT JOHNNY'S EYES ON HIM AS HE WALKED TOWARD the back of the bar in the direction of the restrooms. He also felt himself missing the control he had in prison. And he wanted that feeling back. He walked past the restroom doors, looped around to the other side of the bar, and walked right up behind the unsuspecting Johnny De Luca.

"Pick up your chips."

Johnny turned quickly, his face like a child caught with his hand in the cookie jar.

"L-Lawson. Hey man! Weird seeing you—"

"Don't." Lawson cut him off. "Pick up your chips, or lose them."

Johnny started to protest. Lawson got a grip on his shirt collar with his left hand and took hold of his belt with his right. As he lifted him off his chair, Lawson noticed a look of astonishment on Cassie's face across the bar. He practically carried Johnny out the front of the casino and onto the crowded promenade just outside. He tossed him forward, then got right in his face.

"This ends right here, right now."

"Lawson, I swear, it's a coincidence! I gamble here all the time!"

Lawson drew back his right arm, swung it forward, and slammed Johnny in the stomach. Johnny dropped to the ground, gasping for air. The crowd of people walking around them gasped and widened their walk to avoid the two of them.

Lawson said, "I thought we were going to be friends, me and you. Now you're just going to lie to me? I've got enough to worry about right now. I don't need this."

Even though Lawson was using force, he was also using the angle of feeling betrayed. He got the sense Johnny was the type that didn't like disappointing people. He used this angle a lot in prison. A lot of the men locked up with him were subservient. Used to taking orders and being punished when they didn't do what they were told. It had become ingrained in them to want not to disappoint, even when they were being physically abused. It actually helped make them loyal to him. In his time with the FBI, it also became clear that a lot of mob offspring were sheltered and didn't have a lot of their own friends, because their fathers didn't trust anyone. Lawson was hoping what he saw in Johnny was the same sort of thing. The tactic didn't come without risk, however, because pummeling the son of a powerful mob boss wasn't the sort of thing people would usually call "productive".

Lawson stalked forward, lifted Johnny up by the collar, and shook him.

"Are we not going to be friends?"

"Wait. Wait!"

Lawson let Johnny go.

"You're crazy, Lawson! You know who my dad is. He'll kill you if—"

Lawson grabbed his shirt with both hands and lifted him off his feet. This was it. If after Lawson gave it one last try Johnny was still spouting about his daddy, Lawson was in trouble.

"Friends trust each other, Johnny. Real friends do anyway."

Johnny searched Lawson's eyes. After a moment of contemplation, his expression finally changed.

"You're right. I'm sorry. I was just following orders."

Lawson let Johnny down. Either Johnny was smart and playing along until he could tattle or Lawson had read him right. Unfortunately, only time would tell. This was the hard part about this dangerous game. You never knew if you could really trust them until they proved it. And no one can prove their loyalty without you letting them go and show you.

"It's fine. You just have to understand where I've been and what I've been through. I'm used to trusting no one. If I have to, that's the way it will be out here."

"You can trust me. I won't follow you again. But you have to work with me. My dad will be expecting updates."

"We can give him updates. Tonight Lawson went out for a drink and tried to get some ass. Sounds like what any newly free man would do, right?"

Johnny smiled. "Right. It's what I do most nights, and I've always been free."

Lawson knew that the poor kid had been more on lock-down than Lawson ever had, but it wasn't worth the conversation. He was tired. He needed to get some rest. He had a long day ahead tomorrow of shaking down scumbags, and he planned on getting an early start.

Lawson tried to speak Johnny's language. "Let me know next time you're going to be around. Just text me or something. Cool?"

"Cool. And maybe we can work out together soon? I can't put on muscle to save my life. Maybe you could show me some tricks?"

Lawson nodded. "Talk to you soon, Johnny."

Lawson started back toward Caesar's. Without food, he could feel the bourbon flame in his bloodstream. So far, he had been out almost an entire day and had only managed a couple of drinks, a new suit, and a tagalong Italian puppy. The meet-up with Cassie was fruitless, and it was time he quit trying to let information come to him. He recorded many conversations in prison in his notebook. Conversations that he himself had about Sokolov and many that he had overheard. Men discussing a lot of Sokolov's dealings or talking about their favorite places to find a little trouble on the Strip. Lawson knew he could start there and work his way up the food chain. Starting with Sokolov would kill two birds with one stone for him. It would placate De Luca by working on taking care of his biggest rival, and it would also assure the FBI that he was doing what Cassie had told him he had to do to remain free: investigate the apparent spy situation involved with the Russian's organization.

The only problem with those two birds was that the stone Lawson was throwing did nothing for the real reason he wanted to run free in Vegas: to find Lauren's killer. And while it was too late in the evening to investigate, he could at the very least open up his notebook and study his list. Not that he needed to see it. The names he had written on that page were burned into his memory. Every day for the last 3,650 days, he had been obsessing over those names. He didn't know for sure if any, or all, of those names were guilty, but he sure as hell was ready to find out.

11

LAWSON OPENED THE DOOR TO HIS SUITE AND MADE HIS WAY back to the closet. He opened the safe and breathed a sigh of relief when the notebook was still there. It was silly that he cared so much about it, but it was the only possession he had. In that moment he knew he could no longer stay in that hotel room. There were too many people who knew he was there, and more people than he cared to know with access. After being out in the ninety-five-degree Las Vegas night, Lawson needed a new shirt. When he went to remove his blazer, he noticed a crinkling sound that wasn't there before. He opened his blazer and reached down into the inside pocket on the left side. He removed a piece of white notebook paper, unfolded it, and immediately recognized his old partner's handwriting.

Lawson, first off, I'm sorry for not being at the prison to pick you up. You know I would have been if it were possible. But we have a serious problem. I couldn't speak freely earlier at the motel, I wasn't sure who was listening. But apparently, I might just be a pawn in all of this. Since I left you at the motel earlier, a lot has been brought to my attention. I think I was lied to, by my own superior. Lawson, I'm not sure the FBI wants you to rejoin them, I think they might want you dead.

Lawson's stomach turned. He walked out of the closet, flipped on the bedside lamp, and took a seat on the edge of the bed, steeling himself before he continued reading Cassie's words.

When they brought me in on this, it was only to ensure your release. I think they tried to get to you while you were in prison, I'm just not sure. But I guess if they did, you took out the men they had make an attempt on your life. Anyway, from what I'm gathering, since they couldn't get to you in there, they thought it would be easier while you were free. I say "they," but it might just be one man.

Lawson's muscles clenched. He flashed to a couple of the run-ins he had in prison where the men were more skilled than he thought made sense. This could explain it. And from what he could remember, those same men were released not long after they came at him. It was all written in his notebook. This was the reason he had made such detailed notes. Every time something seemed a little off in prison, he wrote it down. Adding names to his ever growing list. His blood pressure shot through the roof, and he began to grind his teeth as he continued reading.

I couldn't believe someone in the FBI might want you dead. There is a lot going on that I didn't know about. I'm sorry. They kept me in the dark. Some powerful people must be working together on this. People I thought I could trust. They haven't given me any information. But I heard chatter that Kevin Watson has been pulled in from the field. I don't think anyone was supposed to know, but I've been having my tech guy, Troy, notify me when anyone fishy comes to Las

Vegas. Lawson, I don't know a lot about Watson, but the story told about him is that he takes care of "messes" like you for a living for the FBI.

I'll do my best to keep you as informed as I can, but if he is really coming here for you, you have to leave. Right now. I know a condition of your pardon doesn't allow you to leave the state for another six months, but you have to leave the country. And I know all you want to do is find out what happened to Lauren and get back to Lexi, but that will have to wait until we can figure something else out. I've made a lot of friends in Vegas. One of my former informants is the best at paperwork. He is expecting you, tonight. He'll be able to get you every document you need to change your identity and get out of here. Once you're safe somewhere, you can find a way to contact me and we can try to figure out why the FBI, or someone in it, wants you erased.

Lawson, I know you, and I know you don't want to wait to find out who killed Lauren. But you've waited ten years, we can figure this out, so you can wait a little longer. Don't be your usual stubborn self. This is not a game. From everything I've ever heard, Watson is deadly. So GET OUT OF HERE. I was able to leave some money and a burner phone for you at your room I got for you for the night at the Flamingo. There is a key for room 223 and an address for my informant, Jeremy, so you can get your new passport, hidden behind the ice machine on that floor.

I'll do my best to contact you again if I hear anything, but I hope when I try you're already gone.

I love you, Lawson, you are like my brother. If there was any other way, we would do this. But there isn't.

Be safe.

Lawson stared blankly at Cassie's letter. It was as if

someone had hit the pause button on his mind. He tried a deep breath, but the words on the page in front of him scrambled. He blinked a couple of times to bring them back into focus. His eyes returned to form, but his brain was still on a break. On autopilot, he stood from the bed and walked out to the minibar. He found another minibottle of bourbon, unscrewed the cap, and downed it in one swig.

As the alcohol burned its way down his throat, just as he had hoped, it felt like someone hit the reset button on his brain, and slowly it rebooted, returning his thoughts to him. He knew he had to dust the cobwebs off his old detective mind and get to work. He walked over to the window and stared down at the lights. What in the hell could the FBI possibly have against a man who had been locked up for the last ten years? And according to Cassie, what they thought he knew, or the threat they thought he posed, had to be important enough to want him dead. As the bourbon settled into Lawson's bloodstream, his mind drifted to the notebook. If there was any chance for him to understand what it was the FBI was trying to protect, it would be in there. One of the ways that Lawson curtailed his boredom, as he spent nearly every waking moment in his cell, was to write in the notebook. And most of what he wrote were notes about conversations he had with other inmates. He never knew what he might need to remember in order to take advantage of someone in that prison, so he made notes. Nothing of incredible importance ever really stuck out to him that he could remember offhand, but there were years' worth of notes in there. It was his only chance to understand how he could help himself out of this apparently life-threatening situation.

Lawson turned from the window and made his way to the closet. He tried to flip through the pages of the notebook in his mind as he went to it, hoping something would jump out at him. But it was useless. It was going to take some digging to find something, if there was anything to be found in there at all.

Somewhere at the back of his brain, thrumming all the way down to the bottom of his spine, was a strange sensation. A distant vibration. One that was sending signals to his mind's eye. Faces flashed in front of his eyes. Faces attached to the names he had written on his list. The list of who was to blame.

Faces, plural.

That vibrating sensation began to tingle. And it felt familiar. It was the tingle of his detective mind picking up on a clue. For the first time since he started dreaming of revenge all those years ago, there wasn't just one shadowy silhouette staring at the end of his gun. There were a few.

All that had happened to him and his family may very well be the work of one puppet master, but that still meant that there were a lot of puppets. And just like that, the names on his list took on a whole new meaning.

They weren't just a list of individuals.

They were all working together.

12

LAWSON'S MIND WAS RUNNING IN OVERDRIVE. HE HAD TO SEE those names again. He wanted to look at them in this newfound light. A lot of things were jumbling in his head, but one thing had become crystal clear. If the FBI, or someone in the FBI, wanted him dead, it wasn't because of what happened in prison. It wasn't even because of what happened to Lauren. This started long before all of that. But he had made notes about that too. At the time, he thought he was being crazy. He thought he was turning into a conspiracy theorist. And now he remembered bringing it up to Cassie years ago, and she had thought the same thing. Turns out, his first instinct may have been right. It had to be.

With the buzz of a case coming together, Lawson punched in the four-digit code to open the safe. And just as he was reaching in to pick up the notebook, starting to put everything together in his mind, he heard a distant click behind him. It was faint, but it sounded like the hotel room door in the other room. Lawson moved his reach from the notebook to the stainless steel Beretta 92FS that had been left for him by De Luca. He wanted to shut the safe but couldn't risk the sound it would make. He darted across the hall into the bathroom. He pushed the door behind him to where it was only open a couple of inches, then moved quickly over to the large walk-in glass shower and turned on the water as hot as it would go.

With the rushing of the water in the shower to conceal the sound, Lawson performed a press check, making sure the Beretta had one in the chamber. He then removed his blazer and rolled up his sleeves. The steam from the hot shower began to encompass the large bathroom. Most importantly, it fogged the large mirror opposite the bathroom door entirely. This would allow Lawson to wait behind the door without being seen by whoever would be opening it.

As he waited, he tuned his ears. He hadn't heard anything since that faint click a few moments ago. For all he knew, it could have been one of the maids checking his Do Not Disturb sign or someone mistakenly realizing they were at the wrong room. But with what seemed to be half of Las Vegas after him, he certainly couldn't take that chance. It had been a long time since he found himself holding a pistol, awaiting the move of a potential target. The weight of the Beretta felt good in his hands. All the battles he had been in recently had only involved his fists and of course the occasional makeshift prison weapon. He used to be an expert with a handgun. He hoped it would be like riding a bike. And while he wasn't bad at hand-to-hand combat before being locked up, he would now put his fighting skills against any man in the world. If his gun skills did come back to him, he figured that would make him about as formidable as anyone that could be after him.

That's when the next thought slapped him across the face.

Those skills would make him about as formidable as anyone . . .

Anyone but a professional hit man for the FBI.

The bathroom door began to inch open. The safe move would be to kill whoever was walking through that door as quickly as possible. The problem with that was that dead men can't talk. He would be safe for now, but if Lawson killed the intruder, he wouldn't get any information as to who sent him and why. It would be short-term gain at a long-term loss.

A flood of adrenaline released into his veins as he watched the tip of a black pistol make its way around the door into the steamy mist wafting from the shower. Lawson already knew he had gotten lucky. He knew immediately that this was not a man trained or hired by the FBI. He wouldn't have made a sound at the front door if it was, and he wouldn't be this sloppy coming into the bathroom.

Lawson stepped forward, reached for the wrist holding the gun, and locked it in a death grip. As he forced it toward the wall, the trigger was squeezed and a bullet blasted into the mirror. Shards of glass shattered to the marble floor. Lawson slammed the gun hand against the wall, and the sound of the gunshot in that small space jammed a sharp pain in his ears. The gun fell to the floor, and without turning around, Lawson fired an elbow directly behind him, and the force from the blow to the gunman's nose knocked him onto his back out into the bedroom.

While it was good for Lawson's health that it hadn't been a professional hit man, he also couldn't completely relax. Sure, he'd already bested whoever this was, but small-time criminals like this gunman rarely traveled solo. That's why when Lawson stepped out into the hallway of the bedroom, over the top of the unconscious man sent there to kill him, he already had his gun raised and his finger on the trigger. He squeezed it twice when another man entered the room from the door in front of him on his left. Two bullets in his chest, another man down.

Lawson trained the barrel of his gun straight down toward the unconscious man's head. The man's nose was steadily leaking blood from the impact of Lawson's elbow. He kicked the man's leg, trying to rouse him from the depths of the temporary blackness he was experiencing, while keeping his ears tuned to the adjacent room for another possible attacker. The man lying below him was fairly big, dark hair, wearing a black sport coat. Without hearing the man's accent, it was impossible to know if it was one of Sokolov's men or De Luca's. Lawson stepped over into the closet and checked his phone. He didn't have any messages from Johnny, but that didn't necessarily mean anything either. If this was retaliation from De Luca for the way Lawson had treated Johnny earlier, Johnny wouldn't have texted a heads-up. And if it was Sokolov's men, Johnny wouldn't have known to give him a heads-up text anyway.

Lawson noticed a black duffel bag on the floor to his right. He gathered a few of the wearable clothes that were hanging around him, a pair of sneakers, some sweats, and threw them in the bag. He added his notebook and a stack of cash, readied the Beretta, and walked out of the closet to the man on the floor groaning into consciousness.

Lawson set the bag down and took a knee beside him. He pressed the muzzle of the pistol forcefully into the middle of the man's forehead.

Lawson said, "One, if you lie to me, I pull the trigger."

The man's eyes popped open, wide as half-dollars. Lawson spoke again before the man had a chance.

"Two, if there is another man here with you, other than the man I just put two bullets in, and you don't let me know right now, I pull the trigger."

The man jerked his head back to look behind him. He caught a glimpse of his dead partner just before Lawson grabbed him by the hair and brought his focus back to him.

"He is only one, I swear!" the man said with a Russian accent and a nose stuffed with blood.

One of Sokolov's men.

"Good, you already have the hang of this."

Lawson rose to his feet and gestured by flicking the gun upward for the Russian man to do the same. Lawson knew he didn't have a lot of time. At this point the gunshots had been reported, and at the very least, hotel security would already be on their way to the suite.

"Who sent you?"

The man looked down at his feet, hesitating, shaking his head. Lawson shot him in the foot. As the man dropped to the floor, wailing in pain, Lawson took a step forward and once again placed the gun to the man's head.

"And here I thought you understood how this worked. Let me be clear. The next bullet goes into a much more life-altering place. Who sent you?"

The man started to look down again but immediately jerked his head back up and looked Lawson in the eyes.

"Evelyn Delaney."

13

EVELYN DELANEY PULLED UP TO THE MANSION, THE GATE opened, and she pulled into the secluded driveway. It was just a few blocks from the Strip, but once inside the gate it may as well have been another zip code. That was the only reason she had ever entertained having a meeting here. The district attorney could hardly be seen anywhere near the vicinity of a crime boss's mansion and still maintain her professional credibility. She continued driving to the end of the driveway where she stopped and put her Ferrari in park. She reached for the passenger seat and pulled her Chanel lipstick from her new Louis Vuitton handbag. She reached up and adjusted the rearview mirror so that her face—lips—were in view. She traced the lines of her lips with the bright red lipstick, her usual color of choice. It didn't hurt that it matched the cherry red of her car and the bottoms of her Louboutin heels. It was also the power color, and that turned her on as much as any man had in years.

Her cell phone rang—her old pal Phil Walters, chief of the Las Vegas Police Department. Unlikely friends, unless of course you know the genesis of their relationship. They were nothing alike and would never run in the same circles. Evelyn had far more class than that. But when you come together for a common goal, things you don't have in common tend to become less important. And tonight, their common goal, after ten years of quiet, had once again reared his ugly head.

"Chief Walters," Evelyn answered. "Don't tell me you have more important things to do tonight."

"Hello, Evelyn. No, nothing like that, I'm on my way. I just wanted to make sure we are on the same page before our meeting."

"We don't need a same page to be on, I've already taken care of everything," Evelyn said, full of confidence.

"And just why don't I like the sound of that?"

"Because you worry too much. And while men like you sit around and worry, women like me get things done. See you in a few, darling."

Evelyn ended the call. She knew her decision to go ahead and rectify their little problem wasn't going to be a popular one. But as long as the problem was gone, she didn't really care. Ultimately, she knew they wouldn't care either in the long run. She watched as a large man in a suit approached her car. As with every time she had come there for a meeting, she waited, as instructed, for one of the guards to come and escort her in.

The car door opened. "Ms. Delaney." The man held out his hand.

Evelyn took it, and he helped her from the vehicle.

"Right this way, ma'am."

She followed behind the man as he walked her toward the back entrance to the mansion. They stepped inside a doorway, then he immediately walked her over to the elevator. She stepped inside and when the elevator doors closed, she adjusted her red dress in the reflection of the mirrored wall to her left. She was never the prettiest of women, but power has a way of making you look gorgeous.

The door dinged and opened to the elaborate library-style office, and she was greeted by another large man—his hair more slicked back than the last—and escorted through the walkway of shelved books on either side. The shelving gave way to a sitting area, a table encircled by couches and chairs, and beyond that a large desk in front of her on the back wall. Four men stood on each side of the desk, each more intimidating than the next. A man in a suit behind the desk spread his arms, wearing a charismatic smile.

"Evelyn Delaney. It's been too long. Welcome."

"Nero. You look well," Evelyn told him. She then glanced at the men on both sides of his desk. "Some things never change, I see."

"You can never be too careful." Nero waved his arm toward a door on the wall behind him, and immediately all the men in the room exited, except one. "You've met my son?"

Evelyn stepped forward, her hand stretched toward the handsome young man beside Nero. "I don't believe I've had the pleasure."

"Johnny De Luca," he said, turning her hand over and giving it a chivalrous kiss.

Evelyn smiled. "The apple doesn't fall far, I see."

Johnny smiled. Nero De Luca rounded his desk and embraced Evelyn with a hug.

"You look lovely as always, Evelyn. Shall we?"

Nero gestured toward the sitting area. Evelyn followed him there.

"A drink?" Johnny asked.

"Vodka. Thank you."

Evelyn took a seat as Johnny poured her a drink. Nero poured himself a whiskey in front of her. The elevator dinged again, and when it opened, a large black man walked into the room. Evelyn hardly noticed him out of his police uniform.

"Getting started without me?"

Nero stood, and Evelyn stood along with him to greet the man.

"Johnny, you can go now. This is grown-up business." Nero said, completely dismissing his son. "Chief Walters," Nero said. The two men shook hands.

"Hello, Nero," Chief Walters said, then nodded toward Evelyn. "Evelyn."

Nero gestured for the two of them to sit. Evelyn remained standing.

She finished her vodka in one drink. "Sitting won't be necessary," she said. "I've already taken care of our little problem. I just wanted to give you the courtesy of telling you in person."

Nero De Luca and Chief Walters shared a glance.

"I grew tired of waiting for the two of you to take care of him. Chief, how many times did you try while he was in prison? Three?" She looked over at De Luca. "And you, did you ever try? Or were you too busy using him to further your agenda, having him take out your enemies' men? I'm sure I don't need to remind you what would happen to all of us if he were to put together what really happened."

Nero ignored her last few statements.

"What do you mean you took care of him, Evelyn?"

"Just what I said. I sent two men to kill him at the hotel suite you put him up in."

Nero shook his head.

"That wasn't what we discussed, Evelyn," Chief Walters said.

"No it isn't." She was direct. "I listened to both of your convoluted versions of how we should handle the pardon of Lawson Raines, and both of you failed to understand that we couldn't let him get started on what surely was the only thing the man thought of for ten years. Killing whoever was responsible for the murder of his wife. Something we never should have been involved in anyway, but we let you sway us, Nero."

"Let me sway you?" Nero stood, his debonair demeanor turned sour. "You saw your money train"—he pointed to himself—"was in danger of running dry, so you went along very quickly with keeping him from finishing the case he was building against my father. If he and his partner would have been able to take him down, your pretty little car parked outside, your beautiful home, and your closet full of things, I'm sure, like that purse and those shoes would never have happened."

Evelyn waved him away with her hand. "Either way, it's taken care of."

Nero's demeanor turned even darker. "I told you I needed him. I had everything under control. I was going to use him to put all of us in an even more advantageous position. And you're telling me that you went on your own"—he made air quotes with his fingers—"and 'took care of it'?"

Nero picked up his phone. "Johnny, get back in here. Now."

Nero didn't say anything while they waited for Johnny to

make it back to them. He just stared a hole through Evelyn. After an awfully long awkward silence, the door to his office finally opened.

"Yeah, dad?

"Johnny, call Lawson. Tell him I need to meet with him right away." He looked back to Evelyn. "You better hope he isn't dead."

"Or what, De Luca? You going to hurt me, right here in front of the chief of police?"

Nero took two steps toward her and looked her dead in the eyes. "No, Evelyn, if Lawson doesn't answer that phone, I'm going to kill you."

14

"EVELYN DELANEY," THE GUNMAN HAD SAID. LAWSON contemplated this as he crossed Las Vegas Boulevard on his way to the Flamingo Hotel. He had managed to walk into the elevator at Caesar's just as security was on its way to investigate the gunshots in his room.

Hearing Evelyn's name wasn't a total shock. After all, she had been as responsible as anyone for him being sent to prison. However, hearing her name out of a man's mouth who had been hired by her to kill him was a bit shocking. How deep does this thing run? The only reason someone in her position would get involved with killers for hire would be because she had a secret that she wanted to keep hidden. But as far as Lawson knew, she was just doing her job by pinning Lauren's murder on him. Why would she want him dead?

It had always been suspicious to Lawson that she never uncovered anything that would exonerate him. If she had been good at her job at all, she would have seen that he had nothing to do with Lauren's murder. But that is why Lawson had added her name to the list. He didn't think she had direct involvement with putting him away, but now that she had tried to have him killed, he was going to have to rethink that stance.

Lawson walked into the lobby of the Flamingo and headed straight for the elevators. He got off on the second floor and found the ice machine/snack room. He opened the door, set his bag down beside the vending machine, and knelt down beside it. The door handle moved behind him, and he slammed his foot against the door, not allowing it to open. Through the fogged glass he could see the outline of a woman trying to enter.

"Hey, come on. I need some ice." She knocked a couple more times. "Come on, let me in!"

Lawson just held his foot in place.

"Are you passed out in there?" The woman huffed, "Vegas." And then she walked off.

Lawson squeezed in between the vending and ice machines. No small feat for a man his size. He reached as far back as he could and ran his fingers along the back wall. After a few inches, his hand found what he was searching for. Cassie had indeed taken care of him. He got back to his feet with the key to room 223 in his hand.

He heard a knock at the door again. "Hey, asshole." It was the ice lady again. "I brought my boyfriend this time. I suggest you open the door so we can get some ice."

God forbid princess doesn't have ice in her vodka soda. Lawson picked up his bag and opened the door. When he did, both the woman and the man took two steps back. Lawson towered over them.

"We . . . we can come back," the man said, looking up at Lawson.

Lawson took a step forward, and both of them backed up

even farther. His cell phone began to ring. After another moment of holding the couple's frightened glare, he turned and headed down the hallway toward his room. The two of them didn't bother pushing the envelope. He was glad, because he didn't need anyone else raising suspicion about his presence. He pulled his phone from his pocket, and the caller ID said Johnny De Luca. Lawson had other things on his mind at the moment, and another conversation with Junior wasn't on his radar. He ignored the call and swapped the phone for the room key.

Lawson opened the door and immediately felt this room was more his speed. It was a much smaller square room, two queen beds, a dresser with a TV, and a small desk near the door. It felt more like home. He knew this was an odd thought, but it was true. He was used to confined. He set his duffel bag on the bed, and finally he had a chance to take another look at the notebook. He flipped through the pages to the very back. Back to the page that he'd spent hours staring at. Thousands of hours. The only thing on the page was a list of names. Five of them, to be exact. But it was the last name on the list that he had always felt guilty for writing.

Cassie Foster.

His partner and friend.

The first time he considered writing her name on his list of possible people who had tried to bury him, he immediately hit the floor and did another two hundred push-ups. Even he knew it was an outrageous thought. But sometimes all the mind needs is a seed. Once that seed has been planted, the detective brain has a nurturing way of watering that seed with terrible thoughts, and before you know it, you've grown a tree of doubt. Complete with long hanging branches strong enough to tie a rope and hang yourself.

As he stared at her name on the page, Lawson thought about what happened earlier. How it had been so easy for her to lie to him. Had meeting him at the rundown motel been a way to gauge where his head was? A way to get him to trust her so he would tell her everything, so she could find a moment to bury him for good? Is that why she brought a picture of Lexi? Is that why at the bar she pointed out Johnny, then slipped him the note, ensuring that he in fact would trust his old partner and only his old partner?

Seed planted.

Terrible thoughts watering it.

The tree of doubt was on the rise.

The only thing Lawson knew for 100 percent fact was that he himself was the only person in the world he could trust. And that being the case, everyone else would have to be suspected. And if everyone is a suspect, he had to take precautions to make sure that even Cassie wouldn't give him up.

Lawson heard a woman laugh through the walls. Probably the ice queen.

Ice.

Lawson shut his notebook, grabbed the silver ice bucket beside the bathroom sink, and walked down the hall. He checked both ends of the long hallway, making sure he knew where the elevators and exits were. The ice queen from earlier had given him an idea, so he went and filled the ice bucket. On his way back to his room, he knocked on the door beside his, the one that shared the adjoining door inside. He gave it a few seconds, and when no one answered, he went back to his room.

He pulled the armless desk chair over beside his door, then placed the overflowing ice bucket on the very edge of the seat. So much on the edge that it teetered over a couple of times and he had to reset it, ensuring that even the slightest knock against it would send a loud crash to the carpet below. Then he made certain that if the door happened to be opened, even if done extremely slowly, the bucket would fall from the chair. It was no high-tech ADT security system, but it would do the trick.

So he hoped.

15

FOUR A.M. IN VEGAS WASN'T LIKE MOST OTHER CITIES. Ninety-nine percent of other places in the world, the people were almost all rolled up in bed. Here, a lot of people were just catching their third wind. So it seemed quiet on the second floor of the Flamingo Hotel. Sure, Lawson heard the occasional slamming door, bass reverberating from the walls of a room a few doors down, and the occasional drunken singing as a successful night of partying staggered down the hallway past his room. But all things considered, not much noise at all.

That's why it was incredibly easy to hear the ice bucket fall from the chair and slam onto the floor. Lawson squeezed the Beretta in his hand. He of course had hoped that no one would come for him in the night. Especially since there was supposedly only one person in the world who knew he was there. If the doubt tree about Cassie had been growing earlier, it was now a full-grown redwood. He heard four silenced bullets being shot into what he supposed were the pillows he'd made look like someone sleeping in his bed. So he pushed the anguish of realizing his only friend had turned on him out of the way and kicked in the adjoining door going back into his room.

Before the man that had just tried to shoot him could fully turn to face him, Lawson smashed him in the forehead with the butt of his pistol. The gunman's finger involuntarily squeezed the trigger, and dropping unconscious, he shot a bullet into the bed beside him. Lawson immediately took a knee on the floor next to the gunman, and after a search turned up only a tactical knife, zero identification, no money, not even a stick of gum, he knew this was a professional.

Cassie had turned on him.

She must have. Cassie was the only person that could have told this man about this room.

He sat back against the bed behind him. His stomach was in knots. How could she do this to him? And why? Why would she do this to him? Memories flashed in front of his mind. The first time he'd met her. The way she shook his hand as she made fun of his tie. To the time they made their first collar, and the way they'd gotten hammered drunk at the Golden Nugget to celebrate. To Lexi's birth and how Cassie had been so happy to see her in that hospital, and the way she took care of Lauren in those first couple of weeks.

Lawson thought the people who had done all of this to him had taken every ounce of hurt out of him. But there is always more. This pain was as bad as any he had experienced, and he had experienced a lot. Anger swelled inside of him.

Rage.

There were no more tears to be shed.

Only blood.

Lawson tucked his Beretta into his pants and hoisted the

hit man up onto the bed. He removed the sheets from the second queen bed and tied the man's arms to the bedpost. He then went to the bathroom, grabbed a towel, soaked it in water, then took it and laid it over the unconscious man's face. He removed the shoelaces from the extra pair of oxfords he'd packed in his bag and tightly tied down the top of the towel over the man's forehead and the bottom of the towel at the top of the man's neck. That way when he was doing everything he could do to escape the water flooding his mouth and nostrils, the towel wouldn't budge.

Lawson went and filled the ice bucket with water, then the plastic trash can from the bathroom, and finally the wastebasket from the room, and set them all on the night-stand, keeping them within arm's reach. As he slapped the man in the face, trying to rouse him, he heard music start up and laughter coming from the nonadjoined room next to him. What a completely different night they were experiencing.

What a different experience this was for Lawson as well. He would never have been doing something like this ten years ago. In fact, he may have even had a problem with torture being performed at all. But as he already knew, and was finding out more and more the longer he was free, he couldn't be further from the man he used to be. Was that easygoing guy still inside him somewhere? As he slapped the man under the wet towel again, he couldn't imagine that he was. The old Lawson Raines was dead.

As soon as the man whimpered, Lawson grabbed the ice bucket of water and slowly poured it over the towel as he sat on the man's legs, clutching his jaw in his hand so he couldn't move. The man writhed and choked on the water, desperately gasping for air. The thing about waterboarding is, you can only exhale for so long. And once your lungs are empty, the body automatically sucks for air. And when all that is there is water, it is as painful a few seconds as a man can experience. So much so that Lawson knew he wouldn't be needing that third container of water. This man—any man —would tap out before then. The only reason some people say that torture doesn't work is because a man will say anything to keep from having that water poured down his nose and throat again. So the information could be a total lie. But Lawson already had a good idea of what the truth was, so as long as this man's story was close enough to confirm it, he would end the torture.

The man jerked and bucked under Lawson. But Lawson held his head still. The man sent there to kill him took every ounce of water meant for him.

"You can make this stop," Lawson said in a calm and calculated tone. "All you have to do is tell me exactly who sent you. Nothing more."

The man continued to choke on the water, until finally the ice bucket was empty. Lawson released his grip on the man's jaw and removed the towel. After the man violently spat water, gasped for air, and finally took a breath, Lawson gave him a little reminder.

"Now that you know what I want, just know that the trash can holds a lot more water than the ice bucket. Now's not the time for games."

16

_____

THE MAN LOOKED AT LAWSON IN A WAY LAWSON COULDN'T believe. He looked surprised that Lawson could possibly be doing this to him. Like *he* was the bad guy, even though this hit man meant for Lawson to already be dead.

"I don't hear you telling me what I want to hear," Lawson growled.

"You're crazy, man. I am FBI! You can't do this!"

"I didn't hear an answer to my question, so I'll assume you're still thirsty."

Lawson covered the man's face again with the wet towel and tied the towel down. The man was screaming now. If not for the towel dampening the sound and the music playing next door, there was little question that someone would have heard him.

"What I asked you was very simple. Who sent you? And just so you know"—Lawson picked up the trash can filled with water and began pouring it over the man's covered face —"if you think this torture isn't worthy of someone who just came in my room and tried to kill me, you'd better keep that to yourself. Because if I see that same judgmental face again when I remove this towel, I'll use your knife to cut your balls off and feed them to you. Because that's what you really deserve."

As Lawson spoke to the man getting his holes filled with water, he wasn't sure the man had even heard him. Not that it mattered. Lawson would have his answer after this second bucket. He was certain of that. The water poured slowly over the man's face. His struggle against it was becoming weak. He had had enough. Lawson placed the bucket back on the nightstand, untied the towel, and sat back, waiting for the man to clear his airways, waiting for the man to clear the air.

Sure enough, between deep inhales and coughs, the FBI hit man wasted no more time outing who hired him. "Director Adam Billings."

Lawson's mind's eye immediately saw that name written on the list in his notebook. However, Adam Billings was merely the head of the Las Vegas FBI ten years ago.

"Director?"

Cough. Cough. "Yes. The head of the FBI. Please don't pour any more water on me. Please! That's all I know. This wasn't sanctioned by my handler. And I was told to tell no one. As far as I know, Director Billings and I are the only ones who know. I'm sorry. I'm just doing my job. You know how it is. I swear—"

"Stop talking," Lawson interrupted.

The man closed his mouth immediately and nodded emphatically. Lawson got up from the bed and paced the room. This information wasn't surprising to him, but the secrecy of it was. This meant that this was personal for Adam Billings, but Billings and Lawson had always gotten along. Lawson and Cassie were helping Billings make a name for himself with the good work they were doing. And why would Cassie tell Billings where to find him? Why would she set him up?

Lawson stopped pacing and looked the hit man dead in the eyes. "I have one more question. If you answer it honestly, I'll let you go."

The man began nodding even before Lawson had the chance to finish his sentence. At this point this man would tell Lawson all the classified information he'd ever come across. He just didn't want any more water.

"Is Cassie Foster involved?"

There was zero hesitation. "Who? I've never heard of her. I swear. I would tell you if I had."

Lawson believed him. When a question catches a man off guard, it's hard for him to hide knowledge of the subject. And when Lawson said Cassie's name, if this guy knew of her, it would have registered on his face. But it hadn't. Lawson took a minute, walked over to the window, and though his eyes were looking out, he only saw the problem at hand. He was now sitting directly in the middle of a moral crossroad.

This man had been sent there to kill him. But this man isn't a criminal. He is trained in much the same way that Lawson had been. Probably started as a cop, then maybe a detective, then the FBI sent him to Quantico where he learned to be a well-rounded agent, then possibly some more stealth training, specializing in tracking. He may or may not have a family. A man like him is on the road a lot, doing a lot of secretive things, so that does make a relationship difficult but not impossible. The hardest part about this was that this man, like he said, was just doing his job.

It was Director Billings who had stepped over the line.

If Lawson killed this FBI agent, he was drawing a line in the sand. One which once crossed, he could never go back. In his own mind at least. Lawson had been a prisoner for ten years, but he wasn't a criminal. Never had been. And he would be damned if he let these people who are after him turn him into one. Even as he had that thought, he realized its hypocrisy. He did just torture a man for information. But the man was fine now, already breathing normally, no long-term effects, except the conviction that if he ever crossed paths with Lawson again, he would more than likely steer clear.

Lawson looked back at the man tied to the bed. The man pleaded with his eyes for Lawson not to kill him. But he knew that now was not the time to speak. Lawson looked back out the window. This time he saw the lights on the High Roller Ferris wheel spinning against the black of night. He imagined this is what his brain looked like at the moment, swirling inside as he contemplated what kind of man he was going to be. This was the moment that would shape the rest of his life. And instead of seeing the sheets under this man filled with blood, he saw Lauren's face. He often thought about what she would think of him now. She would probably have understood why he had to become what he did in prison. It was a matter of survival. But she would be disappointed in him if he carried it into the real world. She wouldn't want what happened to her to turn him into a monster on the outside. She would want him to forget all of this and do whatever he could to work his way back into their daughter's life.

But she also didn't find the love of her life lying dead on the deck of a boat.

Lauren didn't have Lexi ripped away from her like he had.

And Lauren wasn't blamed for something that she would never have done in a million lifetimes.

Still, there was a line. And as furious as Lawson was at this man for trying to kill him, an action that would have ultimately taken him from his daughter for good, it was a line he couldn't cross. Lawson wasn't willing to live up to what he thought Lauren would want as far as letting everything go. But he couldn't deny her voice when it came to killing this man. Her voice may very well be the only conscience he had left. She always was a better person than he was anyway, so he knew he should probably listen to her.

17

THE SUN HAD BEGUN ITS ASCENT INTO THE CLEAR LAS VEGAS sky. It had still been dark when Lawson finished his five-mile run down Las Vegas Boulevard, but as he did the last of his four hundred push-ups, streaks of light worked their way around the curtain against the far wall of his hotel room. His new hotel room at Bally's just across the street from the Flamingo. After Lawson let the FBI hit man go free, he knew he couldn't hang around the same hotel. And after checking into his new room, he also couldn't sleep. Thoughts of his daughter, his beloved dead wife, and all the people that seemed to be working together to betray him kept churning through his mind. For him, there were really only two ways to work through those types of thoughts: exercise, or drowning them with drinks. The latter wasn't an option, because today, more than any other day in his life, he needed clarity.

Lawson finished his shower and took a seat at the end of the bed. The run helped him organize his thoughts from a jumbled mess, but he still had little clarity. He grabbed the notebook beside him and once again flipped to the last page. He needed a place to start, and this list of names would help. The first name on the list was Tony De Luca. Father of Nero. This was the most obvious place to start, it always had been. He knew that it couldn't have been a coincidence that as he and Cassie were closing in on Tony and his operations ten years ago, everything went haywire. And even though it was obvious that the De Luca family had every reason in the world to do something about Lawson, he never fully suspected Tony of masterminding the crimes against Lawson and his family, because he would have had no idea that Lawson had been so close to nailing him all those years ago.

However, now that it was clear that Billings, Lawson's former superior and now the head of the FBI, wanted him dead, Billings could have also informed Tony De Luca that they were close to bringing Lawson down. It was really the only thing that made sense, but why would a man who was clearly ascending the ranks of the FBI feed De Luca information? Lawson had never been naive, he knew that money rules the world, but he never saw Billings as that type of man. But could he even trust his own radar anymore? His partner and best friend hadn't seemed the type either, but now he just didn't know. And the thought of her also being against him made him nauseous.

Lawson got dressed in his all-black attire once again, fitted the Beretta in the back of his belt line, and began to brew a small pot of coffee. He needed a place to get started today, and while all he wanted to do was go and take out his rage on everyone that ever worked for the De Lucas, he wouldn't be able to do anything until he knew for sure whether or not Cassie was his enemy. He pulled his phone from his pocket, the one De Luca had given him. He left the one from Cassie at the Flamingo for obvious reasons. He grabbed the phone book in the dresser drawer, found the number he was looking for, and dialed it.

He knew it was a long shot, but he literally had no one else in the world that he could try.

"High Desert State Prison, how may I direct your call?" a female voice answered.

"John Simpson, please."

"Is he in the office or in the prison?"

"He's a guard."

"I'll page him, whom shall I say is calling?"

Lawson smiled to himself. "The next UFC champ."

"Whatever you say. Please hold."

As the coffee continued to brew and Lawson waited for John to come on the line, he grabbed the remote and flipped on the television. Four terrible commercials later, the line clicked over.

"Lawson? Is this really you?"

"It is. You miss me?"

"Miss you? With all these wonderfully engaging people surrounding me all day, how could I?"

"I need your help."

While it was good to hear a familiar voice, Lawson didn't have time to waste.

"Uh-oh. I don't like the sound of that."

"It's nothing big," Lawson explained, "I just want to get a hold of my old partner in the FBI. Go see her actually. Any way you can find out where she lives?"

"Did you google her?"

"I don't have access to a computer."

"You have a phone, don't you?"

Lawson paused for a moment, pulling the phone from his ear and looking at it.

"Lawson? You still there?"

He put the phone back to his ear. "This thing has internet, doesn't it?"

"Sure does, it is 2018, ya know. But that doesn't mean it will show her address. I'm close with some people at the police department. Let me make a call. Give me your number and I'll call you back."

Once again, Lawson stopped and looked at his iPhone. Clueless. "I have no idea what this number is."

"How'd you get the phone? You sure I should be looking up this address for you? You're not going to get me in any trouble, are you?"

"I won't. Can you help me out?"

John walked Lawson through the steps for how to see what his own phone number was. Then John sent him a text from his cell phone so Lawson would have his personal number. They ended the call, and just as Lawson was walking over to get a cup of coffee, he heard the words "District Attorney Evelyn Delaney" on the television. When he glanced over, the video on the television was of a crime scene. Lawson rushed over to the remote and upped the volume.

Police Chief Phillip Walters confirmed just a few moments ago that it was in fact the body of District Attorney Evelyn Delaney that was found by a jogger just over an hour ago. There are no further details at this time as to cause of death or suspects, but she was found dead in a ditch just outside her home in palatial Falcon Ridge. Chief Walters said he will be holding a press conference later this afternoon to give a statement about this tragic apparent murder.

Lawson stared blankly at the television. He couldn't believe what he was seeing. Just a few hours ago he had a hired gunman tell him that Evelyn Delaney wanted him dead, and now it was her who had been killed. This couldn't be a coincidence. Lawson's old detective senses were tingling. But he didn't have time to indulge them because the reporter once again grabbed his attention when she moved on to her next story.

Chief Walters also gave a brief statement about what happened at Caesar's Palace last night, saying, "It is confirmed that there was in fact a shooting in one of the suites last night. Two people were killed. We do have video of the suspect leaving the scene . . . "

Lawson's stomach dropped. He knew exactly what was coming next, and when he saw video on the TV of him entering the elevator at Caesar's Palace, it confirmed to him that yet another one of the names on his list, Chief Phillip Walters, was in fact in on everything that happened ten years ago. It was the only way they would have shown Lawson so quickly to the public.

"His name is Lawson Raines. He is six-foot-four, two hundred and thirty pounds. If you see him, consider him armed and very dangerous. We do have reason to believe that the murder of DA Delaney and the shooting at Caesar's Palace are connected. That's all I can tell you at this time."

So much for his new hotel room.

The screen flashed back to the reporter, and this time there was a still photo of Lawson's old mugshot over her right shoulder. Fortunately for him, that was ten years, a longer haircut, and about thirty pounds less muscle ago, so the photo didn't look exactly like him. Lawson knew the reason they used his mugshot was because the one taken at

Caesar's Palace when he got on that elevator would have been indistinguishable. Lawson knew there was a camera recording him, so he had kept his head down in case someone was looking. He also knew that it would be just a matter of time before they pulled another, better image off another camera that he passed last night. Once that photo was out, he would have a hard time *not* being noticed. So he needed to work fast.

Lawson turned off the TV and stood quiet for a moment, staring at his dark reflection on the blank screen. He was really in a tight spot now. He should have listened to Cassie. He should have gone to see her contact to get new paper-work. He should have never indulged his thirst for revenge, there were just too many people working against him. He had always thought so, but now he knew for sure. And now all of Las Vegas would be on the lookout for him. He had blown his chance to get his daughter back. He would never be able to get out of these new crimes they were accusing him of. Chief Walters had too many people in his corner to cover up what really happened to Delaney, and he would pin it on Lawson. That was obviously what was going on. In no investigation would you tie two seemingly completely different crimes, like the shooting in his suite and Evelyn Delaney's murder, together. They would need to gather much more substantial evidence. But when the chief of police has an agenda, like he did against Lawson, and you want someone found, this is exactly what you do: you get the entire city looking for him.

Lawson's only defense if he got apprehended would be that everyone was setting him up, but who would ever believe that? He had zero evidence. And there was no way he could find a way to prove it to anyone. And anyway, unless it was irrefutable proof, no one would believe a convicted murderer over the chief of police. Pardon or no pardon. The case that Walters was building against Lawson now would just confirm to everyone that he was guilty not only of these new crimes but the murder of his wife as well.

He was done.

18

LAWSON TOOK A DEEP BREATH, CRACKED HIS NECK, AND began to take off his sport coat. But before he got it off, a thought stopped him. If all these people were working together, they had to be communicating somehow. So maybe there was some sort of trail to that knowledge. Lawson pulled his sport coat back on and walked into the bathroom, propping himself up on the sink as he leaned into the mirror to take a hard look at himself. It was time for what his father would call a "come to Jesus meeting." With himself.

The way he saw it, he had two options. One: if he continued down this path of vengeance, it would most likely lead to him either dead or back in jail. Almost a 100 percent chance in fact. Which would still leave Lexi without her father. At this point he didn't know if that was a good thing or a bad thing. Two: if he left Las Vegas right then, he could get to Lexi in about a day. But then what? Take her from the only home she's ever known and make her live a life on the run with a father she doesn't even know? A father she probably thinks killed her own mother? No matter how much

Lauren had disagreed with her sister, Lexi's life had to be better there than on the run with him. Even if he somehow convinced her he didn't kill her mother. Eventually that scenario would also lead to him dead or in prison. And maybe scarring Lexi even further in the process. Plus, everyone that conspired against him would get off scot-free. Well, except of course for Evelyn Delaney.

Option two wasn't an option at all.

A lightbulb went off in his head.

Even if there was just the slightest possibility in the world he could bring all of this down on the people out to get him, he had to take that chance. All it took was just the slightest opening. And the lightbulb moment was maybe just the minuscule piece of thread he needed. Maybe if he could pull the string just right, this entire garment of betrayal would unravel.

Lawson poured himself a cup of coffee, sat down on the bed, and opened his notebook. He took a Bally's ink pen from the end table and drew a line through Evelyn Delaney's name. Above her name was Phillip Walters, Tony and Nero De Luca, and Adam Billings. If Evelyn hired two men to kill him last night, then ended up dead herself before anyone knew whether Lawson was still alive or not, that meant she had gone against someone, and they punished her for it. Chief Walters was definitely in on it, but Lawson doubted he would do something as brazen as having her killed. And it was clear that if FBI Director Adam Billings had put a hit on Lawson for the same night Evelyn had, they obviously weren't on the same page. So one of the two of them was working on their own. And it made sense that if Evelyn was still connected in Las Vegas, it probably meant that Director Billings was the one out of the loop. And since Evelyn was dead, he figured there was only one person who would be so public about dealing with her in the way he had.

Nero De Luca.

It had been right there in front of his face the entire time. He had always sensed that Nero stepped up for his father, Tony, to make Lawson go away. Billings must have let the De Lucas in on how close Cassie and Lawson were to taking them down. And Nero must have made the moves to make sure Lawson's case against him disappeared for his dying father.

Lawson was furious with himself. Just last night he was in the same room with the man who murdered his wife, and he did nothing about it. In fact, he had agreed to help him. And that is when another realization hit him. Nero's organization must really be weak at the moment. So weak that instead of just having Lawson killed, he wanted—*needed*—Lawson to help take down Sokolov for him. The only reason he would risk that was if he felt like the De Luca stronghold was about to die.

"The balls on that son of a bitch," Lawson said to the empty hotel room.

Nero must have been so confident he could manipulate Lawson that he risked everything to get his help with Sokolov. And that is why Evelyn Delaney was dead. Nero knew that her actions in hiring a hit man for Lawson could expose him, just like it had. He knew Lawson would be able to put it together if he found out. And Lawson knew then that was why Johnny tried to call him last night. If Lawson had answered, Evelyn would probably still be alive. But because he didn't, Nero assumed that Lawson was dead, and that meant Lawson couldn't help Nero take down Sokolov, which would ruin his plan to stay on top, and Evelyn paid the ultimate price for it.

What Nero De Luca didn't know in that moment, however, was that he should have been praising Evelyn. And he should have prayed that her hired guns actually had killed Lawson. Because Lawson still being alive now meant Nero De Luca's fate was much worse than losing the organized crime race.

He was going to lose his life.

Lawson knew that Nero was now aware of that too, so he would be pulling all his men to find Lawson first. Same reason Chief Walters was so quick to put Lawson on blast in the news this morning as well. The two of them were preparing for war. And there was no way one man could survive Walter's police force, and De Luca's army of gangsters. Not even Lawson Raines. He needed help, and the only way a man without friends can find help is to get it from someone who wanted the De Luca family gone as much as he did.

Serge Sokolov.

19

LAWSON FINISHED HIS COFFEE AND PACKED UP HIS DUFFEL bag. He wanted to be ready to move as soon as John got him Cassie's address. All the revelations that had occurred in the last half hour meant nothing to him until he found out for sure if Cassie was on his side or not.

His cell phone dinged. Sure enough, John had come through.

Thank you, Lawson texted back. He had to retype it three times to get the words spelled right. His thumb kept hitting two keys at once.

A half hour later, a taxi dropped Lawson three houses down from Cassie's address. Lawson had left his bag behind in the hotel room, and he had decided to destroy the notebook as well. He had run the bath and made sure the pages were destroyed before he left. He didn't need it anymore, but he had to make sure no one else got their hands on it either. It felt good to be rid of it. It was the only physical thing left to remind him of his time in prison. Besides, the names on the list were burned into his memory at that point. Cassie's being the only question mark left.

He adjusted his sport coat and quickly walked toward the backyard of the house in front of him. There was a car in Cassie's driveway. He hoped he could catch her before she left for work. He also needed to hurry to her house because he stood out like a sore thumb. A man in a suit walking a quiet suburban neighborhood wasn't a common occurrence. No way he would pass for a Jehovah's Witness. He would just go up to the front door and knock, but if Cassie wasn't the woman he had always thought, she may try to evade him in some way. Better to catch her off guard.

He hurried to the back deck of Cassie's house and sidled up to her back door. He was already sweating. It was only 8:30 in the morning, but it had to be in the nineties already. As he peered inside, the decor reminded him of Cassie immediately. You could see the Tennessee in all the furnishings. It also reminded him of his home with Lauren. Their home was in a neighborhood just like this, and Lauren and Cassie had similar Southern styles. He swallowed the longing feeling that had crept up to his throat and kicked in the door. The time for subtleties had passed.

He stepped inside the kitchen and immediately disliked how quiet it was. He pulled the Beretta from his waistline and perked his ears. He hoped that the silence was because she wasn't home. But the car in the driveway suggested otherwise. He knew he should at the very least be hearing her footsteps as she raced to see what made the loud noise, but there was no movement at all.

Not good.

Lawson crept toward the hallway that led to the front door. There was a set of stairs that went up just inside of it.

He walked down the hall and saw that the wood was splintered around the lock in the door. Someone had forced their way in. And that someone had just made a floorboard at the top of the stairs moan under their weight.

A gunshot rang out in the house, Lawson threw himself backward, landing with his back on the sofa. He pointed his gun up the stairs and fired off three rounds at the shadowed figure that darted behind the wall, averting his bullets. He heard a woman scream from a room upstairs. Cassie was still alive. He wasn't too late.

An arm reached around the wall, and just as two more shots were fired, Lawson rolled off the couch onto the floor, picked up the solid oak coffee table as he rose to his feet, and used it as a shield as he started up the stairs. The gunman fired a few more shots, two of them splintering the table, but Lawson kept charging. If Cassie was in fact upstairs, he had to get to her before these men could accomplish their mission. Whatever that might be.

The gunman fired two more errant shots, and Lawson heard the click of a gun with an empty magazine. He tossed the table over the rail, and as it crashed on the hardwood floor below, Lawson took the last five steps in two long strides. Just as he heard the gunman's spare magazine lock into place, he rounded the corner and pinned the pistol against the wall. The gunman's eyes were wide, and his breathing was heavy. This wasn't a man who was used to these kinds of situations.

"Brandon!" the skinny, wide-eyed gunman managed, just before Lawson drove his forehead into the man's nose.

The man shrieked and dropped to the floor clutching his face. Lawson grabbed his pistol.

"Cassie!" Lawson shouted as he tucked the extra pistol into his pants.

Cassie shouted back, "Watch out, Lawson! He's got a gun!"

Upon Cassie's cue, a much larger man with a bull neck rounded the wall of the far bedroom. By the look on his face, this man had seen situations like this far more frequently than his partner. He extended a pump-action shotgun in front of him and squeezed the trigger. Cassie giving Lawson the heads-up saved his life. He had managed to dive into the bedroom at the top of the stairs just in time to avoid the oncoming slug. Lawson jumped to his feet immediately after landing, and it was fast enough to catch the barrel of the shotgun before the muzzle made it down to his body. The blast filled the small room, sounding like a bomb had gone off.

As he gripped the business end of the man's shotgun, he fired off a knee meant for the man's groin, but he missed left, hitting him in the hip. It only managed to knock the big man backward, giving him separation to train his shotgun once again on Lawson. But Lawson leaped forward and caught the gun again, and he and the big man were now nose to nose. A tug-of-war for the shotgun. The red in the big man's face showed surprise, he wasn't used to having his strength matched. Lawson had the upper hand in this scuffle because his right hand was closest to the tip of the barrel. In a quick, upward motion, Lawson lifted the tip of the shotgun high in the air and twisted it left with all his might. It was enough to free the big man of the shotgun, but the power of the move sent it crashing against the wall.

Lawson didn't hesitate. He surged forward and caught the big man in a Thai clinch, wrapping both hands around the back of his neck, controlling the man's posture and movement.

"Big mistake, asshole," said the big man as he pounded down, both his arms on top of Lawson's arms in a smashing motion. The big man was shocked when it didn't break Lawson's grip. Lawson pulled down on the man's neck as he jumped up and smashed his knee into his forehead. As the big man staggered back, Lawson kicked the man's skinny partner in the ribs as he reached for the abandoned shotgun. Then Lawson caught the big man under both his arms as he charged into him. Lawson lifted him up, keeping the man from tackling him, then whipped around 180 degrees, throwing the big man toward the stair rail behind him as hard as he could. The man crashed into the rail, which buckled but held its ground. The man turned toward Lawson with a "that didn't work" smirk on his face, but Lawson quickly closed in on him and front-kicked him through the rail.

Lawson only heard the big man land, he didn't get the chance to see it. He pulled his Beretta, spun toward the skinny partner, and shot him twice in the chest as he raised the shotgun to shoot Lawson.

"Lawson! Are you okay? Lawson!" Cassie shouted from the back bedroom.

Lawson took two steps back, looked down where the rail used to be to the first floor, making sure the big man was in no condition to continue. His neck was turned in a manner that suggested he was finished, so Lawson moved toward the back bedroom.

"Lawson!" Cassie cried out again.

Lawson entered the bedroom and found Cassie standing with her hands tied to a post on the left side of the bed. Her face turned from elated to see him alive to horrified when he raised his gun toward her.

"Lawson, what the hell? That isn't funny, put the gun down."

Lawson didn't lower his gun.

20

"LAWSON, SERIOUSLY. WHAT THE HELL IS WRONG WITH you?" Cassie stared down the barrel of Lawson's Beretta.

He ignored her question. "I had a visitor last night. At my room at the Flamingo. You know, the room that only *you* knew about."

In the sunlight that poured in through the window to her left, Lawson watched Cassie's face turn from shocked to hurt.

"Are you kidding me right now?"

"Does it look like I'm kidding?" Lawson stepped into the center of the room, gun still stretched in front of him.

"Why the hell would I give you the heads-up that someone was coming if I was just going to turn around and send them right to you?"

"For this very reason, Cassie. So in case I survived, you could have plausible deniability."

Cassie's face scrunched up in anger. "Plausible denia— Lawson, have you lost your damn mind? It's me. Your only friend? Your old partner . . . remember?"

"Why didn't you go after Adam Billings for setting me up while I was in prison?" Lawson continued to fire away. These questions had been swimming in his head for years.

"You mean *Director of the FBI* Adam Billings? And where—if I had any at all—would I take proof of one of the most powerful men in the country's involvement in an organized crime scandal? *If* that is even what this is."

"You know that's exactly what this is, Cassie. The only thing that makes sense is that Billings fed the De Lucas information that we were about to shut them down. The only thing I can't figure out is why he would do it and why nobody ever came after you. They only came after me. Pretty convenient, wouldn't you say?"

"Lawson, since you have everything figured out, why don't you just go ahead and shoot me. That *is* what you came here to do, isn't it?"

Lawson didn't like that question. Because he really didn't know the answer. Did he really believe that Cassie could be involved? No. But that didn't mean that he didn't need to hear her say it. And it didn't mean that he didn't want some answers to some very pertinent questions. Lawson lowered the gun.

"Just answer my questions, Cassie."

"I'm going to chalk this up to your mind being messed with all these years. Untie me, and I'll answer your questions. Then we need to get the hell out of here. This is a quiet neighborhood. Someone definitely heard all the ruckus you just caused." Cassie smiled.

Lawson wasn't there yet. "You're welcome, by the way."

"Just untie me."

Lawson did as she asked, and the two of them sat on the bed.

Cassie went to take Lawson's hand, but he moved away. "Listen," she said. "All the thoughts that you are having, I promise you I've had them. All the scenarios you are running in your head? I've run them. I can't answer all your questions. If I could, I would have taken the people down that did this to you. You understand that, right?"

Lawson didn't respond.

"I can't tell you why they didn't come after me, Lawson. I've thought about it a thousand times over the years. If I had to guess, they knew you were the lead agent. Maybe they thought without you, I wasn't much of an agent myself. Clearly I proved them right, 'cause I haven't made a damn bit of progress since you went away. Now, as for why Director Billings might have tipped the De Lucas off that we were closing in? I can definitely answer that. I did at least try to get answers."

"And?" asked Lawson.

"Remember Billings's son, Joe?"

"The poker player?"

"Yep. But poker wasn't all he bet on, and he racked up an insurmountable debt with Tony and Nero De Luca."

Cassie paused for a minute, letting Lawson process.

It didn't take Lawson long. "So Billings gave Nero the information he needed to know we were closing in, in exchange for letting Joe off the hook for his debt."

"That's what I'm thinking."

That made perfect sense to Lawson. He knew Billings wasn't the type of man to let money keep him from doing his job. But saving his son, what man could blame him for that? Lawson knew he would do anything if it came to saving Lexi's life. Trying to have Lawson killed in a hotel room ten years later, however—Billings was going to have to answer for that.

"All right," said Lawson, "but that didn't mean you had to stop pursuing the case we were building against De Luca just because of what happened to me."

"Lawson, you know better than that. I know you read the papers."

Lawson had in fact read the papers, and he knew exactly what Cassie was referring to. After Lawson was sentenced to life in prison, the three confidential informants who were going to turn on the De Lucas and testify against them for Cassie and Lawson all ended up dead.

Cassie continued. "After Nero had our informants killed, our case was dead. I had nothing left to go on. And after learning from Billings that the FBI was scrutinizing their business so closely, Nero really tightened everything up. It was the perfect cover-up. Well, except for you."

"What do you mean?"

"They should have killed you is what I mean. And I'm pretty sure that was exactly their plan on the boat that day. But since you weren't there, they called an audible and decided that putting you in jail forever would be just as good. Hell, they already knew they had the chief of police and the brand new DA in their pocket. How could they lose?"

It hurt Lawson even further to know for sure that he was the reason that Lauren died that day. He had always suspected it, but hearing Cassie have the same thoughts only confirmed it for him.

"So that leads me to exactly what I *did* do to help while you were in prison."

Lawson snapped out of his trance. "Which was what exactly?"

"I know you think it was the favor you did for the governor that got you that pardon, Lawson. But just how in the hell do you think he came to know that you were in there and could help him out?"

Lawson didn't have an answer.

"I heard what you were doing in there. Doing favors for De Luca and others. And I knew exactly why you were doing it. It was smart. You were playing the long game. On the off chance you were ever going to get out of there, you wanted an 'in' wherever you could get one to find answers on the outside."

"So what does that have to do with the governor?" Lawson asked.

"Well, I heard about him getting his mistress pregnant from someone I am friends with in his office. And I thought it was awfully fishy how his mistress's husband went to prison on that unrelated drug charge. So . . . I managed a meeting with the governor and convinced him that maybe this guy in prison needed a little convincing not to tell everyone that the governor was the father of his wife's baby."

"And you helped get word to me to tune him up so he wouldn't talk. Thus putting the governor in my debt."

"Right. I knew you would find out that this guy was a real scumbag anyway. Dealing drugs to kids, running prostitutes. If he wasn't, you would have never done the favor that got you out of prison. You would have never hurt him."

"Wow, Cassie. Talk about working the angles."

"Just using what I learned from you."

Lawson stood up and took a peek out the window. The sun was blazing down on Cassie's little backyard. Instead of grass, of course, her yard was rock and sand. Grass in the desert was too much upkeep for a single woman who worked all the time. He turned back to her.

"So where does that leave us now?"

Cassie stood. "It leaves us exactly where we were when I slipped you the letter. You have to get the hell out of town, and apparently"—she motioned toward the hallway with her hand—"I have to get this mess cleaned up."

"I'm not leaving, Cassie. An FBI hit man tried to kill me last night."

"What?" Cassie was shocked. "Kevin Watson already came for you? He must have been watching you for longer than I thought he might be. How are you still here?"

"Honestly? Because I wasn't sure I could trust you. That's what saved my life."

"You thought I may have told him where you were, so you were ready. At least you not believing in me saved your life, you prick."

"Whatever. Water under the bridge. Like I said, I'm not leaving town. A crime boss colluded with the chief of police and the district attorney to kill my wife and frame me for it. These people have to pay for what they've done."

"Someone already has."

Lawson knew Cassie was referring to Evelyn Delaney being found dead in a ditch.

"Yeah, about that . . ."

Cassie's face turned white. "That was really you?"

"What? No. Well, not the Evelyn Delaney thing."

"But the killing in your room at Caesar's?"

"Hey, they came after me. And it was Evelyn Delaney who hired them."

"What?" Cassie was flabbergasted. "How could you

know that? . . . Never mind. So if you didn't kill the DA, who did?"

Lawson's face hardened, and his jaw clenched. "The same son of a bitch who's been behind everything this entire time . . ."

"Nero De Luca."

21

LAWSON LEFT CASSIE'S HOUSE IN HER SPARE CAR, AN OLD Honda Accord that she hadn't driven in months. The two of them searched the men who broke into Cassie's house but didn't find anything that could link them to who sent them. At this point, however, there was little doubt in both of their minds that they were De Luca's men. They certainly weren't undercover police or FBI. Lawson figured De Luca sent them to see if he was hiding out at Cassie's house. Lawson imagined that Nero had grown quite worried by that point. He was sure that was the reason for all the missed calls and texts from Johnny. They were desperately trying to figure out Lawson's location.

Nero must have been wondering if his plan to use Lawson for his own gain before he killed him had backfired. Probably up all night trying to decide if Evelyn's little hiring blew it for him. Nero was a powerful man, but the last thing he wanted was for Lawson to put everything together. He obviously had an idea of what Lawson was capable of, or he wouldn't have asked him to help bring him back to power by taking down Sokolov.

Sokolov.

Twenty-four hours ago, Lawson thought Sokolov would have been the last person on earth he would want to see on the outside. Now, it seemed like a must. The old adage "an enemy of my enemy is a friend" had never rung more true than in that moment. Lawson was being hunted by everyone in Las Vegas. Sokolov included. But if anyone could appreciate Lawson's situation, and possibly benefit from bringing down De Luca, it was Sokolov.

One of the many things written in Lawson's notebook was the inner workings of Sokolov's operation and where his people gathered. Whispers in prison from their men over the years gave Lawson more information about these crime bosses than he could have ever learned with the FBI. And now was the time to put these secrets to good use.

Lawson pulled up to the D Casino downtown. He had heard on a number of occasions that Sokolov worked out of a suite at the top of the hotel and that several of his degenerate employees were always drinking and hanging out at the Sports Book there.

By Vegas standards, the D's interior wasn't overly gaudy. They weren't pulling people in with promises of Italian marble and Roman statues. Nor were they using gimmicks like pirate ships and shark tanks. Most people who stayed there wanted to be downtown—old Vegas—and the D was known for loose slots, and that would always bring in a steady clientele. The Fremont Street Experience just outside was a nice draw, and Lawson heard from many imprisoned Italians that Andiamo Steakhouse was "delicioso!" Lawson passed through all of that, following the signs to the Sports

Book. Which wasn't much of a sports book at all, so it was very easy for him to get the attention of Sokolov's men in the small room.

"My name is Lawson Raines," he announced. "And Serge Sokolov wants me dead."

Again, the time for subtleties had passed.

Two men sitting in front of a small wall of televisions and one man at the betting counter turned immediately when Lawson announced himself. They all reached for their sidearms, but Lawson stopped them before they could pull.

"I come in peace," he said, holding both hands up. "It seems your boss and I have a common enemy."

The red-haired man at the betting counter stepped toward him. "What makes you think Sokolov cares who you are, or who your enemy is?"

"You already know he cares who I am. That's why the three of you reached for your guns. And he cares who my enemy is because I'm going to kill the son of a bitch. Thus giving your boss the keys to Las Vegas."

Five minutes later, Lawson was walking off the elevator on the top floor of the hotel, heading toward Serge Sokolov's suite. *This could possibly be the worst decision I've ever made*, Lawson thought. Cassie spent five minutes trying to convince him of that very fact before he left her house. But if fortune favors the bold and Sokolov doesn't kill him, he might buy himself enough time to think of a way to bring the entire ten years of pain directly down on Nero De Luca's head.

Two of his escorts from the Sports Book opened the door to the suite and ushered Lawson inside. Directly in front of him was a row of windows with a sweeping view of the Las Vegas mountains in the distance. The walls were grey, the carpet was a red-speckled black, and a large grey sectional sofa sat in front of a long dining table. At the table a grey-haired, fake-tanned man in a black suit sat having brunch.

"Lawson Raines." The man stood. He walked around the table, wearing a smile on his narrow and wrinkled face, his hand stretched out in from of him.

Lawson did not expect this sort of greeting.

Lawson shook his hand and nodded. "Sokolov."

"Please, sit. Would you like some brunch?"

"Is that an invitation for a last meal?"

Lawson sat with his back to the windows, and Sokolov sat in the adjacent section of the sofa.

"My men told me that you announced that I wanted you dead. And I must admit, after hearing what you did to a couple of my best men yesterday in the desert, I was a little put off, but they weren't coming to hurt you. They were there to request that you meet with me."

Lawson sat back. "They ran me off the road, flipped the car I was riding in on its head. There are better ways to make such a request."

"Yes, I should have informed them that one of De Luca's men might be escorting you. When they saw that, they took unfortunate measures. An automatic reflex, if you will. Seems as though you made it out all right."

Lawson shrugged. "So why would you want to meet with me, Sokolov? After I didn't help you out at all on the inside."

"That *was* unfortunate, Mr. Raines. I tried many times to get to you the information I had in my possession, but they never hit their mark, I take it."

"A lot of people say a lot of things when every day is spent behind bars. What information are you talking about?"

"We will get to that in a moment."

Sokolov's English was exceptional. Only the slightest Russian accent could be detected. If Lawson didn't know better, Sokolov's cordial demeanor might suggest he wasn't a bad man at all. But he did know better. And on a longer look into his beady little eyes, a darkness could be found there.

"First, I would like to propose a partnership of sorts."

Lawson leaned forward. "You already know I have a partnership with De Luca."

"Yes, well . . . we also both know why you have that partnership. You are a smart man, Mr. Raines. I knew why you refused to help me while you were in prison. If De Luca found out you were doing favors for me, you could never get in his good graces. Which you thought was where you needed to be in order to get your revenge. Correct me if I'm wrong."

Lawson played dumb. "Revenge?"

"For your wife."

Hearing Sokolov talk about Lauren cut to the quick.

"Why else would you be here now?" Sokolov continued. "You came to me because we both will benefit from Nero De Luca falling from grace. You certainly can't go to the police. You *have* seen yourself on the news today?"

He had Lawson pegged, no sense prolonging the inevitable. "How can you help me with De Luca? If you could take him down, you would have already," Lawson said.

Sokolov stood and walked past two of his men over to a laptop computer that sat on the dining room table.

"That is why we will make such great partners."

Sokolov motioned for Lawson to join him at the table. When Lawson walked over, Sokolov turned the laptop's screen in his direction. On the screen a video was cued up. It looked like some sort of service hallway. Concrete block walls, nothing else. The video was in black and white. Sokolov hit play. Nothing appeared on the screen.

"It's a gorgeous hallway, Sokolov. But what the hell am I looking at?"

"Be patient."

Another couple of seconds went by, and finally a figure appeared at the far end of the hall.

"Johnny De Luca," Sokolov offered before Lawson could ask.

Where the hell was this video going?

Then at the opposite end of the hallway, another figure appeared. This one was clearly a woman. Her long hair showed up white on the screen. Lawson assumed she was a blonde. The two of them hurried toward each other and locked in a sensual embrace. They continued kissing while Lawson tried to figure out just what in the hell Sokolov was trying to show him.

Lawson didn't get it. "So, Johnny De Luca has a girlfriend. Is this big news in the Mafia Herald Leader? How does this help us?"

"That, Mr. Raines," Sokolov explained, pointing at the woman in the video, "is my granddaughter."

22

As Lawson walked out of the D Casino, he ended his call with Cassie explaining how the meeting went. He could feel the slime lingering from his time with Sokolov. But it was a small price to pay. That meeting went as well as it could go. Better than he imagined actually. Sokolov's plan was good, but Lawson's contribution had made it genius. The Russians might not be good at a lot of things, but espionage was apparently built into their DNA. Sokolov had been training his twenty-one-year-old granddaughter all her life for this. And Lawson was going to jump on the train with him to help bring De Luca down.

It was a perfect plan for Lawson as well. If he could maintain his relationship with Johnny De Luca, and Johnny was as in love with Kiara Sokolov as she had told her grandfather he was, Lawson had a chance. The key factor was that Johnny needed to hate his father, Nero, as much as Lawson suspected he might. If not, all of this would be for naught. And that aside, Lawson felt safe about Sokolov for now, because his plan couldn't work without Lawson setting it all up. So at least out of all the people gunning for him, Lawson had been able—at least for the moment— to take Sokolov off that list.

Time to set things in motion.

Lawson dialed Johnny's number as he got into Cassie's Honda. He was finally starting to figure out this iPhone thing.

"Lawson! I've been calling and texting for hours! Where the hell have you been?"

Lawson could hear the stress in Johnny's voice. He imagined that over the last several hours Johnny had really been getting it from his father—since watching Lawson was his only responsibility. This couldn't hurt in helping to persuade Johnny to see how awful his father was.

"Calm down, Johnny. Everything is fine."

"Fine? You promised me you would check in. Dad is furious!"

Perfect.

"You have to come in right now. My father wants to speak to you immediately."

"I can't meet with your father."

Lawson kept it vague to further stretch Johnny's frayed nerves.

"Lawson, don't do this to me. He will *literally* kill me if I don't get you here."

"I don't doubt that, considering he just tried to kill me."

The setup begins.

"What? Why would—this is exactly what he was worried about. He knew you would think it was him that tried to kill you."

"It *was* him. I don't care what he told you, Johnny. You are apparently not in his inner circle."

"Well, no shit on that one. He thinks I'm nothing. But you have to come and talk with him. Otherwise it will blow back on me."

Lawson stayed quiet for a moment.

"Lawson?"

"Why should I care if it blows back on you?"

Now it was Johnny who was quiet.

Lawson continued. "I like you, Johnny. I see a lot of potential in you, you have a lot of charisma. It's a shame your father doesn't see it. But if you think I am going to walk into a meeting with a man who just tried to kill me, just so he doesn't take it out on you, you are out of your mind."

Lawson knew that there was a lot going on in Johnny's head at the moment, so he let him think. He knew Johnny was trying to find a way to get Lawson to trust him.

Johnny broke his silence. "Look . . . I give you my word that he doesn't want you dead."

Lawson turned off the Strip, onto a side road, and put the car in park.

"I'm sorry, Johnny, but why should I trust you? I barely know you."

"Lawson, PLEASE!"

Johnny was panicking.

Now was the time to go for broke.

"Maybe you are no different than your father," said Lawson.

"Wha-what?"

That caught Johnny off guard.

"You and him both seem to like to keep secrets."

"What are you talking about, Lawson? If I knew why he wanted to see you, believe me, I would tell you."

"So it's just your father you keep secrets from?"

A pause.

"I would never keep anything from him. Is that what he told you? Have you been watching *me*?"

Enough beating around the bush.

"I know about Kiara Sokolov, Johnny."

"What? Who?"

"See, I knew I couldn't trust you. Good luck, Johnny."

Lawson ended the call. This would send Johnny over the edge. Thoughts of Lawson telling Nero about Johnny's secret rendezvous with a Sokolov would drive him crazy. Maybe, just maybe it would drive him crazy enough to do what Lawson needed. His phone began to ring immediately. Johnny. He called several more times as Lawson took the time to grab a couple of protein bars at a gas station. Then Johnny sent the text that Lawson had been waiting for.

Johnny: *Please, Lawson. Don't tell my father. I'll do anything.*

Bingo.

Lawson called him back.

"Lawson, thank God."

"Okay, Johnny. Looks like we're going to have to trust each other."

"What do you want?"

This was it. This would tell Lawson exactly how far Johnny was willing to go. It was a huge ask, but Lawson learned a long time ago that if you never ask, you'll never know. And sometimes, it's all how you word the question.

"I already know that your father has District Attorney

Evelyn Delaney and Police Chief Phillip Walters on his payroll. What I need from you is proof."

Silence from Johnny's end.

Lawson stepped into his car and blasted the air conditioning.

"So you're asking me to rat on my father? For what? So you can have him arrested?"

Time for some finesse.

"Johnny, I told you, we are going to have to trust each other."

"I can't put my father in prison. Are you out of your mind? Even if I wanted him gone, he would have me killed before they ever even read him his rights."

"Who said anything about putting him in prison?"

"Why else would you want proof of something so incriminating?"

"Look at it from my perspective. Come on, you're a smart guy."

Lawson wanted Johnny to get there on his own. Almost making it seem like his idea. Empowering him to take control of this situation.

"You want it in case my father really does want you dead. You need it as leverage."

Lawson couldn't help but smile. Johnny had taken the bait.

"Leverage that I have no desire to use." *Lie.* "If what you're saying is true, and Nero really doesn't want me dead, why would I use it?" *Because your father murdered my wife and pinned it on me.* "Your father is paying me very well to help him. Whether I am actually guilty or not, where else would a convicted murderer like me be able to make that kind of money?"

Come on, Johnny. Reel yourself in.

After a moment, Johnny agreed. "You couldn't."

"Right, I couldn't. And I need money to find out what happened to my wife. And I shouldn't have to tell you what that means to me."

Johnny took another long pause. Lawson could hear him let out a long, resigned exhale.

"So how did you know? About me and Kiara?"

Lawson knew this question was coming. And after his speech to Johnny about trust, he had to make it good.

"I really shouldn't be telling you this, but since you are showing trust in me, I'll do the same. But you aren't going to like it."

"I don't like any of this, so how much worse can it be than sharing incriminating evidence on my father with you?"

"Much worse."

Lawson let that sink in. He obviously couldn't see Johnny's face, but he didn't need to. He knew it was filled with fear.

"Good God, what is it?"

"Serge Sokolov is how I know about you and his granddaughter."

"What?" Johnny said without hesitation. "He knows?" Terror filled his voice.

"And he's hired *me* to kill you."

Silence.

This was going to jumble young Johnny's mind.

"That can't be true," Johnny finally said, his voice choked by emotion. "Why would he hire you to do it?"

"He's blackmailing me too. He's hiring me to be a double agent of sorts."

Johnny was pretty quick to the punch. "Because he

knows you work for my dad now, and he wants inside information on him from you."

"That's right. I obviously have no intention of giving him anything on your father, but when he told me he needed me to kill you, I had to take the job."

Johnny was buying what Lawson was selling. "Because if you didn't, Sokolov would just have someone else kill me. You knew at least if it was you, you could buy Kiara and me some time."

"I knew you were smart."

"Well then, that's not as bad as it could be."

Lawson let out an overly dramatic, audible sigh. "It gets worse."

Johnny cleared his throat. "Worse than wanting me dead?"

"I'm sure you know from listening to your father how terrible a man Serge Sokolov is."

"Y-yeah?"

"After I kill you, I'm supposed to kill Kiara next."

"What?" Johnny shouted. "His own granddaughter? Lawson, you have to help me—no, I have to tell my father."

Lawson was prepared for this reaction.

"And let him find out that you have been running around with the granddaughter of his mortal enemy? You sure that's the direction you want to take?"

Silence again.

"You have to help me, Lawson. You wouldn't kill me and Kiara, would you? I love her. I know it was stupid to get involved with her, but she is the one. The way we met, it was just so perfect—"

Poor Johnny didn't have a clue. Lawson had been right about him all along. He was lonely. He was never allowed to make his own friends. And just as Lawson was trying to take advantage of that fact, Sokolov had seen the opportunity as well. He knew Kiara could bring Johnny in without much effort at all. All the kid wanted was someone to care about. Someone to make him feel like he belonged.

"Johnny, relax. We're friends, right?" Lawson almost felt bad . . . almost.

"R-right. Yes!"

"Friends don't kill each other. They help each other. Remember, Sokolov hired *me* to kill you. So you are good. Kiara is good. For now. But I can't stall Sokolov forever. He wants this done today. *Today*, Johnny. So I need you to get the information I asked for. And it has to be hard evidence."

"I'm not saying I know that my father was working with those people, but if he was, I'll find proof."

"Johnny, now is not the time for games. I need it before I can meet with your father."

Johnny wasn't stupid. "Okay, so that protects you. Then what about me? After I give you the proof you need, what happens to me? And Kiara? Sokolov will still want us dead. How does me giving you leverage keep me and her safe?"

"Johnny, I know this has all been a lot to take in, but what was the reason your dad hired me in the first place?"

"To help him take down Sokolov."

Time for Lawson to put the finishing touches on Johnny. "That's right. When I know that I can trust your father, which is why you are getting this proof for me in the first place, then I can resume my responsibilities."

Johnny couldn't wait for Lawson to say it. "And kill Sokolov."

Lawson repeated for effect, "And kill Sokolov. He can't

still want you dead, Johnny, when he is dead. You see how this all works out for me and you, my friend?"

"Thanks, Lawson. You're saving my life."

"Johnny, I need that proof, sooner than later."

The pep in Johnny's voice returned. "I'm on it."

23

AFTER ENDING THE CALL WITH JOHNNY, LAWSON DROVE PAST Cassie's street. With a glance down the road toward her house, he could see several police cars and a couple of ambulances. Cassie was in full cleanup mode. That would keep her occupied for at least a couple more hours. He hoped she would have time to get away for a few minutes later if he needed her. He felt bad for having questioned her loyalty. But he had just been through so much. He had just lost so much.

It felt good to be doing something normal like driving around in the car. Even though he had nowhere to go. There was nothing for him to do until Johnny got back to him with some sort of proof that everyone was colluding with Nero. Johnny's failure to protest made Lawson think Johnny already had an idea of where to go to get that proof. If he came through, it would change everything. Lawson just might have a chance to have his cake and eat it too. Revenge could be his redemption.

And then maybe he could finally see his daughter.

Lawson drove aimlessly through the suburbs of Las

Vegas. The farther he got from the Strip, the more it felt like Lexington to him. Though the foliage, the lawns, and the style of houses still couldn't be more different, it began to feel more like a place to live. Home. Home, which he desperately missed.

His mind, as it had a million times over the years, floated back to that day on the boat. The worst day of his life. He thought about the way Lauren smelled, the way she felt. He savored Lexi's laugh, he could still hear it echoing in his mind as he saw himself tossing her in the air. How soft her two-year-old cheeks were. How curious and inquisitive she had become. Mocking everything her mommy and daddy did.

Before he knew it, he had driven back to his old neighborhood. He and Lauren had only lived in one home while they were in Las Vegas, and now there it was, right across the street from him. He pulled off the road, parking next to the curb. He squinted through the sunshine at where his family made so many memories. The only home that Lexi had ever known until that tragic day. So many feelings and emotions were running through Lawson in that moment. So much of the last ten years had been spent numbing himself to emotion. To pain. It was a matter of survival. But now it felt good to let nostalgia for his lost family wash over him. He had never loved anything more than his girls. And he knew he never would again. The thought of Lexi living the rest of her life without him being able to share in it was the most terrifying thought imaginable. It wasn't lost on him just how much weight that fear carried. Because as far as terrifying goes, for anyone else the next twenty-four hours would be far more frightening. But not for Lawson. What lay ahead, all the terrible things he was about to do, that didn't scare him at all. He was numb to violence. That part of his humanity was dead. For him, it was just something that had to be done.

As he stared at his old home, the front door opened. A man wearing a business suit, probably in his late twenties, walked down the driveway toward his car. Much the way Lawson had done every day for three years. Then the door opened again. This time, a young girl with bright blonde hair, maybe five years old, came running out after him. A brown paper sack in her tiny little hands. The man turned around, and his smile matched the wide one that his daughter wore on her face as he picked her up, kissed her cheek, twirled her around, and looked back toward the front door. His wife stood there, watching. Smiling.

Was Lawson really seeing this? Or was this a daydream of what his life would have been like if his horrific nightmare had never happened? As he watched these strangers interact with each other in such a blissful way, Lawson began to feel the opposite. His first thought was that he wanted a piece of his old life back. He wanted more than anything to see Lexi grow up. And he was going to do everything in his power to make that happen.

He watched the dad take his daughter back to the front door and hand her off to his wife. She rewarded him with a long and heartfelt kiss good-bye. And as Lawson watched her wrap her arms around him, giving him an extra squeeze, Lawson's blood ran cold. The warm thoughts that had been passing through his mind were washed away and replaced with the thought that it should've been him. That woman should have been Lauren. He didn't realize it, but he was squeezing the steering wheel so hard in his hands that the tattered thing was beginning to crack. A rage unlike any he had felt through all his pain found him there in that car. And the next image that flashed in front of his mind's eye was of Nero De Luca.

That smug son of a bitch thought that his money and his power made him untouchable. People that believe that way begin to get sloppy. And though Lawson didn't think that De Luca had necessarily been sloppy about covering his tracks suggesting he was involved in Lauren's murder, he did feel like Nero was sloppy with him. Far too overconfident that he could pull the wool over Lawson's eyes and actually have Lawson help him regain his foothold in Vegas. Nero's biggest problem was that he thought he was smarter than Lawson. He saw Lawson as a brute force, the smash-your-way-through-people kind of man. But Nero didn't know the other side of Lawson. The side that uses brute force to gain favor. The side that, as a detective and FBI agent, was not just good at putting things together but good at manipulating situations. Situations like finding weak spots. Finding that one link in the chain that was ready to break. And in this instance, that link was Nero's own son.

Nero's biggest mistake was the one thing that should have been his strongest link. But a man like Nero doesn't have time for his actual family. Because his work is his life. His power is his legacy. And his neglected, unimportant son, who doesn't want anything to do with the criminal life, is left swimming in the ocean all alone . . . sad . . . angry . . . vulnerable. Vulnerable to a shark like Sokolov. Vulnerable to Sokolov's beautiful granddaughter. And Lawson was the only one who could take full advantage.

Lawson's phone began to ring.

Speak of the devil.

Before he answered Johnny's call, he took a deep breath and let the rage fall from his mind. "That was fast."

"I didn't need a lot of time, Lawson. Besides, you didn't give me much."

"So you have proof?"

"He just met with Delaney and Walters last night. The only reason I knew was because he wanted me there to serve them drinks. It's like he thinks I'm his servant or something. Then he kicked me out before they started talking. I have no idea what was said. There is no audio."

"So what is the proof?" Lawson persisted.

"Oh, right. Dad has a security camera in his office because he doesn't trust anyone, including me, to be in there without him. But he wasn't around when the system was set up. I was. He thought I was at school, so he thinks he and the head of his security are the only ones who can access it. I overheard them discuss the passcode that day and I wrote it down just in case. I can access the hard drive from any computer. So how do I get the video to you?"

This was too easy. There must be some sort of catch.

"I have an email address you can send it to," Lawson said.

"That won't work. The file is too large to email. I can't just cut the meeting you want proof of, the entire day's video had to be downloaded. I put it on a flash drive."

And there was the catch. No matter how clever Johnny thought he was being, Lawson knew a man like Nero, who had secrets floating around all the time, would never be so cavalier with a security video. Lawson knew what Johnny didn't, that his father's head of security would undoubtedly be alerted when someone accessed the terminal.

"Where are you, Johnny?" Lawson's tone had turned more serious. And Johnny could hear it.

"What? I'm in my room. Why? What's wrong?"

"You have to get the hell out of there. Right now."

"What's going on?"

"Meet me at Battista's Hole in the Wall. It's a little Italian restaurant on the back side of the Flamingo's parking garage."

"I know where it is. But what—"

"Johnny, go now. Or I won't be able to save you."

24

"WHERE THE HELL WAS JOHNNY DE LUCA TEN YEARS AGO when we needed him?" Cassie asked.

"Middle school," Lawson said as his car went sideways onto Las Vegas Blvd. He mashed the gas pedal and swerved around three cars that were in front of him.

"Was that your tires I heard squealing, Lawson?"

"I have to get to Battista's. There is no doubt Nero's men will be close behind Johnny. This is it, Cassie. This is the break that helps me clear my name, and the break that helps us finally take down De Luca. If this is what Johnny says it is, I could actually get Lexi back."

"Well, we're not going to be able to take down anyone if you are in jail. You realize that you are public enemy number one right now. Let me handle this, Lawson. I can have Johnny picked up by a local cop and have him brought to me. You don't need to go anywhere near this."

Lawson swerved around a couple more cars. His heart was pounding. Not because of the frantic drive, but because he was so close. He thought it would take weeks, maybe even months to get to this point with De Luca, and now he's only minutes, hell, only a few blocks away!

"I can't take that chance, Cass. I have to get that flash drive!"

"Lawson, listen to me—"

"There's no time. The police are after me, the director of the FBI is after me, and my in with Nero is gone. If this doesn't work, I'm dead, and so are you. You think Nero won't send more men for you? You and I are the last link to his involvement in all of this. He made the mistake of letting me live once, he won't do it again. And if the police get to me now, he won't have to. I'll be locked up forever."

Cassie's voice went up an octave. "That is what I am trying to tell you! If the police see you now, this is all over. The proof will be gone, and Delaney's murder will be pinned on you too. Let's do this by the book and—"

"To hell with the book!" Lawson slammed his fist against the dashboard. "The book is why I am in this situation to begin with! I'm not leaving this in someone else's hands this time, Cassie. Not again. This time I'm ending it once and for all."

Lawson ended the call.

His blinders were on. There was nothing else in the world that mattered more than getting that flash drive. He would worry about De Luca, the police, and everything else after it was in his possession. Until then, he knew he was a dead man walking, and Cassie's plight wasn't much different.

He tried to calm himself as he pulled into the parking lot of Battista's. He couldn't go inside. He couldn't risk someone recognizing him from his picture all over the news and calling the police on him. He just hoped Johnny could make it before Nero had him picked up.

Lawson's phone alerted him of a text.

Johnny: *I'm at the bar. Did you know you are all over the news? And listen, there is something else I have to tell you. But you're not going to like it. I put something else on the flash drive that you need to see.*

An SUV swerved into the parking lot and four men jumped out of the car.

De Luca.

Lawson pressed call on Johnny's contact.

Johnny answered, "I just sent you a—"

"Johnny, go out the back door, right now. And run!"

"What? I don't—"

"Now! I'll try to distract your father's men. GO!"

Lawson stepped out of the car and shouted at the men as they hurried toward the entrance to the restaurant. "You guys looking for Johnny?"

The bald guy in the front of the pack pulled a pistol immediately and started firing on Lawson. Two bullets clanked into the hood of Cassie's car. Then one of the men behind him pointed over Lawson's shoulder and shouted, "There goes Johnny!"

Lawson turned and saw the back of Johnny De Luca sprinting down Audrie Street toward the massive High Roller. The man shooting at Lawson was distracted by his man shouting just long enough for Lawson to pull his Beretta. There were three cars and a pickup truck that separated him from De Luca's four men. Lawson's first shot missed, and the four of them dove behind the cars for cover. Lawson used the moment of opportunity to jump back in his car, throw it in reverse, swerve out onto the street, and pull away just as a few more bullets hit the trunk of his car. Johnny was just a couple of blocks ahead of him, still making a run for it. Lawson was closing in. He was going to get to that flash drive after all.

Then a black Chevy Tahoe coming toward Johnny from the opposite direction slammed on their brakes, and three more men jumped out. Johnny noticed them and darted left before the men could get completely out of the truck. Lawson floored it, then slammed on the brakes when he reached the Tahoe and bolted out of the car. It was time to use all that running he'd been doing for something more than just exercise.

Johnny had turned left just in front of the High Roller, which meant he was running up the LINQ Promenade, where they were last night. Lawson could see Johnny up ahead and the three men right behind him in close pursuit. Lawson kicked into another gear and sprinted up the back side of them. The men weren't shooting at Johnny, most likely per Nero's orders. This gave Lawson a chance. If they were going to try to bring him in without killing him, Lawson would be able to wait for the right time to move in.

Lawson couldn't see Johnny now, but he was closing in on De Luca's men. They were bowling over the crowd that was strolling down the promenade. Oversized drinks were spilling from their hands, ladies were screaming, and bystanders lunching on the patios were shouting for people to watch out. Lawson was just a few yards behind them now, when they all turned right into O'Sheas, the bar where Lawson had met Cassie for drinks and pulled Johnny out of last night. Lawson rushed through the door. One of De Luca's men had just run over the craps table that greeted patrons at the front, and gambling chips were scattered everywhere on the floor. De Luca's man had managed to get back to his feet, but not fast enough to get away from Lawson.

Lawson reached the back of the man's collar and yanked him backward. He thudded to the bar floor on his back, and before he could register what happened, Lawson drove his elbow down on the bald man's forehead. The lights instantly went out.

"Lock the entrance, there are more of them coming!" Lawson shouted to the bartender as he bolted to his feet and raced for the back of the bar. If they did as he said, maybe it would slow the other four of De Luca's men down who were coming up behind him.

The back of O'Sheas opened into the LINQ Hotel. Lawson sprinted left and could just make out the other two men chasing Johnny as they entered into the casino. Lawson lowered his head and continued to chase. He could tell the men in front of him were starting to slow. This was a lot of running and adrenaline dumping. If you weren't in good shape, this would be exhausting.

Good thing that wasn't a problem for Lawson.

25

LAWSON RAN ONTO THE CASINO FLOOR TO A SLOT MACHINE chorus of bing-bing-bing-bong-bong-bong-bong. He saw the men on the main path, following the signs to the exit out to the Strip. Lawson decided to try a shortcut through the rows of slot machines. Halfway through them, he could see that it was going to pay off because he was now closing in on Johnny. But when Johnny tried to slow his momentum and take a left toward the exit, the slick marble under his feet took its toll, and Johnny went sliding on his side into a rail that separated the gaming area from the slick surface of the entrance. The two men slid to a stop right in front of Johnny, and one man pulled his pistol and shouted at Johnny to get up. Lawson closed the distance, hurdled a trash can, and dove at the gunman, taking him to the ground with a double-arm tackle.

"Run, Johnny!" Lawson shouted. "Out to the Strip! Blend in with the crowd!" Lawson raised himself off the man, holding the man's wrist in his hand, and slammed the man's hand down on the marble. The man's gun skittered across the floor.

Lawson glanced back over his shoulder, and De Luca's other man had managed to grab Johnny before he could get away.

"Where's the flash drive, Johnny? I know you have it," the man shouted as he shook Johnny by the shirt.

Lawson punched the man below him in the forehead, then grabbed him by his dark hair and slammed the back of his head against the marble.

"I . . . I don't know what you're talking about!" Johnny answered.

The man punched him in the stomach. Johnny bent over at the knees and gasped for air. Lawson rose to his feet and turned toward Johnny's attacker.

"Why don't you try hitting me like that?"

The man straightened Johnny up and held him in place by the front of his shirt. Then he turned to look at Lawson. Lawson recognized the man's face from the meeting with De Luca at STK.

The man's expression was smug. "Thought you were supposed to be working for us?"

Lawson shrugged his shoulders. "Things change. Let him go, and I'll let you live."

"Who the hell do you think you are?"

"Right now?" Lawson stalled. "I'm the man who's going to stop you from getting that flash drive. Later? I'll be the man standing over your boss's dead body."

"You'd have to get by me first, Raines. And there's no chance in hell you're man enough for that."

The man smirked as he reached for his waistline.

Lawson shouted, "Knee, Johnny!"

The man looked back at Johnny, giving Lawson's words enough time to register. Johnny shot his knee toward the man's groin. He missed, but still hit him in the lower midsection hard enough for the man to flinch and let go.

"Give me the flash drive!" Lawson shouted to Johnny. But the man had already recovered. As Lawson closed the eight-foot distance between them, the man once again reached for his gun.

"Hey!" The bald man Lawson knocked out back inside O'Sheas had caught up with them.

"Just go, Johnny!" Lawson told him. "Meet me at Carnival Court!"

Lawson caught the hand of the man pulling his gun and drove his forehead down on the bridge of his nose. Johnny looked at Lawson, then up at the other man coming his way, then did what Lawson asked and ran out the front entrance. As the gunman reached for his nose, he dropped his gun, and Lawson delivered an overhand right to his temple with enough power to knock him off his feet. Lawson grabbed the waist-high, gold-domed trash can, wheeled it around 180 degrees, and hurled it at De Luca's oncoming goon. The man stopped, then stepped around the trash can, continuing toward him. When Lawson turned back around and stomped the heel of his shoe down on the neck of the bloody-nosed gunman, a crack reverberated in between the dings of the nearby slot machines.

Only one man to worry about now.

The man who had dodged the trash can finally pulled his pistol, and Lawson dove behind the Wheel of Fortune slots just as two bangs from the gun sent everyone nearby into hysteria. Lawson pulled his Beretta as he pushed up off the ground. He could feel the eyes of all the cameras on him as he aimed around the slot machine. The media was going to love the next video clip in the ongoing saga that was Lawson Raines: pardoned prisoner turning once again to murder.

The end of Lawson's gun found its target, and before the man shooting at Lawson could react, Lawson shot him twice in the chest. He rounded the corner of the slot machine just as Pat Sajak was asking another player to spin the wheel, dodged several terrified passersby, and walked toward the exit. The first man he tackled and knocked out finally came to, and as he began to sit up, Lawson didn't break stride as he shot him in the forehead and walked out the door onto the Strip. No sense leaving these men alive to take another run at him later. Thinning De Luca's herd now could only pay dividends when he finally went after the son of a bitch.

The temperature change on the sidewalk immediately exhausted him. It was oppressive heat at this point in the day. The Forum Shops at Caesar's Palace were across the street in front of him. He turned to his right, in the direction he told Johnny to run, and up about a block there was commotion in the middle of the street. Lawson ran down the crowded sidewalk, and up ahead he could see an SUV stopped in the right lane and a crowd of people curved around some sort of commotion beside it. The closer Lawson got, the more he knew it was trouble. Sure enough, he maneuvered around the gawking crowd just in time to see two men stuffing Johnny in the backseat. There was nothing he could do. There were far too many people to start shooting.

Then he heard tires squeal, but not from the truck they were putting Johnny in. He looked to his left, and four men jumped out of an SUV and started shooting at the truck taking Johnny hostage. Lawson recognized the four men, they were De Luca's men who had shot at him in front of

Battista's just a few minutes ago. But if they were shooting at the people taking Johnny, then who was taking Johnny?

Lawson took a step back into the crowd for a moment. The truck with Johnny inside roared to life, the back tires started spinning, and in a cloud of smoke it propelled forward away from the oncoming gunfire. Lawson pulled out his phone and called Cassie.

"What the hell, Lawson?" she answered in a panic. "My radio is calling shots fired at the LINQ Casino!"

"I don't have time for this, Cass. I need to know who owns a navy-blue Ford Expedition with the Nevada license plate 212-ZAN."

"Are those gunshots?" Cassie ignored Lawson's request. She was hearing De Luca's men firing the last few shots at the escaping Expedition before they jumped back in their Tahoe and sped off after them.

"Cassie! 212-ZAN! I need it now!"

Lawson ended the call before getting confirmation from Cassie that she had heard him. He didn't have a choice. Someone was getting away with Johnny, which meant they were getting away with the flash drive. He couldn't let that happen. Lawson pulled his Beretta and walked around the front end of a Black Mercedes Benz S500 that sat closest to him in the road. He pointed his gun at the already frightened brunette woman in the driver's seat, and when she opened the door he hurried her out and hopped behind the wheel. He put the sedan in drive and mashed the pedal to the floor. The car shot forward like a rocket.

He swerved around a few slower-moving cars and zoomed past Harrah's, then the Venetian, and finally the Palazzo when he saw De Luca's men making a right just in front of the Wynn. Lawson arced his right turn around two stopped cars, slid sideways onto Sands Avenue, and as his back tires gained purchase on the pavement, he veered across two lanes and three cars to put himself in position to run down the first of the escaping SUVs. What he was going to do once he reached them was another thing entirely.

26

ABOUT TWO FOOTBALL FIELDS IN FRONT OF DE LUCA'S MEN in the black Tahoe, Lawson could see Johnny's captors' Ford Expedition. The Mercedes that he had "commandeered" was much faster than the Tahoe, so he closed in fast. Lawson was no wheelman, far from it in fact, so he really didn't know what to do. He didn't care about De Luca's men. All he cared about was not losing sight of that Ford Expedition. He had to know who was taking Johnny. And more importantly *where* they were taking him.

Lawson decided that since his car was much faster than the Tahoe, he would just go around it and pursue the Expedition. He accelerated to go around the Tahoe on the right side, but before he could pass, the driver swerved over and cut him off. Lawson slammed on the brakes, swerved left, floored the pedal once again, but the SUV swerved to block him. As this little automotive dance was taking place, the Expedition up ahead began to put even more distance between them.

Not good.

Then the driver of the Tahoe slammed on the brakes, and

Lawson was too close to keep from hitting it. When the front end of the Mercedes smacked into the back of the Tahoe, metal crushing metal echoed all around him, the airbag deployed, and a burning sensation seared into Lawson's skin. As he tore at the airbag, muffled sounds of gunshots reached Lawson's ears just before the bullets penetrated his windshield. Lawson instinctively ducked as glass rained down on him. He reached down for the shift knob, threw the car into reverse, and hit the gas. His tires squalled as the Mercedes began moving backward, but his escape was short lived. He heard someone lay on the horn just before he heard the metal-on-metal clash once again. His body was whipped back against his seat from the jarring impact. In front of him, De Luca's men exited the Tahoe and began to walk toward him. Guns raised.

Lawson noticed his cell phone ringing on the console. It was Cassie calling. But instead of reaching for his phone, he reached for the Beretta tucked in the front of his pants. He fired two shots before he could really even take aim. Hitting them was a priority, but keeping them from coming any closer before he could get out of the car was imperative. As soon as the men heard the shots, they took cover behind the Tahoe. Lawson took two more shots through the open windshield at the man's feet on the left side as he took cover behind a door. He missed both, but it gave him a moment to push the start button on the car.

Nothing.

Several gunshots rang out and Lawson again took cover. This time, he stayed low and crawled between the two front seats to the back. He only had a couple of bullets left in his magazine. There were four of them, and he had no way to get cover. If he expected to live through this little shoot-out, he was going to have to get creative. His mind flashed to one of the first run-ins with the underground crime world he and Cassie had when he first arrived in Las Vegas. Cassie had been tipped off by a local DEA agent that one of their informants in a smaller drug ring was on his way to execute someone for infringing on their turf. Cassie didn't want to run it down because the DEA agent had given them faulty intel before, but Lawson always looked to get in the middle of the action. The info-gathering and building-a-case portion of his job nearly drove him mad day to day. So any shot at finding some trouble and Lawson was all over it. Even when it wasn't the smart thing to do. Cassie tried to warn him, but he didn't listen.

The two of them had pulled up to the warehouse where the execution was supposed to be happening, but it wasn't an execution. It was a large cocaine sale, and the informant had flipped on them. The men were waiting for Cassie and Lawson to show up. After a defensive shootout, the two of them barely made it back to their car. After a chase much longer than the one Lawson had just been through, they ended up in a similar position: outmanned, outgunned, and no cover. As the men closed in on them, Cassie's panicked suggestion was to put the car in drive, climb out the back, and shoot the gas tank to blow the car up when it got near them. It sounded good, and Lawson knew she thought of it because it happened in movies all the time. But Lawson knew from experience that even if you were a good enough shot to hit the gas tank on a car that was rolling away from you, it still wouldn't work.

When he first made detective in Lexington, Kentucky, to celebrate, one of his buddies on the police force bought an old junker car. It still ran, barely, and they drove it out in the country to have some whiskey and shoot it up for fun. They ended up challenging each other, betting a night handcuffed to the car on who could make it blow up first. After many errant shots, several did actually penetrate the gas tank, but there was no explosion.

However, when Cassie suggested it that day, it gave Lawson an idea, which he put the idea to use and it actually worked. And it was that flash of a memory that gave him the creative idea he needed to give himself a chance to get out of the near impossible situation he found himself in now. This little trick working twice for him would be nothing short of a miracle, but when you're out of options, a miracle was still something to hope for.

Lawson reached back toward the front dash and depressed the cigarette lighter. He then shot through the open windshield a couple more times to buy him the valuable seconds he needed. De Luca's men once again took cover behind the Tahoe. Lawson wiped the sweat running into his eyes on his blazer sleeve, and opened the glove box. The paperwork to the car was there. Lawson pulled it out, wadded it into a long cone-like shape, and when the cigarette lighter popped up, hot, he grabbed it and opened the back door. A couple more gunshots rang out from the Tahoe. Lawson popped open the gas cap, stuffed the paper down as far as it would go, shoved the hot lighter in behind it, and shut the gas cap to hold it in place. He then quickly opened the driver-side door, held his foot on the brake, jammed the shifter into neutral, and as a few more bullets clanked against the front of the car, he hurried toward the back end of the Mercedes. This would have been a lot easier, and a whole lot safer, if the car would have started. But since it wouldn't, he would have to push.

Mercedes S500s, thankfully, were made like tanks, and it absorbed the oncoming bullets with ease. But with a car made like a tank, that meant a lot of weight. Fortunately for Lawson, the road they were stopped on was on a gradual decline. But if the car didn't get enough momentum as he pushed it forward, he was a dead man. And if it did get enough momentum but for some reason the paper in the gas tank didn't catch fire, he was also a dead man. They would have him in the open behind the car, dead to rights. His odds weren't great—they were terrible, actually—but he didn't have any other choice.

Lawson started pushing with all that he had. He drove his legs down into the hot pavement. He pushed forward on the mangled trunk with as much force as he could muster. The veins in his neck were bulging, sweat poured over every inch of his body, and it was all he could do to breathe in and out as he struggled against the weight of the car. The bullets kept coming, and Lawson kept pushing. There was commotion all around him—other cars laying on their horns, people screaming and panicking to get away from the gunfire—but Lawson heard none of it. All he could hear in his mind was his little girl laughing. The smile on her face that day on the boat. He dug deep within himself to find power that only the thought of living for his daughter could bring. And after what seemed like far too long—long enough for that paper to have burned up—finally, his push paid off.

The car slowly started to become easier to push. Once he felt that momentum, another shot of adrenaline gave him another gear, and he roared forward, the car moving faster and faster now. He drove forward with all his might, and when he thought it had enough speed to make it to the Tahoe, he let go, dove toward the sidewalk on his right, and looked up to see if he had just saved his own life or sealed his own fate.

Lawson rapidly squeezed the trigger to buy him enough cover time for the explosion, but the last few presses of his finger did nothing. The slide on his pistol locked back, his magazine was empty. The men walked out from behind the cover of their SUV as the Mercedes bumped into the back of it.

Nothing.

De Luca's men looked at each other, then to the Mercedes, then to Lawson, then back to each other. Then they began to laugh. All of them. Gut-laughing at Lawson's failed attempt to save himself. Lawson thought about making a run for it. But he knew there was no time. As the four men continued to laugh, each of them trained their guns directly on Lawson as he lay on the ground. It was all over.

Then, in the blink of an eye, they were all gone.

27

THE BLAST WAS MUCH LARGER THAN HE REMEMBERED IT being all those years ago. But it worked all the same. The Mercedes was a much larger vehicle, maybe that was the reason the ball of fire reached so high into the blue sky above. Regardless, it blew the men back off their feet, and if they weren't already dead, the chain reaction of the Tahoe blowing sky high certainly did the trick. Lawson was lying about a hundred feet from the explosion, but the heat from the fire was so intense, it felt as if his face was melting.

Pieces of both of the vehicles rained back down to the ground in a chorus of bangs, and Lawson managed to push himself up to his feet. He was soaked with sweat, from the hundred-degree sunshine, from the exertion of pushing the Mercedes, and from the frying pan that was the asphalt he had been lying on. People were still screaming from various places around the explosion. The crackle of fire continued in front of him. He bent down and picked up his Beretta. Knowing it was empty, he began to walk toward the fiery blaze. On his way there he pulled his phone from his pocket. Five missed calls from Cassie. One voice mail.

In the distance he could hear sirens, fire truck, ambulance, and police were all on their way and arriving in minutes. There was no time to go to jail now. He had a flash drive to retrieve. Now all he needed was to know where to go get it and a way to get there. Just like the rest of life, problems never end. Lawson had always known this of course. Being in law enforcement, there are days that are so dark it seems that all you will ever see again is problems. So you either don't fight it and give up, or you do what Lawson had always enjoyed most, get to solving them.

As he approached the first dead De Luca gunman, he thumbed around in the phone and pressed on Cassie's voice mail.

Nevada license plate number 212-ZAN is registered to Sandy's Laundromats, a business owned by Sokolov Enterprises. As cliché as it gets. Lawson, please call me ASAP. Las Vegas is on the verge of going on lockdown from all the havoc you and De Luca are wreaking. I'm trying to throw the authorities off your scent, but you're making too much of a stink. And since I am the only person who knows you, they are all up my ass about it. Please at least let me know you're okay. And please tell me you aren't caught right in the middle of a Mafia turf war. I wish I could say I was surprised.

The voice mail ended. Lawson bent down next to the severely burned gunman and confiscated his weapon. A Glock 17 pistol. He went around to the other three dead gunmen and did the same. All told he had enough ammo for two guns and an extra magazine. The sirens were closing in, and the heat next to the mobster bonfire was positively unbearable. With a quick glance at his surroundings, he had his choice of vehicles. Several cars that couldn't get around the crash site were abandoned by their owners when things got explosive. Lawson walked over to a white Toyota Camry, still running, got inside, and took a long deep breath of cold, conditioned air. Then he put the car in drive and pulled away.

Just like that, his questions were solved. He now knew where to go—back to Sokolov's room at the D casino—and this wonderfully cooled Toyota was his *how* to get there. As he considered earlier, however, problems in life never ceased. He just solved two of them, and now he already had another. How in the hell was he going to get through Sokolov's men to get to his room? And once he got there, how the hell was he supposed to save Johnny, retrieve the flash drive, and get out of there alive?

Problems were never-ending. You chose either to solve them or to give up. Lawson was a lot of things, but a quitter wasn't one of them.

He started back down Sands Avenue toward old Vegas, and the D Casino. He put his phone on speaker and dialed Cassie.

"You're alive," she answered dramatically.

"And so are you. Now that we have that cleared up, I'm going to need your help."

"Asshole. What the hell do you think I've been doing?"

"Listen," Lawson said, "Sokolov has Johnny, and Johnny has the flash drive. You can bet by now that the original video of his meeting with Delaney and Walters has been deleted by Nero from the security system's hard drive."

"So the flash drive is the only thing left that can completely clear your name." Cassie finished for him.

"Right."

"So let me have a team go to Sokolov's—"

"Cassie," he interrupted. "You know that won't work. You'll have to have a warrant to get in there. And even if you didn't, Sokolov would have the flash drive hidden by the time you could pull a team together to get to him. I am the only person that can clear my name."

Cassie let out a long sigh. "So, what, Lawson? You're going to go in there and take care of this all by yourself? An entire team of gangsters will just, what, cower at your presence and let you walk right in?"

"I expect quite the opposite, Cass. But it doesn't matter. I'll die before I let that proof get lost. Because if I lose *it*, I lose Lexi. And if that happens—"

"You might as well be dead. I get it. I'm on my way to the D Casino. Do not go in there without me. And by the way, you've become quite the drama queen since you got out of prison. So morose. Morose means—"

Lawson ended the call. Cassie was doing that thing again where she resorted to humor when she was nervous. The last thing Lawson needed on his way into the lion's den was someone else's nerves rubbing off on him.

28

LAWSON PULLED THE CAR UNDER THE LARGE RED D SIGN AND into the valet tunnel of the hotel casino. He handed the Toyota keys to the valet attendant and hurried in through the sliding glass door. He had a little over a thousand dollars in cash on him from De Luca's stipend. As he walked into the gaming area, he gave a quick scan of the tables. He saw old and young, large stacks and small stacks of chips, but what he was looking for was very particular. Lawson and some of his friends used to come to Vegas when they were young. They barely had enough money to afford the drinks, but they always managed at least a short amount of time at the tables before they went out to the pool. The drinks were free while you played, and if you got a little lucky at all, the hundred dollars you brought to gamble with could last you long enough at a five-dollar table to get a few drinks in you. Albeit drinks that were light on alcohol, but drinks all the same.

Lawson found the five-dollar-minimum tables, and at the far end, he could see a group of three young men wearing board shorts, sunglasses atop their heads, and party T-shirts to boot.

"You guys having any luck?" Lawson asked.

By the way the three of them looked at him, he could see in their eyes that he must look worse for the wear.

"Not too bad, bro," Spiked Hair answered.

"You want to make a thousand dollars?" Lawson went with the direct approach.

Turns out they did want to make some extra drinking money—shocker—so they said they would do as Lawson asked. He didn't know if they would actually go through with it, but it was a risk he had to take. He would know in a matter of minutes if the grand he handed over to them had been well spent.

Lawson picked up a newspaper sitting in a nearby slot machine chair and walked over to the elevators where they had taken him up to see Sokolov earlier. He texted Cassie to meet him there. This was all taking longer than he would have liked, but it was the smart way in. Just outside the elevator hallway, Lawson leaned back against the wall and turned the paper to the sports section. He saw Cassie walking up out of the corner of his eye.

"Could you look more suspicious?" she said.

Lawson just held his finger to his lips. A few seconds later, an elevator dinged behind him, and three men in suits went sprinting by.

Lawson tossed the newspaper on the floor. Cassie still looked confused.

"Was that Sokolov's men? How did you know they would be coming?"

"You took too long to get here, so I had time to create a distraction."

Lawson pulled one of the Glock 17s he took off De Luca's men and turned the corner for the elevators.

"So we're doing this now, are we?" Cassie followed behind him into the elevator. She pulled her pistol from her shoulder holster that was tucked beneath her navy-blue blazer. "At least tell me the distraction."

"I paid a couple of young guys a thousand bucks to have a loud conversation over by the Sports Book."

"That's where Sokolov's men hang out, I assume?"

Lawson nodded. The elevator moved past the tenth floor on its way to the thirty-fourth and top floor. "I told them to shout to each other that they couldn't believe how the guy that's been on TV all day for killing the district attorney is in a fight with the security guard in the lobby."

"Nice," Cassie checked the magazine on her pistol. "And they weren't worried about why they were doing this?"

"I told them it was a prank. That it's my bachelor weekend and my buddies who are hanging out in the Sports Book were scared to go over to the Strip because this crazy guy was on the loose. They thought it was funny, so they agreed to do it."

"Glad *they* thought it was funny," Cassie ribbed. "So how'd you know Sokolov's men would come running from the elevator?"

"I didn't. But I thought Sokolov's men at the Sports Book might call for backup. Or at least get confirmation that they should go and get me. We were just lucky they did. Best thousand dollars I ever spent."

This really was not the time for jokes, but it was almost like a reflex being with his old partner. They had always done their best to lighten the mood when going into a serious situation. Some habits die hard. The elevator moved past the thirtieth floor.

"You realize I am probably going to lose my job for not calling this in?"

"Yeah." Lawson pulled back the slide on his Glock, chambering a round. "But the benefits are terrible anyway."

"So how many men can we expect in here?"

Cassie was fearless. She always had been. Lawson's frozen heart thawed a bit at the thought of her willingness to put everything on the line for him. He was also angry with himself for ever doubting her.

"Two just inside the door. Maybe five more inside, not counting Sokolov."

"Seven men? Who do you think we are, Lawson, Batman and Robin?"

"Maybe only four total since three of them ran past us on their way out of the elevators."

"Oh, only four. Well, in that case . . ." Cassie glanced at the numbers lighting up on the slow-moving elevator.

Lawson tried to focus her as they reached the top floor. "You're going to have to lure the men at the door out into the hallway."

"Right, 'cause I'm a beautiful temptress and all."

"Just knock on the door, flash your FBI credentials, and tell them you need to speak with Sokolov."

"They're not going to open the door for that," Cassie explained as the elevator door dinged open.

"Then make something up, you are an FBI agent, right?"

Cassie rolled her eyes and walked out toward Sokolov's suite.

It was always an odd mix of feelings when walking into a situation like this. When you are on a case that you have spent months, and sometimes years on, the weight of everything working out the way you've planned is a heavy burden of anticipation. Then you have the excitement of the adrenaline rush mixing with the nervousness of how dangerous what you are about to do really is, and often it leaves you with a sickening high. For Lawson, after spending ten years churning over this moment where he could actually get his hands on proof that he didn't kill Lauren, it was different. There were zero nerves. Only the shot of adrenaline that made him feel like he was floating behind Cassie. It made him feel like he could achieve anything. And if he didn't control it right, things could go very wrong once that hotel room door opened.

"I'll be just out of sight when you knock on the door," Lawson said.

"Roger." Cassie pulled her FBI credentials from her blazer pocket. "Just try not to make a mess. I've already spent the entire morning cleaning up after you."

Lawson didn't answer, and Cassie didn't expect one. She approached the door to Sokolov's suite and gave it a confident knock. The door cracked open to the length of the chain lock.

A man's voice with a Russian accent reached Lawson's ears. "We are busy. Go away."

Lawson watched Cassie present her credentials.

Then he heard the door shut.

Cassie glanced over and shrugged her shoulders, then gave a more forceful knock.

"FBI, open up. We know you have a hostage in there!" she shouted.

The door opened to the chain again. And once again the Russian man spoke calmly.

"You have warrant?"

"We don't need one. We—"

The door slammed shut.

This wasn't the first time Sokolov and his men had been through this routine. Law enforcement had most likely been a regular occurrence there. Cassie stepped back and gave Lawson the look of knowing what was coming next. Lawson moved around the corner of the door. Cassie drew her weapon, ready for whatever came next. Lawson and Cassie could only hope that Sokolov and his men were not.

29

LAWSON READIED HIS PISTOL IN HIS RIGHT HAND, TOOK A long step forward with his left leg, then brought his right leg forward as hard as he could. The bottom of his black oxford shoe connected with the door, right beside the lock, which shattered as the door crashed inward. Lawson pointed his pistol at the red-haired man's midsection while simultaneously dropping down to one knee so Cassie would have a clear line of sight from behind him. Since Lawson had previously visited the room, he knew exactly where everything would be and where every potential target could be standing. He had expected some sort of volatile situation between Sokolov and Johnny. What he found was quite the opposite.

"Mr. Raines." Sokolov calmly rose from his seat on the couch in front of the wall of windows. Johnny was seated beside him, and Kiara on a chair to the left. Johnny showed no signs of fear or anxiety. Lawson was confused. The two men at the door had both pulled their guns, one on Lawson, the other trained on Cassie. Two more men stood to the right of Sokolov, both reaching for their weapons. "You know you are welcome here." Sokolov glanced at the busted door. "Why the theatrics?"

Sokolov motioned for his men to put down their guns. Lawson rose from his knee and lowered his but kept it down by his side.

"I told you I would handle Johnny," Lawson said.

"Yes. And you did. You coerced him into giving you criminal evidence, and now I have it. Our business has concluded."

"How long were you following me?"

Sokolov gave a pitying smile. "Long enough to watch you reminisce at your old home. Such a shame. Your wife was a very beautiful woman."

Lawson took an angry step forward. Sokolov's man put his hand to Lawson's chest, stopping him from moving any closer. Lawson went to raise his gun when he felt Cassie's hand wrap around his wrist.

"I think we can settle this without violence," Cassie said. "Sokolov, you seem like a civil man."

Sokolov's pitying smile morphed into one more befitting a snake. "Yes, of course . . . As I was saying, our business together has concluded. I'll see to it that this video will reach the proper hands. Benefitting both of us greatly."

Lawson moved his eyes from Sokolov to Johnny. "Are you all right?"

Johnny nodded.

"Does he have the flash drive?"

Johnny nodded again, this time with a sorrowful look on his face.

"Did you manage to best the security guard in the lobby?" Sokolov asked, changing the subject. His tone had a humored edge.

Lawson heard the sarcasm in his question, and didn't much care for it. "I need the flash drive, Sokolov."

"And I need you to leave." The smile was gone. "Now. . . . And take Johnny's body with you."

Before there was any time for reaction, Sokolov pulled a pistol from behind his back, raised it out to his right, and shot Johnny De Luca in the forehead. Kiara screamed from the chair beside him, Johnny's blood a mist upon her face. As Sokolov's men were raising their weapons, Lawson kicked backward and knocked Cassie to the floor back out into the hallway. He immediately grabbed the man to his left and bull-rushed him into the bathroom that was just inside the door. He heard several gunshots behind him, a couple of which he hoped were Cassie's.

The image of Johnny's head exploding flashed before Lawson's eyes as he drove the big red-haired man in a black suit all the way to the back wall of the bathroom, slamming him hard against the solid marble. The man wrapped both hands around Lawson's neck and began to squeeze, but all that did was make him completely vulnerable. Lawson delivered a nasty knee to the man's groin. As the man dropped to the ground onto his knees, Lawson took a step back and put a hole in the top of his skull with one of the twelve bullets in his Glock's magazine.

The sound in that tiny room was deafening.

Outside the room, through the ringing in his ears, he heard more gunfire. That meant, at least for the moment, Cassie was still alive. The other man guarding the door was lying facedown just outside the bathroom. Cassie must have shot him first.

"Idti!" Lawson heard Sokolov shout in Russian. "Go! Kill them both!"

Lawson picked up a porcelain toothbrush holder from the bathroom counter and threw it out the bathroom door, smashing it against the entryway wall. Sokolov's men reacted to it by blasting off a few more bullets, and Lawson reached outside the door with his pistol to take advantage of the intended distraction. With only his right eye peeking around the bathroom door frame, he squeezed the trigger three times. Two of his bullets broke the glass on the wall of windows, and one found its mark in the shoulder of one of Sokolov's gunmen. The shattering of the glass was so loud that the other of Sokolov's men instinctively looked toward the loud noise, and Lawson quickly put two bullets in his side.

"Stop!" Sokolov shouted.

"Lawson, are you all right?" Cassie called from the hallway.

During the shooting, Sokolov must have moved into the bedroom off to the right. However, in true scumbag fashion, he left his granddaughter out in the main room. Lawson moved his gun and pointed it at her.

"I think you forgot something, Sokolov."

Kiara was in the fetal position on the couch, physically shaking from all the commotion. Lawson took a step forward. The entryway wall extended another couple of feet in front of him on his right. This blocked Lawson's view of the bedroom where Sokolov was hiding.

Sokolov answered from the bedroom. "I didn't forget anything . . . Now!"

On her grandfather's command, Kiara's entire demeanor changed in an instant. In a blink, she had turned toward Lawson, her arm swinging upward from underneath a cushion. A cushion that had been hiding a gun. Lawson had time to squeeze the trigger, plenty of time to take Kiara down. But he didn't, even though he knew she was attempting to kill him. He wasn't sure if it was her blonde hair, reminding him of how Lexi would look as a young woman, or what it was, but his instinct instead shouted at him to duck.

Lawson dove forward toward the base of an oversized leather chair. He heard two shots from Kiara's gun, followed immediately by two shots from behind him.

Cassie didn't see Kiara as Lexi. She saw her trying to kill her old partner. And she didn't let that happen.

When Lawson dove forward, it gave him a clear line of sight into the bedroom, where Sokolov stood in the doorway. Lawson never dropped his arms when he dodged Kiara's bullets, so his gun was pointed right at Sokolov's chest.

"Don't shoot!" Sokolov shouted. "I'll destroy this flash drive!"

Lawson heard Kiara's body thump against the floor. Sokolov didn't so much as flinch.

"You just killed your granddaughter. And you're worried about a flash drive?"

"Put your gun down or I will destroy it."

Sokolov stepped into the main room, and the light from the glassless windows revealed a glass of water in his right hand. The flash drive dangled above it from his left. Lawson rose to his feet, his gun still trained on Sokolov. Cassie moved in beside Lawson.

"Your own granddaughter?" Lawson said.

"I have another. She is much more competent than this one."

The level of cold-bloodedness in that statement chilled the entire room, even as the Las Vegas heat flooded in from the broken windows. Lawson had been more willing to save Kiara than her own grandfather was. Right then and there, something shifted inside Lawson. He physically felt a change come over him. There, standing in that room in front of a man so vile that his own flesh and blood meant nothing to him, Lawson realized that he had been wrong about himself after all. This man, Serge Sokolov, was a monster. Nero De Luca was a monster. Lawson knew for the first time in years that he definitely was not. Instead, Lawson was just a man fighting for what was right. Always had been, always will be. The moment of clarity took Lawson by surprise. But just because he knew now that he wasn't a man—a monster—like Sokolov, it didn't mean he wasn't capable of doing what was necessary.

"There is no way out of this, Sokolov."

"If that is the case, then why wouldn't I just go ahead and drop this flash drive into the water—"

Lawson squeezed the trigger and a dark hole appeared in the middle of Serge Sokolov's forehead. As his body swayed, before it could hit the ground, Lawson raced over to him, and when Sokolov finished his backward collapse, Lawson snatched the flash drive from his dead hand before any of the water could get to it and ruin it.

Lawson looked back at Cassie who was taking inventory of the carnage around the room.

"Yep, my career is over."

Lawson left Cassie to her thoughts as he walked over to the man he had shot in the shoulder earlier. The man's eyes were filled with fear. However, just because Lawson now knew himself not to be a monster didn't mean he was the kind of man who was going to let someone get away with doing terrible things. So before the man on the ground could protest, Lawson put him down with two more bullets to the chest.

"Lawson," Cassie huffed, "you can't just kill a man like that in front of me. I'm still an FBI agent, and I still have rules."

"Yeah, but I don't."

Lawson moved his eyes from Cassie's to Johnny's bloody remains. Then back to Cassie. He knew she understood. He walked over to Johnny's body lying facedown on the floor. Dead. All because Lawson had brought him into his own quest for revenge.

As if Cassie could read his mind, she said, "This isn't your fault, Lawson."

He turned toward her and held up the flash drive. "He wouldn't be dead if I hadn't forced him to get this for me."

"Wrong." Cassie switched out the empty magazine in her pistol for a fresh one. "He wouldn't be dead if Nero De Luca, his father, wasn't a criminal scumbag."

Though Lawson knew that was true, he couldn't help but feel responsible.

"Johnny was a good kid," he said.

"Maybe so, but his father is a bad man. A bad man now gunning for you . . . and me. It's time we get you out of town. Now that we have proof to clear your name, this thing is finally over."

Lawson dropped the flash drive down into his suit jacket's inside pocket, pulled the second Glock from behind his back, and chambered a round.

"This isn't over until Nero De Luca is dead."

30

Cassie didn't like what Lawson was saying, he could tell that by looking at the scowl on her face. He understood where she was coming from. But he wasn't going to leave Nero's fate—his wife's murderer—in the hands of the system that kept Lawson wrongfully locked up all those years.

"So, what, Rambo?" Cassie waved her gun as she spoke. "You're just going to charge into De Luca's home and take out all his men, even though they are all there waiting on you? That the plan?"

Lawson didn't answer for a moment. Mostly because that *was* the plan. But the way she said it, it did sound like suicide. Lawson glanced back at Johnny's body. Cassie could see Lawson's mind working.

"I won't let him get away with it, Lawson. Can't you just let me handle this?"

He glanced up at her as he kneeled over Johnny's body. "You know I can't do that."

Lawson reached down in Johnny's pocket and pulled out

his iPhone. He pressed the home button and a keypad popped up, asking for a passcode to unlock it.

"Damn this new technology."

"Whatever you're doing, we don't have time for it. I hear sirens, and you know the rest of Sokolov's men have to be on their way up here."

"Is there any way to bypass this passcode?"

Cassie walked over. "No." She glanced down at Johnny's dead body. "Well, maybe."

Cassie bent down and rolled Johnny over.

"What the hell are you doing?" Lawson was lost.

Cassie picked up Johnny's hand, grabbed hold of his thumb, and pressed it against the home button. "Breaking yet another law for you. But at this point, what the hell does it matter?" She stood up and turned the phone's screen toward Lawson, showing him it was now unlocked.

Lawson's face scrunched in confusion. "You unlocked it with his thumbprint? How long was I in jail?"

Cassie took a second to punch in a few things on the screen. "Tech changes fast. Wait until you see someone unlock their phone just by looking at it. I disabled the passcode function in case you need to get in the phone again later."

Lawson snatched the phone from Cassie and opened the messages app. He scrolled down to "Dad" in the text thread, clicked on it, then tapped inside the typing line.

"Lawson, I wasn't joking when I said we have to get out of here."

He ignored her. She walked over to the doorway and checked the hall. Lawson hardly noticed, he was busy concocting.

Lawson typed a message to Nero from Johnny's phone:

Dad, Sokolov kidnapped me. He thought I had evidence against you. But it was just a plan Lawson and I came up with to get Sokolov. I thought it backfired, but Lawson just texted me that he is here, and coming to get me. I'm not sure he can handle all these men. We are at the D Hotel. Send help now!

Lawson knew it was a long shot, but worth it. Nero already knew that Johnny had been taken. His men would have messaged him that immediately during the car chase out in the street earlier. Nero also knew that Johnny had done something in the security system, which is why Nero's men were trying to stop Johnny from handing the flash drive over to Lawson in the first place. So while the text may not be easy to believe, it was, at worst, somewhat plausible. And if all it did was make Nero let his guard down just a little, maybe that would be enough to take him down.

"The hallway is still clear, but it won't be for long." Cassie walked over to him from the doorway. "What did you do?"

Lawson handed her the phone. She read the text.

"Smart, but you really think he'll buy it?"

"Not the point. Just trying to gain any edge I can."

"I think that ship has sailed, partner. And so should we."

Lawson nodded, readied his gun, and took the lead over to the doorway. With a glance, he could see that the hallway was still clear. As they rushed toward the elevator, Cassie started to get skeptical.

"You really think that flash drive has evidence that will tie Nero to Chief Walters and the recently deceased Evelyn Delaney? You think Johnny would do that to his own father?"

"I don't know, Cass. But if he didn't, I'm done. So it

doesn't change what I am going to do now. If I'm going back to prison, I'm going back with Nero De Luca planted firmly in the ground."

"Right, so take down an entire organized crime ring all by yourself," Cassie said, her tone full of disbelief.

Lawson pressed the button on the elevator and glanced back at Cassie. "I don't give a damn about the entire operation, I only want De Luca."

"There isn't anything I can say to stop you, is there?"

"Not a damn thing."

"Damn it, Lawson. Well, at least let me help you then."

"Not a chance. I'm not going to lose you too."

Cassie smiled. "What happened to the hard-ass that couldn't even accept a hug yesterday at that motel?"

"You're not coming with me."

The elevator was almost to them now. As the two of them watched the number rise, so did their anticipation. But that moment of silence helped guide Lawson to an important thought. If he did die trying to get De Luca, which was highly likely, and he had the flash drive on him, De Luca would still get away with everything. Lawson reached down into his lapel pocket, and just as his fingertips touched the flash drive, the elevator door dinged and opened to two men who looked an awful lot like some of Sokolov's men who had rushed past them near the downstairs elevator earlier.

Sokolov's men registered danger at the same time Cassie and Lawson did. The wiry, pale-skinned man in a dark suit on the right raised his gun toward Lawson. Lawson instinctively snap-kicked up with his left foot and knocked the gun from the man's hand. But there was no time to get to the other man's gun. Both Lawson and Cassie dove in opposite directions in the hallway outside the elevator. Two shots came from inside it, both bullets carving into the hallway wall. Lawson glanced to his left, and Cassie was in the same position he was: lying prone on the floor, gun fixed on the open elevator. Neither party could move without the risk of being shot.

Lawson brought himself up to a knee, not moving his gun, and hit the button, calling the second elevator.

"You can come out if you want," Cassie said to the men. "We promise we won't shoot."

"Put guns down," a Russian accent demanded from the elevator. "Or we kill you both."

The second elevator was almost there.

"You can quit now if you want. No need to die. Your boss is dead." Lawson told them.

"You are liar. He just message us three minutes ago."

Lawson motioned to Cassie with a point to the second elevator, and a thumbs-up, letting her know it was arriving. "A lot can happen in three minutes. You're about to find that out firsthand if you keep coming after us."

Lawson took a step toward the back wall, and could barely see the left shoulder of one of the men in the elevator. He raised his gun just as the elevator dinged. With just a shared glance, Cassie understood the plan. Lawson shot three times at the shoulder, missing all three times, but it gave Cassie the cover she needed. She dove into a front roll across the opening of the first elevator, then jumped into the empty one. Lawson rushed in behind her, and as she held the "door close" button, she fired a couple of rounds into the hallway, keeping Sokolov's men back until their door closed. And just like that, they were alone in the elevator, only Frank Sinatra's buttery voice to accompany them down.

"This is ridiculous, Lawson."

"I know. But it's necessary."

"I'm not sure it is."

"Here's how you can help." Lawson handed her the flash drive. "When we get out of this hotel, you go and make sure what Johnny said was on it is there. If it is, get it to the right people to see that it doesn't get lost. Obviously, make a copy."

"Obviously. And then when I call you to confirm it's all on there, you'll stop what you're doing, right?" Lawson had a blank look on his face. "Hello?" Cassie waved her hand in front of his face. Lawson snapped out of it. "Where'd you go there?"

"I just remembered something Johnny texted before things got crazy outside Battista's. He said he put something else on the flash drive that I needed to see. Said I wasn't going to like it."

"Hmm, well, I'll check on that too, but right now we have to make it the hell out of this hotel."

The elevator hit the lobby, and the door slowly slid open. Before they could exit, the elevator beside them dinged. Sokolov's men had also reached the lobby. Cassie glanced up at Lawson as they both readied their guns.

"This is about to get hairy."

31

WITH THE CASINO FLOOR JUST AROUND THE CORNER, HE wanted to make a run for it. Lawson knew the police were closing in, and even though he was with an FBI special agent, Cassie wouldn't be able to keep them from taking him to the station. Even if the evidence did pan out to be on the flash drive, by the time they cleared Lawson, Nero would already be in custody. And his fate would once again be in the hands of people who didn't really give a damn what happened to him. Not the way Lawson gave a damn anyway.

However, running was too risky at this point. Even if they made it past the two bozos in the elevator next to them, it was highly likely he and Cassie would run into more of Sokolov's men before they could exit the hotel. Lawson reached down and hit 2 on the elevator's button board. The elevator doors shut just as Sokolov's two men came out of their elevator with their guns drawn.

"You think they won't know we are going for the stairs?" Cassie said.

"I think they will, but I'd rather have a shootout in a stairwell than on the floor of a casino around a hundred innocent people."

"You know, for a hardened criminal you're proving to be an awfully big softy."

"Instincts never die."

Lawson readied his pistol, and when the doors opened, he rushed to his left and found the door to the stairs. As he raced down the stairs, he could hear Cassie following closely behind. He kept his gun trained in front of him with both hands. As he was descending the last few steps, the door to the casino swung open. Lawson moved the end of his gun to a terribly frightened lady who was at the wrong place at the wrong time. Her hands shot up as her purse dropped to the floor.

"Take it! Just don't hurt me!"

Lawson peeled his finger away from the trigger. He had come a hair from squeezing it. He waved his gun left, telling her to move that way.

"It's okay, ma'am," Cassie said. "I'm a federal agent."

The woman shuffled to the side, and Lawson gave a sweeping glance into the casino floor. He didn't see anyone. He looked back at Cassie.

"Be careful getting out of here. Let me know when you confirm the info on the flash drive."

"Lawson, just come with me. Please don't get yourself killed."

Lawson had already moved out into the casino before she could even finish her sentence. He tucked his gun back into his pants and tried to walk casually yet quickly for the front exit. He didn't see any suspicious movement. Sokolov's men must have already gone back up to the suite. They were in for one hell of a surprise.

He walked toward the main entrance, hoping to be able to hop in one of the taxis that always stood on standby at every casino on the Strip. He rounded the corner, and before he even fully walked around the last row of slot machines, three uniformed officers hurried in through the large revolving door.

"Freeze!" the first cop shouted, reaching for his piece in the holster on his hip.

The cop had recognized Lawson's face immediately. No doubt, every cop had been shown his picture before they started their daily beat. Lawson darted back the way he had come and sprinted for the exit out to Fremont Street. He knew it was on the opposite side of the casino. As he ran, dodging hotel patrons, he followed the signs posted every hundred feet or so, directing the way. He was getting close. He glanced back over his shoulder, and the three officers weren't far behind him. When he looked back in front of him, two of Sokolov's men were waiting for him at the exit. Both had guns extended out in front of them.

Lawson dove left into one of the last rows of slot machines, his momentum carrying him into the brass swivel chairs, his ribs slamming against them. Gunshots banged loudly over the ding-ding-ding of the slots. Several of the bullets clapped against the other side of the slot machines.

"Freeze! Drop your weapons!" one of the officers shouted from the opposite direction.

More gunfire came from Sokolov's men, followed by return fire from the officers. Lawson, the reason everyone was shooting, was caught directly in the middle. People all around them were shouting in fear. Lawson looked down the row of slot machines, and on the floor facing him, about four machines down, was an older lady. The look on her face, sheer terror.

Lawson motioned downward with his hand and mouthed the words "stay down." The lady nodded frantically. Lawson pulled himself up and took a peek toward the exit through the gap between machines. Something blurred by on the left just as he looked, and before he knew it, one of Sokolov's men tripped over the lady lying on the floor. The man skidded on his stomach, rolled onto his side, pointed his gun at the woman, who shrieked in terror, and Lawson shot his gun before he could fully get turned around. The lady screamed again as the gunman moved his pistol toward Lawson. But Lawson's gun had already found the man, and two squeezes later the man collapsed dead to the ground. The lady screamed even louder.

Lawson moved to the gap in the machines once again. The other of the two gunmen was lying dead in front of the exit. That meant the cops were—

"Don't move!"

Lawson stepped up on the chair, pushed off with all he had, and launched himself up and over the row of slot machines, just as several shots were fired behind him. He hit the ground hard but immediately rolled to his feet and sprinted for the glass doorway. Shooting at it twice, he watched the glass fall down in front of him like rain. The last of the glass was still falling as he covered his head and ran through it out into the suffocatingly hot air. More shots were fired behind him, but he didn't feel the burn of any of them on his skin. Out on Fremont Street, the sidewalks and street were packed. And though there weren't any cars allowed under this massive awning-covered path through the down-town casinos, the first thing Lawson saw were two officers on bicycles, and when they saw him run out of the D, their feet twisted their pedals forward, launching them toward him.

"Freeze! Stop right there!"

Lawson had the advantage here. There were too many people for the bike cops to catch him. They couldn't weave through the crowd the way he could. But Lawson knew that if he didn't hurry, all the roads that led out of this covered stretch of carless walkway would be sealed off at any minute. No way out. Lawson launched himself into the crowd, bowling over everyone in his path. He made a right at the flashing Fremont Casino sign and sprinted past a souvenir shop. He could see the next street just out in front of him. But at the intersection, two police cruisers skidded to a halt, their blue-and-reds flashing above them. Lawson skidded to a stop as well, the slick bottoms of his oxfords sliding on the smooth concrete below him. The last thing he saw were two officers exiting each vehicle, pulling their guns and aiming at him.

Lawson turned back toward the crowd and took a right, sprinting down Fremont. The bike cops were right on him now, but they still had too many people to swerve around. So much so that when he looked back, Lawson saw them abandon their bicycles, and the cops from inside the casino were right beside them. He sprinted toward the iconic Binion's and Golden Nugget up ahead under the covered intersection. The cross street that ran through this section allowed cars. This was Lawson's chance.

About fifty feet in front of him, a large man wearing a florescent yellow vest with the word *security* written in black down the front stood in a ready stance. The man was as round as he was tall, but unfortunately for him, Lawson had momentum. Lawson would have just run around him, but a car was stopped right behind the security guard at a light. And Lawson needed that car. Just as the security guard began to move forward, Lawson lowered his shoulder, like a fullback running through a stationary linebacker. The impact jarred Lawson but lifted the big man right off his feet. As the security guard slid on his back, Lawson slid to a stop and opened the door of the neon-yellow Toyota Prius. He immediately reached in across the young man in the driver's seat and unclipped his seatbelt, then pulled him by the arm out of the car. Lawson slammed the door shut, laid on the horn, and put the accelerator to the floor. The people opened like the Red Sea in front of him. The front tires squealed, and a couple of seconds later Lawson was passing the Golden Nugget's main entrance, then running a red light, swerving left onto Carson Avenue.

He lifted his foot off the gas and brought the car down to the speed limit. If he drove out of there like a maniac, all that would do was draw attention to what was for the moment an otherwise inconspicuous car. A few blocks down, he would be able to step up the pace again and get away for good. As maddening as it was not to race away from so many people chasing him, slow and steady was the smart move until he got out of the immediate vicinity. Two police cruisers zoomed past him going the direction he just came from.

Now the only problem he had was that he had nowhere to go.

32

LAWSON PICKED UP THE PACE AS HE DROVE AWAY FROM downtown, away from the unbelievable series of events that had just taken place. He couldn't help but feel frustrated. Even though he managed to elude death and capture on several occasions, he still was no closer to ending this entire thing. Especially if Johnny's flash drive didn't hold the proof that he promised. Lawson knew he couldn't let his mind wander down that path. He had to focus on what was ahead of him.

The sun was beginning its drop from the sky, and the lights of the Strip a couple of streets over were beginning to sparkle. He knew where Nero lived. Everyone did. He stayed in the same mansion his father had lived in when Lawson was trying to run him down. But Lawson doubted that Nero would be there right now. With everything going on, he was most likely lying low in a more secure, secluded location. Thus the reason that Lawson was driving in the direction of the Pink Kitten at the end of the Strip. It wasn't well known that De Luca owned the place, much less that he kept a secure office there. Again, Lawson's time behind bars was paying dividends in insider organized crime information.

Though organized crime had been *mostly* phased out of the casinos, there were still plenty of ways for crime bosses like Sokolov and De Luca to make their money. One of the largest current ways was narcotics. Most of the wars between crime syndicates in modern Vegas were waged because of turf trading violations. The large amount of strip clubs and other various seedy businesses lends itself well to cleaning the dirty money coming in from drug sales. However, one of the most popular ways a boss sells his drugs is through illegal prostitution. Contrary to popular belief, prostitution is only legal in the twenty-one designated brothels throughout Nevada. The vast majority of money spent on prostitutes is illegal. And it is a nice side income to the drug trade for these organized crime rings.

The Pink Kitten was the largest strip club in Las Vegas. Its reputation for the "extra" benefits a patron can receive was legendary. Lawson knew of it from all the chatter in prison. Mostly from De Luca's own men. Nero had figured out that letting his men have their own prostitutes to run as a side business kept them happy. That way they made plenty of extra money while still doing all the things he needed for his breadwinner, drug sales.

The women were a perfect way to sell a lot of the drugs as well. Even if they weren't selling themselves every time they went out, it was easy for them to push the party drug, Molly, to partiers in clubs. They could make as much money or more, selling drugs than when prostituting most nights, and didn't have to let someone have sex with them. Lawson had heard of Nero building offices of sorts in the two stories above the Pink Kitten. He had also heard, on more than one occasion, that it was crawling with security. The rumor was that Nero kept lots of cash hidden in the walls of his office. Prison is a lonely and boring place. A few well-timed questions and normally non-talkative thugs can become quite the Chatty Cathys. Especially if you just saved them from an anal assault in the showers. How much truth there was in those rumors, no one really knew. But usually if you hear something more than once, you could bet there was probably something to it. Smoke; fire.

Lawson parked across the street from the Pink Kitten. It was early, but places like these had a steady clientele all day in Vegas. Lawson picked up his phone and dialed Cassie for the third time. Even though he knew how capable she was, he was beginning to worry.

Finally she answered. "Do you want me to see what's on this flash drive or not?"

"Oh, am I disturbing you?"

"Lawson Raines, if I didn't know better, I would think you were worried about me."

"Hardly. I just need to know what's on the flash drive."

"Right." Cassie paused. "So does that mean you are reconsidering taking this matter into your own hands?"

"No. I just don't want to be surprised. Johnny mentioned something else was on there. I need to know what that is."

"Hold your horses. I'm pulling it up now. This would have been a lot easier if I could have gone into headquarters. But I'm just as wanted as you are now thanks to the party we threw in Sokolov's suite."

Lawson watched as several scantily clad women walked

toward the back of the club, while a few groups of rowdy men walked in the front entrance. His biggest obstacle would be getting in. His mind processed the options. They were few. Lawson would most likely be persona non grata, whether Nero believed the text message from Johnny's phone or not. A text message that was never returned. And that gave Lawson an idea.

"Damn it," Cassie blurted just as Lawson was formulating a plan.

Lawson's stomach dropped. "I don't like the sound of that."

"It's passcode protected. Smart of Johnny, but he died with the code."

"Where does that leave us?"

"I'm not at the office, but I think it's only a small roadblock. Our tech guy owes me a favor."

Lawson said, "Can you trust him not to turn you in?"

"Like I said, he owes me. I'll have him come see if he can crack it. Hold tight, I'll call you as soon as I'm in. Don't do anything until—"

"Hurry up." Lawson ended the call. Frustrated. He knew he was going to have to go in regardless of whether the evidence was there or not, so he put the flash drive out of his mind completely.

Several minutes of tapping on the steering wheel, waiting impatiently for Cassie to get back to him, and Lawson's patience had run out. He couldn't wait any longer to do something—anything—even if it was wrong. He reached over to the passenger seat and picked up Johnny's phone. It wouldn't be long before Nero got word about what really happened in Sokolov's hotel suite. Lawson needed to take advantage of that now, if he was ever going to get the chance. He swiped until he found the option to call Nero and pressed the button to do so.

It only rang once before Nero answered.

"Hello, Mr. Raines."

33

LAWSON WAS TAKEN ABACK FOR A MOMENT. HE WASN'T ready for Nero to know already that Johnny was dead. It had only been a little over an hour. But then again, the chief of police was on his payroll.

Lawson recovered. "Looks like your plan has failed miserably, Nero. You got your own son killed."

"You think you have this all figured out, don't you, Lawson?"

Lawson wasn't sure where Nero was going with this, so he said nothing.

"You think you are smarter than me," Nero continued. "You think manipulating my naive son to give you incriminating evidence would be enough to bury *me*?"

"I don't think, I know."

"That was sloppy of my head of security. But a man like me always has a backup plan."

Lawson didn't like the sound of that.

"It's been a busy twenty-four hours, Mr. Raines. For both of us, I'm sure. I must admit, I didn't see it coming, you turning Johnny on me. But when Evelyn Delaney's ignorant attempt to have you killed failed, I knew if you hadn't already put all of us together, that you soon would. So I had to be prepared for something like this."

"Am I supposed to be taking notes, Nero?"

Lawson could feel that his breathing had become labored. He didn't know where all of this was headed, but he knew wherever it ended up wasn't going to be good.

"No, no notes. I think you'll be able to remember this. You see, Johnny is—*was*—a smart kid. But he was soft. His mother sheltered him far too much."

"This is heartwarming, Nero, but get to the point."

"The point, Mr. Raines, is that you have no evidence against me. Your friend at the bureau will be notifying you of this fact at any moment."

Lawson reached over and checked his phone.

"You see, I bought Johnny those flash drives that he uses. They are made by a company called IronKey."

On the phone's lock screen, it showed a missed call from Cassie and a text message.

Nero continued. "The special thing about an IronKey flash drive, Lawson, is that when an unauthorized computer attempts to unlock the passcode, it automatically alerts the administrator, and all I have to do is press one button to wipe the data from the flash drive."

As he heard Nero tell him this, Lawson was reading confirmation of it from Cassie's text message.

"Clever little devices, no? It also tells me where the computer is that the flash drive was inserted into, that's how I know it was your FBI friend who has it. She tried to unlock it from her government-issued laptop. From a Starbucks."

Lawson didn't know what to say. Nero knew it too, so he just let silence fall between them.

Another text came in from Cassie: *I'm sorry, Lawson. Our tech says there is no way to recover it. But we are reverse tracing where the command to erase it was sent from. This is the first time the tech has done something like this, so it could take some time. Don't move. Hopefully I'll know where Nero is shortly.*

Lawson took a deep breath. The fact that he would never spend another moment with his daughter washed over him. The fact that no matter what happened, he would never outrun what has happened in the last twenty-four hours settled in. Without that evidence, he was going back to prison. So there was only one thing left to do before the police came for him.

"Mr. Raines, I know that was hard to hear. But I still haven't gotten to the good part. I have an even better story to tell you."

Lawson was through listening to Nero feel proud of himself. "Story time is over, De Luca. And I'm about to make sure that there's no chance you'll live happily ever after."

Lawson ended the call and got out of his car. He stalked toward the entrance of De Luca's strip club. The big man at the door held up his hand. "I need to see your ID."

Lawson walked right by him and through the entrance of the strip club. The bass was thumping, the all-open, over-sized room was dark, except for the spotlights shining down on the massive square stage where all of the women were dancing. Lawson felt a hand on his shoulder.

"I told you I need to see your—"

Lawson wheeled around and bludgeoned the man in the

mouth with a straight right hand. The man dropped to the floor. Lawson scanned the room, then walked over to the bar on his right. Out of the corner of his eye, he saw two more security guards moving toward him. They had seen him knock the doorman out.

"Can I get you a drink?" the bottle-blonde bartender with obnoxiously fake breasts asked Lawson as he approached.

"Where is De Luca's office?"

She raised her painted-on eyebrow. "I just work here, buddy." She noticed the two security guards coming his way in a hurry. Then she pointed at Lawson.

Lawson turned away from the bar and squared up to the oncoming muscle. The first bouncer threw his tree-trunk arm in a slow right hook toward Lawson's face. Lawson stepped in, parried the punch with his left arm, and punched the man directly in the throat. The other security guard, even bigger than the first, grabbed Lawson by the lapels of his jacket and brought his big bald head forward, slamming Lawson in the forehead. This knocked both men backward. The force of the blow was like few Lawson had taken. He saw purple stars shooting in front of his eyes, and he nearly blacked out. The music in the club swirled in his ears, taking on a swimming sound.

Lawson shook his head left and right to clear the cobwebs and stumbled left as he did so. When he put his hand down to catch himself, it landed in an ice bucket that was chilling a bottle of liquor. When he looked up, the bald man was already coming at him again, this time with a punch. Lawson brought the bucket up in a defensive move, and the man's hand slammed into its metal bottom. The man staggered back, and Lawson windmilled the bucket around and slammed it down on his head, knocking the man out.

When Lawson looked up, two more bouncers were right in front of him. He went to pull his pistol from his waistline, but someone caught his arm from behind. Lawson turned, bringing a left hook around with him. It found the temple of a short, round man, but as the man went to the ground, he took the sleeve of Lawson's suit jacket with him.

One of the two bouncers was on him now and threw the first punch. Lawson's right arm came free of the jacket, but his left was still tangled, so he spun and used the part of the jacket that was coming off to catch the bouncer's punch. He squeezed with his left arm around the bouncer, holding him in place while delivering a right hand to the man's jaw, then immediately front-kicked the stomach of the second bouncer coming at him. This backed him up. Lawson freed himself of the suit jacket completely with one more 180-degree turn, picked up a chair, wheeled around, and smashed it over that second bouncer's head.

By this time, most of the club was dialed in on Lawson and the Pink Kitten staff. Lawson was on fire. From the inside out. There was something burning in him at that moment, a rage that was so hot nothing short of a bullet to the head was going to stop him. He took two steps over to the bar, where the bartender quickly extended a handful of napkins to him.

"For your head," she shouted over the music that had yet to stop.

Lawson hadn't realized he was bleeding. Must have been from the head butt. He took the napkins and pressed them to his forehead. When he pulled them away, the napkins were soaked in crimson.

"De Luca's office is through that door on the back wall," the bartender pointed. "There's a stairway back there. It's all the way at the top. You've got some set of balls coming in here like this . . ."

Lawson didn't hear the rest of the sentence. He was already halfway to the door she had pointed out. Every eye in the bar was on him now. The people at the tables looked on in fear. But Lawson never saw one of them.

All he could see was red.

34

LAWSON KNOCKED ON THE METAL DOOR THAT THE BARTENDER said led to the stairway up to De Luca's office. Yet another large meathead of a man opened the door, and Lawson greeted him with a stiff hand around his throat. When Lawson pushed forward, the man was caught so off guard that he was easily driven back against the wall. Lawson slammed him in the stomach with a hard right, then stood him back up and once again grabbed him by the throat.

Lawson growled, "Tell me what I want to know or I rip out your Adam's apple."

The man knew this wasn't the time to act tough, probably because of the strength he felt in Lawson's grip. So he nodded emphatically.

"How many men are upstairs?"

Lawson relaxed his grip so the man could answer.

"Two at the door, that's it."

Lawson grabbed him by the back of the neck and forced him out the door, locking it behind him. Two men? With everything Lawson had heard over the years about the notorious security here, something was off. It made him wonder whether all of this was for nothing and De Luca wasn't there. He should have waited for Cassie. He knew that. But he couldn't sit in that car and listen to that smug son of a bitch any longer.

Regardless, Lawson had to know for sure, so he started up the stairs. As he was coming to the top, he slowed, trying to see over the last step. Down a long hallway, he could see the two men he was told would be there, and both of them were already running toward him. They stopped to pull their guns when they saw the top of Lawson's head. Lawson went back down a few steps and let the men fire off their warning shots. Bits of the concrete block wall were dropping on him from the bullets landing over his head. He waited until the shooting stopped, then walked right up the stairs, firing straight in front of him.

One of the men had already swapped out his magazine and began firing back. The bullets were hitting the ceiling, however, because Lawson had already shot him twice in the torso, and he was falling backward. The other man dove into a room to his left, immediately pleading for his life.

"Please don't kill me! I just started here, I'm an ex-cop!"

Lawson walked forward and swung around the open door with his gun out in front of him.

"Please don't shoot!"

But the man didn't have his hands up, he was sliding a fresh magazine into his pistol. And Lawson recognized his face immediately. He was the man standing next to De Luca at the meeting at STK. Lawson knew because he had a long scar running vertically down his left eye. This man was no ex-cop. He was just another of De Luca's cronies. Lawson squeezed off two shots, stopping the man as he cocked his pistol.

He turned toward the door the two men were guarding. A moment ago, he had it figured that Nero wasn't there. But these two men were guarding this door for some reason. And Lawson couldn't help but hope it was for Nero.

Lawson looked down at his Glock, the slide was locked back. He was out of bullets. He pried the pistol from the dead man's hand, chambered a round, and walked toward the now-unguarded door. He didn't know what he expected to be on the other side, but there was no sense in waiting. He walked up and put his hand on the knob. It wasn't locked. Two armed gunmen must have figured they would be enough. He pushed the door open and nothing on earth could ever have prepared him for what he saw.

Lexi.

35

LEXI STOOD FROM BEHIND THE DESK WHERE SHE WAS SITTING. Pure terror on her face. There were two reasons Lawson recognized his daughter immediately after all those years. Of course, from the picture that Cassie had given him the day before. But he wouldn't have even needed that to know it was her, because standing there before him was a younger version of his wife, and instantly he fell in love with her.

"Lexi? I . . ." Lawson didn't have words.

Lexi backpedaled slowly until her back was against the wall. She was horrified. But did she even know who she was afraid of?

"D-Dad?"

The word *Dad* from her sweet trembling lips brought a wave of emotion that nearly took Lawson to his knees. He stepped forward, slowly. Lexi had nowhere to go, but she did her best to sink further into the wall behind her.

So many things to say, but so many things he couldn't. All he wanted to do was run to her and squeeze her, hold her, for the first time in ten years. But he couldn't.

"Are you all right?" It was the only thing he could think to say.

Lexi visibly swallowed her rising emotions. "Am I all right? Am I all right?"

Apparently, that was the wrong starter.

Lexi pushed off the wall and stood up straight. "Of course I'm not all right. Yesterday, I'm in my room, writing a new song, and here I am today, all the way across the country, the only mother I've ever known taken away by some scary guys with guns, and I'm left here all by myself with armed guards at my door. Oh, and the father I've never met, who murdered my real mother, is standing in front of me with blood running down his face. No, I am not all right!"

Apparently she was twelve going on twenty-five. And she writes songs?

Lawson took a step toward the desk. "I didn't kill your mother. I loved her more than anything in the world . . . other than you, of course."

Lawson could see emotion rising up inside his daughter. But she choked it back.

"Just stay away from me, okay? Just stay away!"

"I can't stay away, Lexi. I have to get you out of here. It isn't safe."

"It's not?" Her face held an incredulous look, her tone saturated in sarcasm. "I thought with all the gunshots, surely everything was fine."

She was her mother's daughter. All the way down to the smart-ass. She was feigning strength in the face of fear. A coping mechanism hardwired in her DNA. It was a Lauren Raines specialty.

"It's okay to be scared, but I'm going to get you out of here safely."

"I'm not going anywhere with you. How do I know you won't kill me too?"

Ten years of pent-up anger was coming at Lawson full force. How could he blame her? This thing with De Luca ruined her life long before she could ever form memories.

Lawson tried his best to speak in a soft tone. "I guess you're just going to have to trust me."

"Trust you? You just said you loved me more than anything in the world. But you never even tried to write to me. If you'll lie about that, why wouldn't you lie about hurting me?"

She was smart beyond her years.

"I did write, Lexi. I wrote you a letter every month for ten years. But your mother's sister—Erin—would never have let you get them. I can only imagine the terrible things she's told you about me."

Lexi's demeanor turned defiant, her chin held high in the air. "You clearly don't know Erin then. Because she's never had anything but great things to say about you, and my mom."

"Lexi, she kept me from seeing or even speaking to you all these years."

"No she didn't."

"Lexi—"

"She didn't! It was her asshole husband, Dan!" Lexi began to walk toward Lawson. "*He* is the one who said all the bad things about you, *and* my mom." She walked around the desk and straight for Lawson. "Erin had to do what he said, but she used to tell me stories about you and my mom when Dan wasn't around. Good stories. Like, movie-love kind of stories, about how you and mom were." She was standing right in front of him now. Lawson was doing everything he could to hold it together. "But then Dan would come home and beat her. And then he would beat me! And it's all your fault!" Lexi started swinging at Lawson. Furiously punching him in the stomach. Lawson just stood there and let her swing. He thought he was a broken man before, but hearing Lexi say that she was abused growing up demolished him entirely. "You did this!" Lexi continued to hit him. "If you hadn't let the bad men get Mom, then we all could have lived together! She would still be here!"

Lawson dropped to his knees. Lexi continued to swing away, now punching tirelessly at his chest.

"I could have had a mom and dad like everyone else!"

She pounded some more.

"I'm sorry Lexi." It was all he could manage. Even if he could explain, it wouldn't have been enough. Lexi was right. Even though Lawson would have done anything to protect Lauren, he hadn't. She died because of his work, and that *was* his fault.

"I hate you!" she screamed. Tears were flooding from her clinched eyelids. "I hate you!"

"I love you, Lexi. I never stopped loving you, or your mom."

"I hate you." This time she said it through sobs and with a little less shout. She began to cry, and the punches were slowing down. "I . . ."

After a couple more halfhearted blows, the punches stopped and the full sobbing began. And finally, she fell against him and wrapped her arms around his neck. Her body was convulsing she was crying so hard. There was no recoil in Lawson from this hug. The exact opposite. Having his little girl's arms around him pulled at a part of his soul that he thought had been lost forever. Lawson let his daughter cry.

And slowly he wrapped his arms around her and picked her up as he rose to his feet. That was when he felt Lauren there with them. It was so unmistakable that he could smell her perfume as if she were standing right behind him. He could feel her eyes lovingly watching on as this long-overdue embrace finally melded father and daughter together. Where they belonged.

Echoing up the stairs and down the hallway, Lawson heard the door he had locked on the first floor swing open and slam against the concrete wall at the bottom of the stairs. They were coming for him.

They were coming for his daughter.

Lexi pulled her head back, but she held on with her arms. She had heard the door as well. Her face was flush and soaked with tears. "Are they coming for us?"

Us.

Lawson stared into his daughter's aqua-blue eyes. "They are. But I won't let them hurt you."

"We have to save Erin. Those guys with guns took her. Dan is the one that brought us to him. I'm afraid they are going to kill her."

Lawson knew that "him" was Nero De Luca. What he didn't get was where Lauren's sister, and her husband, Dan, figured into all of this. Erin clearly wasn't the woman Lawson thought she was. Lexi made it sound like she was as much a victim in all of this as Lexi had been. And Dan? Was he just giving up Lexi so that De Luca could use her against Lawson? Or did it go much deeper than that? Lawson could hear footsteps coming up the stairs. These questions would have to wait.

"Lexi, I know you don't trust me right now, but I need

you to do everything I say if I'm going to get you out of here. Can you do that?"

He set Lexi on her feet. She wiped the tears from her face with the sleeve of her purple long-sleeved T-shirt, and the wise-beyond-her-years Lexi reappeared. "Erin told me that you had always been good at getting the bad guys, now would be a good time to use that."

Lawson smiled. "Yes it would." He wiped the last of the tears away from her chin with his thumb. "I'm going to have to do some bad things to get us out of here. Promise you won't hold it against me?"

"Only if you get us out of here."

"Right." Lawson pulled his gun from the back of his waistline. Lexi's eyes were wide at the sight of it. He ushered Lexi over to the far wall, farthest from the door. "No matter what you hear, don't move. I'll be right back. I promise."

Lexi nodded.

Lawson moved back toward the door and took a quick look. Two men began shooting immediately, and he just snapped his head back behind the wall when bullets began tearing the books to pieces on the shelf behind the desk. Lexi screamed and held her hands to her ears. If these two guys didn't stand a chance against Lawson before, they sure as hell were walking dead men if they thought they were going to get to his daughter.

Lawson grabbed the rolling chair from beside the desk and pushed it out of the way. Then he took the end of the cherrywood desk and flipped it up on its side like it was nothing. He glanced at Lexi to make sure she was okay, and her eyes widened as she watched him so easily maneuver such a heavy desk. He got behind the desk, which was now only a little shorter than he as it stood on its end, and began scooting it forward toward the door.

Bullets continued his way and were now crashing into the top of the desk that Lawson was crouched behind. As soon as he managed the desk through the doorway, he stopped, reached his gun hand around its side, and fired until the two men firing at him were no longer shooting. He glanced around the desk and both men were on their backs. He listened for a moment to hear if anyone else was coming, but all he heard were sirens off in the distance.

For a brief moment, he had forgotten his situation and felt happy that the police could help him get Lexi to safety. But when he walked back in the office to get Lexi, it once again dawned on him that he couldn't trust them either. Not with the chief of police on De Luca's payroll.

Lawson had to get Lexi out of there, and he had to do it fast.

36

LAWSON PICTURED THE ROUTE OUT OF THERE IN HIS MIND. Because of the commotion he had caused earlier, the club would most likely be void of patrons, but security might have stuck around. And though they weren't armed on his way in, the bouncers certainly could have strapped up by then. He did remember watching the girls walk around the back when he was sitting in his car earlier. He didn't remember seeing a door, but his entry to the back stairs was rushed, so he must have missed it.

"Sounds like the police are coming," Lexi said. "Looks like we're gonna be okay. But what about Erin? Will they save her?"

Lawson took a step toward her. "It's complicated, sweetheart. We can't really trust the police right now. Not all policemen are good guys."

"Tell me about it. I watched this one movie, *Training Day*. That cop was really bad. Are the cops coming here like Denzel in that movie?"

"You've seen *Training Day*?" Lawson couldn't believe

how grown-up she was. "Anyway, no, the cops coming here aren't like him, but their boss is."

"So he may tell them to do something bad, and they don't know it's bad?"

"Exactly."

Lawson reached for her hand. Lexi was reluctant to take it.

"There are more bad guys downstairs," Lawson told her. Then he turned his back to her. "We have to go. Just grab my belt and stay behind me. Got it?"

Lexi nodded. "How will we ever find Aunt Erin? Is she going to die?"

"She's not going to die. And I think I know exactly where she is. Come on, let's go!"

Lawson moved toward the door, and he felt Lexi's hand tug at his belt behind him. They moved around the desk that was still standing in the middle of the hallway, and as they approached the dead men that lay in their path, Lawson knew he had already lost father-of-the-year honors. Lexi had been in his care for all of five minutes and she was already seeing dead bodies.

"Don't look at the men on the floor, Lexi. Just pretend they're sleeping."

"I'm not six, Lawson. I know they're not sleeping."

Hearing the word *Dad* come out of Lexi's mouth again might take a while.

They stepped over the bodies, and Lawson heard Lexi gasp.

"I told you not to look."

Lexi quipped, "Oh, right. So if I say elephant, you're telling me you aren't picturing an elephant right now?"

She had a point.

Lawson still didn't hear anything but sirens. And they would be pulling into the parking lot any second now. Security must have had enough from earlier. Hearing gunshots above them probably made it easier for them to call it a night. They made their way down the stairs, and sure enough, there was a back door under those stairs. Lawson walked over, opened it, and there was zero movement outside. Everyone had cleared out entirely.

"All right, we're going to make a run for it. You ready?"

"Ready," Lexi said.

Lawson pushed the door open, grabbed Lexi's hand, and ran for the stolen Toyota Prius. Halfway there, Lawson was frustrated with himself. He should have ditched that car before he went into the club. He should have had a car ready to go that the cops didn't already know he was driving. He had left the car in a rage, and this is exactly the kind of mistakes you make when you let emotion enter into your decision making. There was nothing he could do about it now because his phone was in that car and he had to talk to Cassie. And the four cop cars that had just rounded the corner only solidified that.

Lawson rushed to the driver's side door and opened it, maintaining his crouched posture.

"Crawl across," he told Lexi.

The police cruisers screeched into the parking lot of the Pink Kitten just as Lawson shut the car door. He dropped as low as he could in his seat, gesturing for Lexi to do the same. Lawson's only hope was that the policemen would be focused on the club and what was reportedly going on inside, not on the cars in the parking lot. The squealing tires all came to a stop along with the sirens. The red and blue lights that were all facing the club were bouncing around the interior of the car.

Lexi whispered, "You want me to take a look?"

Lawson nodded. "Go slow."

Lexi slowly raised her head.

"Tell me what you see."

"Four cop cars. Each one of them has two cops standing with their doors open. Two of them are moving toward the entrance now."

"Any of them looking this way?"

"No." She lowered her head. "But do you hear that?"

Lawson nodded. "More police are coming. Probably a lot of them."

"We should leave."

"I agree."

One of the benefits of stealing an electric car was that they make zero sound when you start them up and almost zero sound when you pull away. When he first took it, he thought the lack of power might be a hindrance. Now, it just might be the thing that would save them.

He started it up. "How we looking?"

Lexi raised her head again, then ducked it down immediately. "Don't move yet," she whispered.

"What is it?"

"I just saw one of the cops start looking around. Want me to check again?"

"Carefully."

Lexi raised up again. "He's moving toward the club. I think you should go now."

Lawson inched his way up the back of the seat. Just high enough to look for himself. He put the car in reverse and eased off the brake.

"We good?" he said.

"All good."

The sirens from the backup drew closer. It was now or never. Lawson took his foot off the brake and the Prius rolled backward, silently, as if it had no engine at all. In a quick move to minimize the brake lights coming on, he tapped the brake and threw the shifter into drive. The Prius moved toward the side exit of the parking lot, just as more police cars sped into the main entrance on the other side. Lawson turned onto the side road without applying the brakes and rolled down an alley with his lights off, seemingly floating away from the fray.

"I've gotta say," Lexi said, breaking the silence. "When I first saw the Prius, I thought it was a really bad car to try to get away in. But you proved me wrong."

Lawson smiled. "Yeah? Well, we're not out of the woods yet." No way he was going to tell her the Prius was just a happy accident.

Lawson hit the lights and turned out onto the main road, heading back toward the Strip. He picked up his phone from the console. The screen was filled with missed calls and texts from Cassie. He called her back.

She answered, "I can't do this anymore. You're killing me. Are you all right?"

"I am."

"You find what you were looking for?"

Lawson glanced over at his daughter in the passenger seat. Before he could answer, Cassie cut back in.

"I know you didn't, because I'm staring at him right now on my computer screen."

"De Luca? How?" That took Lawson by surprise.

"I told you we were running that reverse trace on the kill command for the flash drive."

"Yeah."

"Well, it worked. And, turns out, it gave us a back door into De Luca's security system."

"So he's at his house?"

Cassie sighed.

"What is it?" Lawson couldn't take any more bad news.

"I think I know what the bonus footage Johnny left for you on the flash drive must have been . . ."

Lawson already knew what Cassie was about to say. Lexi's Aunt Erin was going to be there. Just like Lexi said. "Are you going to make me guess?"

"I don't know how to say this . . ."

"Lauren's sister is there with De Luca," Lawson beat her to it.

"How in the hell did you know that, Lawson?" Cassie was floored.

Lawson bypassed her question. "I'm on my way to De Luca's, I need you to meet me there."

"This is a police matter now. We have to let them take care of it."

"Do we really have to keep doing this?"

"No," Cassie resigned. "I'm already on my way. No way we are letting this asshole get out of this."

"Now you're talking. I'm assuming the proof that I didn't kill Lauren was irretrievable?"

Lawson glanced over at Lexi. She looked up at him briefly when she heard her mother's name, but then refocused on something in her pocket.

"Whatever Johnny uploaded to that flash drive is gone.

And I know that is terrible, but we might have an even bigger problem."

"Bigger than a life in prison, problem?"

"Unfortunately. I don't want to, but we have to assume that since De Luca has Lauren's sister, there is a possibility that . . ."

Cassie trailed off. She didn't want to say it. Lawson gave her a break.

"That he could have Lexi too."

"I hope not, Lawson, but it would make sense to use her to get you to stop coming after him."

"Glad we don't have to worry about that," Lawson said.

"How do you mean?"

"Because I have Lexi right here with me."

Lawson ended the call. He hoped Lexi hadn't heard too much. It didn't take but a second to learn that she had.

Lexi cleared her throat. "So, you really didn't kill my mom?"

Lawson went to grab her hand, but Lexi pulled away.

"I didn't. But I'm having a hard time proving who did." He wasn't going to lie to her. Not now.

"But you know who did?"

"I know who is responsible for her being killed. We had proof, but we lost it."

"His name is De Luca?" Lexi asked.

"Yeah. It's not for you to worry about, sweetheart." Lawson didn't know what else to say.

"But you just said we are going there now."

"I am. You are going to stay with Cassie where it's safe."

Lexi shifted in her seat to face Lawson. The lights of the Strip were flashing behind her a street over. "Are you going to kill him?"

"I told you, it's not for you—"

"To worry about," Lexi cut in. "I heard you. But I do. She was my mom, for God's sake, and someone took her from me before I can even remember her."

Lawson's emotions swelled inside of him. He could see in Lexi's eyes what she wanted to hear, and he didn't care if it was the right or wrong thing to do, he wanted to give her what she wanted.

"I'm going to kill him."

Lexi was quiet for a moment. She looked out the window at the passing lights. "If you do, does that mean you don't need proof anymore. All of this will be over?"

Lawson took a moment. He wasn't sure what to say. But he figured sticking with the truth was the only thing he could do. "It will be over for you, Lexi. But I will go back to prison without being able to prove that I had nothing to do with any of this."

Lexi turned back toward him. "Then you need proof."

"I told you, we had it, now it's gone for good."

"Then get more proof, Lawson. You can't go back to prison for something you didn't do."

Lawson stared at Lexi for a second, then looked back at the road. She at least still had some innocence left. He didn't want to shatter that too. "It's not that simple."

Lexi was adamant. "Sure it is. Take this." Lexi turned Lawson's hand over and placed a small recording device in his palm. "Before you kill him, make him confess."

Lawson smiled. "You've seen too many movies. Why do you have this anyway? Can't you record things on your phone nowadays?"

"It was Mom's."

Lawson thought the recorder looked familiar.

"Aunt Erin said Mom used to record herself singing on it all the time. So, it's what I record my song ideas and stuff on."

Lawson wanted to turn the car around and just drive away with Lexi. But he knew she would never forgive him if he left her aunt Erin with De Luca.

"Anyway," Lexi said, "make him confess before you kill him. Then maybe you can hear me sing sometime."

Lawson knew the odds of that were slim, but it warmed him to hear her say the words. "I'd like that, Lexi. If you're half as good a singer as your mom, you'll sound like an angel."

Lexi just looked down, then back to the window. Lawson put the recorder in his pocket. He didn't have the heart to tell her it would never work.

37

LAWSON TURNED THE PRIUS INTO THE NEIGHBORHOOD THAT ran adjacent to De Luca's. Along the way, he was able to avoid a couple of roadblocks that had been set up to catch him, thanks to Cassie guiding him around them. Her tech guy, Troy, was proving to be quite an asset. Up ahead of them, parked in the street in front of a Lot for Sale sign was Cassie's car. She was already out, pacing the street.

"Is this your girlfriend?" Lexi asked.

"No, Cassie used to be my partner in the FBI. And she was very close with your mom. She was at the hospital when you were born."

"She knew Mom?"

"Very well. Have her tell you some stories tonight."

Lexi turned to face Lawson. "I'm staying with you."

Lawson pulled in behind Cassie's car and turned to Lexi. "You know you can't do that. It's going to be dangerous going in there to get your Aunt Erin. Cassie will take great care of you. You'll like her, I promise."

Lexi didn't say anything, she just turned and faced forward in her seat.

"Wait here," he told her. "I'll be just a second."

Lawson opened the car door. Cassie came rushing over. "Where is she? Can I see her? I can't believe you found her!" She gave Lawson a quick hug. He didn't return it.

"I need you to keep her safe."

Cassie stepped back, astonishment on her face. "Lawson, I—you can't go in there by yourself."

"What else would you have me do? She can't sit here in the car while we go in. What if neither one of us makes it? It's not like I have a sitter on call."

Cassie was quiet for a moment.

"You can't go in there alone. Let me find someone to help us. I'm in between partners, but I know a couple of really good—"

"Cassie. Stop. A few hours ago, I wasn't even sure I could trust you. Director Billings wants me dead, you think I am going to trust someone in the Bureau?"

"Then we just let the police handle it. That's it. I'm calling it in."

"He will kill Lauren's sister."

"So? That bitch kept Lexi from you all these years."

Lexi had stepped out of the car without them knowing, and she spoke up from the other side of the car. "She's not a bitch. She's the only reason Dan didn't kill us both. He's a lunatic."

Cassie could only stare at Lexi. Lexi's face was glowing in the red taillight of Cassie's car in front of them.

"Oh my God. You look just like your mom," Cassie said to Lexi. Then she looked at Lawson, her mouth agape. "It's even more uncanny in person."

"I'm not staying with her, Lawson."

Lawson gave Cassie a stern look. Cassie walked back to her car.

Lawson turned to Lexi. "You want me to keep them from hurting Erin, don't you?"

Lexi nodded emphatically.

"Then I have to go in there and do what it takes to get her, and you can't come with me."

"Like you had to do to the guys lying in the hallway of that club, right?"

"I'm going to do whatever I have to, to save her."

Lexi shut the Prius door and walked around the front. "Then I'll stay with her." She turned, walked over to the passenger door of Cassie's Nissan Maxima, and waited for Cassie to unlock the door.

Lawson cleared his throat to get Cassie's attention. Cassie looked at Lawson, he nodded toward Lexi, and Cassie fumbled for her keys and hit unlock on her remote. Lexi got in the car without saying another word.

Lawson joined Cassie by her car. Cassie looked impressed. "Looks like you're a natural at this dad thing. She snapped right to it."

Lawson's mind was on what was next. "Just take her somewhere safe. I don't like going in here alone any more than you do, but there is no other way."

"There is, but I understand."

"You can't take her back to your place, De Luca might have more of his men around. So where will you go?"

Cassie walked around to her trunk and opened it. "It's not De Luca's men I'm worried about. Them I can handle."

"I don't like the sound of that."

"Yeah, well, word—and I'm sure video—from our little

party at Sokolov's earlier got back to Director Billings. I'm just as wanted as you are now."

"For helping me." Lawson said.

Cassie didn't say anything as she pulled out a duffel bag from the trunk. Then she looked at him. "No, no apology necessary, Lawson. It's just my career and life I put on the line for you."

"I . . . I'm . . ."

Cassie saved him the trouble, "It's fine. You know I'd do it all over again." She unzipped the bag, reached in, and pulled out a SIG Sauer P228, a silencer fitted to its barrel, and two extra magazines. "This was the best I could do. I figured when I left my house earlier to meet you at Sokolov's, there might very well be an APB on me afterward. I put this together for just such an occasion. I figured if I'm going down, I might as well give you the best shot I can at taking De Luca with us."

She also produced a bulletproof vest.

"It's one size fits all. I already adjusted the straps as big as it will go."

Lawson removed his shirt, put the vest on, then put his shirt back on. Good thing it was an ultrathin vest, because his shirt was stretched at the seams. He then tucked the gun in his waistline and placed the spare magazines in his pockets. He was happy to see that it was a SIG. It's the gun he spent hundreds of hours on the range with when working for the FBI. It was no coincidence, since of course Cassie knew that about her partner as well.

"Oh." Cassie reached in her back pocket and pulled out her phone. "Troy sent this to me on the way over." She turned the phone's screen toward Lawson. "Remember our old informant, Larry, in the case we were building against Tony De Luca before everything happened?"

Lawson did. "Yeah, they killed him not long after I was sentenced."

"Right. Well, do you remember how he used to always tell us that De Luca built a secret way to get out of his house in case he was ever raided?"

"Yeah, but he never told us where."

"Probably cause he didn't really know. But last year we busted one of De Luca's dealers. He was young and apparently thought it was fun to make videos."

Lawson took the phone from her hand and said, "And he recorded De Luca's escape route?"

"He did."

Lawson watched the dark video. The camera was obviously in a cellar, there was row after row of wine bottles and barrels. He watched as the camera focused on a large wine rack against a wall, eight shelves tall in total. A hand appeared in front of the camera and reached through the fourth shelf and pressed against something on the wall. The next thing the hand was doing was pushing the entire wall in, the wall opening into a tunnel.

Lawson was shocked. "You can't be serious. De Luca ever find out this was recorded?"

"Not that we know of. We couldn't do anything with it, since it's on private property and all. But I kept a copy of it just in case. It is a whole lot harder to get away with things in 2018. The entire world records everything."

Lawson looked up from the video of someone walking down a dark tunnel to find a wry smile on Cassie's face. The only light on the video was the flash that was coming from the phone's camera. Then the man walking the tunnel stopped, his hand out in front of the camera again, this time to grab hold of a string that wasn't visible without him taking hold of it. He pulled, and just like an attic, a door came down out of the ceiling and the hand unfolded the wooden stairs that were attached to it. He walked up the stairs, pushed on what must have been the flooring that covered the door, and just like that, he was standing in a bathroom.

"Looks like the tunnel leads out to—"

Headlights turning into the neighborhood interrupted Lawson's words. Lawson looked right and two beams showered him and Cassie with light. Lawson jerked Cassie by the arm and dove along with her behind the cars, into the small ditch that ran along the road. It was a certainty that they had been seen, but as long as it wasn't the police, Lawson didn't really care. Dust from the rocky ground below them kicked up and swirled about in front of them. The car didn't drive past; instead Lawson heard the brakes squeak as it slowed to a stop behind his stolen Prius.

"Who the hell is it?" Cassie whispered. Both she and Lawson had their hands on their guns.

A man's voice called out after Lawson heard the car door open. "Cass?"

When Lawson glanced over at Cassie, the look he found on her dimly lit face was one of shock. She slowly rose to her knees. "Bobby?"

Cassie's ex-husband.

38

CASSIE GOT UP TO HER FEET AND PEERED OVER THE STOLEN Prius. "Bobby, what the hell are you doing here?"

Lawson stood beside Cassie, his hand not leaving his pistol's grip.

"I saw you all over the news, you and Lawson—"

He stopped talking when he noticed Lawson standing beside Cassie.

"Lawson, I didn't expect you . . . Cassie, what the hell is going on?"

Cassie stepped forward into the lights shining from Bobby's car. "Bobby, tell me right now what the hell is going on, or I will shoot you, right here, right now. How did you know I was here?"

Something was off. Lawson could sense it by Bobby's demeanor, but Cassie's apprehension really made him worry.

"Your phone," Bobby began to explain. "That Find My iPhone app on there. It's still linked to my phone."

"You followed me out here by tracking my phone? We've been split up for a long time now, Bobby. What the—"

"I was worried about you. They're saying you went rogue or something. I tried to call you."

"I'm kinda busy right now, Bobby." Cassie threw up her arms and looked around at the situation. "And I don't owe you anything. You have to leave. Now."

Lawson took a step forward into the light. "I think you'd better listen to her."

Both Cassie and Bobby looked at Lawson.

"Are you—" Bobby looked back to Cassie. "Is Lawson holding you hostage?"

"Is everything okay, Lawson?" Lexi had gotten out of the car.

Lawson shouted, "Lexi, get back in the car, right now."

"What's going on, Bobby?" Cassie said.

"Lexi is with you? What have you gotten yourself into, Cassie?"

"Bobby," Lawson took control of the situation. "I'm only going to say this one time. Get back in your car, drive away, and make believe this was all a dream. You were never here."

"I'm sorry, Lawson. I can't do that," Bobby said. Then he reached for his belt.

Lawson pulled his pistol and trained it on Bobby, but when Bobby pulled his gun, he pointed it away from Lawson. When Lawson looked to his right, he saw that Lexi had walked around the front of the car, and now was planted firmly in Bobby's sights.

Lawson shouted, "Lexi!"

"Put your gun down!" Bobby shouted.

"Bobby, don't! What the hell are you doing!" Cassie pulled her gun as well.

Lexi was frozen in fear. "Lawson, help! I'm sorry I got out of the car!"

Lawson was about to lose his mind. He had come all this way, even gotten his daughter back, and here Cassie's ex also had an axe to grind? He knew he should have just left with Lexi. It was his first instinct and he should have listened to it. She may have never forgiven him for leaving her aunt Erin, but at least she would have been safe.

"I'll blow your head off if you don't take your gun off my daughter. Right. Now."

"Try it, Lawson. Maybe I get a shot off, maybe I don't." There was anger on Bobby's face.

Cassie tried a different approach. "Whatever is going on with you, Bobby, we can help you. But you have to put the gun down, and you have to tell us what is happening."

Bobby laughed. "*You* can help *me*? How do you figure that? Every law enforcement agency on the planet is looking for you. Drop both of your guns, right now, or I'll shoot her."

Reluctantly, both Cassie and Lawson did as he asked.

"So why are *you* looking for me?" Cassie said.

"Because I knew you'd be with this asshole." Bobby glanced at Lawson. "You always did have a thing for him."

"This is about you being insecure? Are you kidding me?"

"No, Cass. Good God, you are as dumb as ever. I can't for the life of me figure out how you ever became an FBI agent. This has nothing to do with you. It has to do with what I should have stuck around and finished ten years ago, but Dan, that moron husband of Lauren's sister, screwed everything up." Now Bobby was looking at Lawson. "Stupid son of a bitch got kill-happy and sliced your wife's throat. You were nowhere to be found."

Lawson's head began to spin. Of all the scenarios, the thousands of possibilities that ran through his mind every day over the last ten years in that prison cell, not one of them involved Bobby. And not one of them involved Erin's husband, Dan. Why would it? Lawson began to see red. His mind flashed back to him standing on that boat, looking at Lauren holding the phone. Cassie's words when he asked if she'd picked Bobby up yet—"he had something come up last minute, he can't make it"—ran through his mind like it was yesterday. Something hadn't come up. He had planned to do this to Lawson all along.

Cassie's voice had a quiver in it. "What? What are you saying, Bobby?"

"It was the perfect plan. But when Lauren saw Dan on the boat, he freaked out . . . Oh, what the hell does it matter now? I'm finally going to be able to quit worrying about this entire thing, and I'll be handsomely rewarded for finishing it."

Cassie turned to Lawson. "Lawson, you know I knew nothing about this. You know I would never . . ."

She trailed off, because it was clear that no words were making it to Lawson's consciousness. He was doing everything he could not to run at the man. But if he didn't make it to him fast enough, Bobby would be able to fire at Lexi, and he couldn't take that chance.

"So what now?" Cassie refocused back on Bobby, who had begun walking slowly toward Lexi. "You're just going to kill us? What's the end game here?"

"The end game is me getting paid. De Luca had already called me to follow you, Cassie. He knew you were at Starbucks, because of some traceable flash drive or something. I almost missed you, you were handing the flash drive off right when I got there. So I followed you, making sure you weren't interfering. But then Dan called a few minutes ago. Said De Luca's men had called from the Pink Kitten and somehow Lawson had managed to get Lexi. That was apparently going to be their bargaining chip for ending this thing. Lawson's life for hers. Dan said De Luca and he would make it a million dollars if I could keep Lawson from getting to them. Now that I can bring Lexi back to them too, I could really make it out of here a rich man."

While Bobby continued talking, Lawson had been talking to himself. Talking himself off the ledge. His emotions were getting the best of him, and he knew that wouldn't do anything to help the situation. "And you think that De Luca will actually pay you?"

"What's the difference to you, Raines? You're going to be dead."

Bobby made a quick move to snatch the back of Lexi's T-shirt, moved her in front of him as a shield, and pointed the gun back at Lawson. "That's far enough right there."

Lexi began to cry. "Lawson, it will be okay. Don't come any closer. I will be okay with Dan. Just don't make him shoot you."

Lexi was trying to be brave. Lawson couldn't believe his little girl. He supposed the thought of losing the only parent she had left would be too much for her to bear.

"Stop moving, Cass. Don't make me shoot you too," Bobby said to her.

"Let her go!" Lawson shouted.

"Or what, big man?"

Cassie held up her hands. "Okay, Bobby. You win. Tell me what you want me to do, and I'll do it. Just don't shoot anyone, and you can still get out of this without doing any major time."

"I'm not doing *any* time. I'm leaving the country with a bag of money. Now, open up your car door, get your keys, and throw them over here on the ground."

Cassie did as he asked.

"Now, get the handcuffs out of your console, and cuff yourself to the steering wheel."

"I don't have handcuffs."

"Did you forget I was married to you? I know they're in there. You always keep them there."

Cassie reached back in the car, then sat in the driver's seat, and Lawson heard the clacking of handcuffs locking into place.

"Now, Lexi, be a good girl and reach into my pocket."

Lawson took a big step forward.

"Ah ah ah. No no." Bobby put his gun to Lexi's head. "Right there is close enough."

Lawson stopped. There was only the length of the car between them now, but it might as well be a mile.

"Go ahead, Lexi, my phone is in my front pocket."

"Do as he says, Lexi."

Lawson was desperately racking his brain for a way out of this. Any way he could save his daughter. But right now the safest thing for her was for him to stay back, and it was killing him.

Lexi hesitated, but then reached and got Bobby's phone and handed it to him. He took it, never moving the gun from her head. He punched some things on the phone's screen, then held it to his ear.

"Yeah, I know where Cassie Foster is, the wanted FBI agent. In the Berkshire subdivision." He paused to listen. "Yeah, that's the one. Hurry, she has a gun!" He ended the call, then looked at Cassie in the car. "I would just kill you, Cass. But if for some reason they did find out it was me, killing a federal agent would bring on a special kind of manhunt. I'll let the people in prison take care of you. As

I'm sure Lawson can tell you, the law isn't very welcome there."

Bobby moved his gun from Lexi's head back to Lawson. "This guy, however, they may give me a medal if they find out I killed him."

Lawson knew what that meant, the bullet was coming. There was nowhere for him to go, so he launched himself forward in a last-ditch effort to save his little girl. Before he could get his hands on Bobby, he heard two gunshots break the silence of the night, followed by a terrible burning sensation, right before his face met with the blacktop below him.

The last thing he heard, as his consciousness was being dragged into darkness, was Lexi screaming.

39

A HEARTBEAT WAS THE ONLY THING THAT WAS REGISTERING. Rapid in pace and pounding in his ears. Lawson felt as if he were swimming. But there was no water, only darkness. Slowly, another sound came to him, but it was as if it were at the far end of a long tunnel. It sounded like a car horn. Finally, he felt something under his fingertips. Rocks? Pavement maybe?

Then there was the burning.

Then there was the recollection of why there was burning.

Then the memory of Lexi screaming.

Lawson's eyes popped open and he jumped to his feet. Just like that, he was back in the middle of a nightmare. Cassie's car was in front of him. That was the horn he was hearing.

"Lawson! Lawson, please get up!" He heard a sobbing cry from inside the car. Then he remembered Cassie handcuffing herself inside, and then, the gunshots.

Lawson stood too quickly, and the dark neighborhood

swirled all around him. He was forced to drop back to one knee. The burning was coming from his left shoulder. He touched his shoulder and his hand brought back a puddle of blood.

"Lawson, please! Please tell me you're not dead!" Cassie continued to scream.

Lexi. Where's Lexi?

Lawson stood once again and found that there was no car behind the stolen Prius. Bobby was gone, and so too was Lexi. Cassie honked the horn a couple more times, but she took in an audible gasp of air when she found Lawson standing in front of the open car door.

"Lawson!" Her face was wide with shock. "I thought you were dead!"

"I moved right before he shot me. Got me in the shoulder just outside of the vest. I probably should have just let him shoot me in the chest." He looked to his shoulder. His black shirt was glistening in the street light. Drenched in blood.

"You've got to get to a hospital. You've clearly lost a lot of blood."

"How long have they been gone?" Lawson was only worried about one thing.

"Four, maybe five minutes. I thought you were dead, Lawson." Tears welled in Cassie's eyes.

"Do you have any other weapons in the car?"

"N-no," Cassie said. He took the guns and the key to the handcuffs with him. "Lawson, you can't go in there. The police are on their way. We can make sure they go to De Luca's home. It's just right there, they'll have time to save her."

Lawson didn't respond. He began rolling up the sleeves

on his button-up shirt, then walked toward the back of Cassie's car.

"Lawson?"

He popped the trunk of the car, lifted up the mat, but there was no spare tire and no tire iron. Sirens were wailing in the distance. A familiar sound at that point. They had been the soundtrack to his entire day, it seemed. The night air had cooled a bit, but it had to be somewhere in the nineties still. Lawson couldn't tell if his shirt was wet with sweat or if it was all blood.

"Lawson, wait for the police, I'm begging you."

"Where's your tire iron?"

"I . . . I don't know. I had a flat a couple of weeks ago. I guess it never made it back inside. You don't have a choice now but to wait for the police."

Lawson walked back to the open door. "And sit in a jail cell while they take my daughter from me again? I've lived that once. I'll welcome death before I let that happen again."

Cassie dropped her head, dejected, but resigned to the fact that she would do the same thing if she were in Lawson's position.

"At least wrap that wound before—"

"Tell the police to get ahold of your tech guy so they can see the feed into De Luca's security cameras."

"Lawson, they've already killed those cameras. Troy called me on the way here. De Luca has taken the entire system offline."

Lawson's fists clenched at another door slamming in his face.

"You know you are just going to get yourself killed."

"Probably, but not before I take at least one of these sons of bitches with me."

Cassie wanted to help. "I think the entrance to that escape tunnel is in the pool house. It's really the only place it could be. That's your only shot at this. If they think you're dead, they at least won't be expecting you."

The sirens were closing in.

"Lauren's brother-in-law slit her throat, Cassie. Why?"

"I don't know, Lawson."

"For money? Then he took my daughter and beat the shit out of her all these years?"

Lawson swung his fist and pounded a large dent in the roof of Cassie's Nissan. His chest was heaving, his anger was boiling over.

"Lawson, calm down. You don't even have a weapon. You can't go in there with all that rage. You have to be smart."

"All I have left is rage."

Lawson's face went blank. The sirens were closing in and his daughter was in the hands of madmen. He didn't say another word. He couldn't say another word. He turned away from Cassie's car, headed straight for the large brick wall that waited ahead of him in the darkness. The wall that separated him from everyone who had ever done him wrong. From the people who had his daughter, and from the man who murdered his wife.

40

LAWSON WINCED AS HE PULLED HIMSELF UP THE BRICK WALL. His shoulder was still leaking, the pain was still burning. He jumped down and his feet landed in soft grass. One of the few lush lawns you would find in Vegas. In front of him was nothing short of a palace. Though it was only dimly lit, he could see a resort-sized pool that sat like a pond in front of the monstrous Mediterranean-style home beyond it. All of this paid for by the pain and suffering of others. The De Lucas were a family that had been profiting off heartache for far too long. It was time to bring that all to an end.

Between him and the pool was what looked like a miniature home compared to the main house. Lawson knew it had to be the pool house. It was the only place that really made sense as to where the tunnel in that video could have led. Lawson stayed low. He knew security would be heightened, but he doubted there would be many eyes on the pool house. He crouched and moved forward to its back wall. A light breeze moved through the palm trees that dotted the pool area. He leaned around the corner, and over fifty yards away at the back door, he could see two men standing guard. He looked over the mansion once again, and crippling anxiety squeezed his heart. His daughter was in there with people who only wanted to do her and her father harm. What if he didn't make it in time? What if they killed her before he could get there?

Lawson swallowed hard. He took a deep breath and let some of the anxiety subside. It didn't do any good to think that way. It's just that he had never gone into a situation like this. Not in all his years of law enforcement where the stakes were so high and so personal. It made it especially worrisome that he was so out of practice. The only thing he had going for him was the momentum of the day. He had seen a lot of action and come out on top. He needed now to have confidence in that. He needed to know he could make it. To believe he could save her.

Think like a detective.

Cassie was right. If he let emotion cloud his judgment, he wouldn't even make it out of the cellar, because he would most likely die of a heart attack from the overwhelming feeling of helplessness. Right now, he needed to focus on what these men were thinking. It would do them no good to kill Lexi now. Not in case Lawson could actually make it to them. Bobby had surely told them about shooting Lawson by then, but De Luca wouldn't believe Lawson to be dead without seeing it with his own two eyes. They needed Lexi alive so that Lawson's rampage would end in giving his life for hers. Something he would gladly do and would most likely be asked to do. But he would have to cross that shaky bridge when he came to it. Because right now, if he didn't focus, he was never even going to make it that far.

Lawson took one more deep breath. The pain in his

shoulder had subsided. Either because his body had relaxed from the shock or his adrenaline had numbed the feeling. He crouched as low as he could and walked along the side wall of the pool house. The men at the back door, as far as he could tell, were generally focused on the immediate area around them. He was glad that he had chosen to wear black. It would offer at least a little more shadow. The sirens had closed in behind him, just beyond the brick wall he'd scaled a moment ago. They were probably listening to Cassie's story just then, deciding what exactly to do with her. He looked back that way and could see red and blue lights bouncing off the surrounding trees. The men at the door must have noticed it too, because they rushed inside, most likely to let their boss know that trouble might be close. It gave Lawson the brief moment he needed to rush around the wall and slide into the door of the pool house.

Once he shut the door behind him, there was only a small trickle of light coming in through the mostly drawn shades. It was enough to see that the place was decorated more lavishly than any home he had ever owned. There was a large bar area, a seating area, and even a few gaming tables. But what Lawson cared about was the door just off to his right. The only one in the entire building.

He walked over to it, pushed open the door, and sure enough, it was the bathroom. He shut the door behind him, and in the complete blackness, he pulled his phone from his pocket. Not knowing about any flashlight feature, he simply made the screen light up and used it to search the floor for a seam. Whoever built the door into the floor had done a great job blending it with the tile. More than likely there was a button, or a latch, but he would need to turn on the light to find it. Instead, he began to bounce on the balls of his feet.

He inched forward, bouncing, until finally there was a slight change in the feel of the floor. A give.

Lawson dropped to his knees and pulled one of the SIG Sauer magazines from his pocket. Since Bobby took the gun, he was going to at least get something out of them. At the bottom of the magazine, there was a small and thin lip that jutted out on one side. He took that part of the mag and began trying to wedge it downward on the tile's seam where he first felt the floor give a little. It wasn't a science exactly, all he needed was a small opening. After a few more presses, the magazine inched inside something. He pushed it forward as far as it would go and turned the end of it upward. He was hoping for a slight movement, and that's exactly what he got.

He set down his phone, and with his free hand he wedged what little fingernails he had under that same small opening that he had created. There was no clock on him, yet he could feel one ticking. This was all taking too long. He needed to step up his pace, but without being sloppy. He dug with his nails and began to lift. This was what he was looking for, this was the door. His fingernails burned at the tips as he raised it up just enough to shove the tip of one of his oxfords in that opening. That was enough. He dropped the mag and wedged all eight of his fingers under the trick floor and pulled. It was a great cover. Heavy enough that anyone not looking for a door in the floor would never have found it. Cassie had really come through on this one. Otherwise, he would have had no chance of getting in this house.

Under the lifted cover was a folded wooden ladder. Lawson pushed down with both feet on top of it, and it lowered. He kicked the tip of the folded ladder, and it extended down to the room below.

He was in.

41

Lawson descended the stairs into complete darkness. He had never been a man of privilege, never had the spare money to go on many wine-tasting vacations. Besides, he much preferred the bourbon trail in his home state of Kentucky if ever the whim arose. That said, he did know the smell of barrels holding alcohol from those many visits to the bourbon distilleries, and the room he was in now had a similar scent. Even though he knew he was only in the empty tunnel, the smell beyond the trick wine shelves had made it to him. He pulled his phone and held the lit screen out in front of him. Just like in the video he watched on Cassie's phone, he reverse-followed the route that it showed. After a short trek, he could see a wall in front of him.

This was where he was most likely going to have to risk making noise. There was no way to get this door open without breaking the bottles of wine on the other side. If someone happened to be in the cellar, this mission was going to be a short one. He got to the wall, and just like the floor of the bathroom, he pushed around until he felt something give.

He readied himself to plow through it, but luckily he realized he had his wounded shoulder ready to bulldoze. That would have been painful. He switched stances, squared up his uninjured right shoulder, and rushed the hidden door like a lineman hitting a tackling dummy.

The wall gave way to his force, and the crash of wine bottles that followed sounded like it could have been heard out on the street. The floor inside the cellar was poured concrete, so the glass breaking was an excellent metaphor for his two days out of prison. A loud and crushing disaster. If there were anyone guarding the cellar, even one floor above him, they had certainly heard his high-decibel entrance. He needed a weapon of some sort, and he had a feeling he needed it fast.

Fortunately, there was some dim lighting around the cellar. As far as he could tell, nothing had really changed from when the video had been made. He walked forward, and on his right, the barrels along the wall opened up into a cave-like sitting and tasting area. Beyond the couches and the round table in front of them, he noticed a cabinet back against the wall, and hopes of an old school wine opener flashed in his mind. As he made his way to the cabinet, he heard the distinct creaking sound of a door opening at the other end of the cellar. The time for exploring was over.

It was time to fight.

He rushed over to the cabinet and opened the first drawer. Nothing. Whoever had entered the cellar was doing a good job of not making noise. It was eerily quiet down there. Only the smell of spilled red wine for company. In a slow and steady motion, trying to remain soundless, he pushed the empty drawer shut and pulled open the second one. Lying amongst a sea of corks, he found the wine opener he was looking for. Lawson grabbed it, extended the corkscrew, placed it in his left hand in such a way that the corkscrew jutted out between the middle and ring finger of his closed fist, and hurried over to the opening in the wall.

Out of nowhere, a calm washed over Lawson. As he stood there in the dark, confined space, he began to feel like himself again. For the first time in two days, there was a familiar feeling buzzing around him. Especially as he held the makeshift weapon in his hand. This was a very familiar scenario for him. One instance flashed in his mind as he waited for his mark to make it to his waiting position.

After almost twelve consecutive months of beatings when he first went to prison, Lawson was being hunted by Carl Sampson, one of the most feared men in High Desert State Prison. Lawson had done his first favor on the inside, and it happened to be one of Carl's closest allies whom Lawson had worked over. Word got back to Lawson that Carl was going to make him pay. After a few close encounters, Lawson knew the man wasn't going to quit coming, so he decided to make a stand. The man Lawson had done the favor for had gotten word to him that he was going to be cornered by Carl and another man in the laundry room. Just before Lawson left for the laundry room, he managed to pry a spring off his bed. He managed to snap it off to a sharp edge, and much like the cork he was holding in his hand in De Luca's cellar, he held the spring in his fist. Carl came calling, just as Lawson was told he would. Lawson took a couple of lumps, but ultimately he sank the spring into Carl's neck and survived the attack. Inmates began looking at Lawson very differently from that moment on. And after that encounter, he knew he could survive anything that prison could throw at him.

Just like he could survive anything he encountered in this mansion in order to save his daughter.

Lawson eased his left eye beyond the wall and jerked his head back when he saw a man walking right toward him with a pistol extended. The man had been focused on the right side of the cellar, or Lawson would have been seen. Lawson closed his eyes and waited, listening for the footsteps of the man against the concrete. A light tap from his dress shoes. With his quick glance, Lawson sized the man to about six feet one. Making his neck about shoulder high to Lawson. When he figured the footsteps to be close enough, Lawson stepped out with his right foot, cranked his hips to his right, and delivered a jarring left hook that landed to the man's throat. The length of the average corkscrew was about two and a half inches. And every single millimeter of that corkscrew made it through the man's Adam's apple.

The force of the blow pushed the man backward, pulling the corkscrew free, and Lawson closed on him, this time slamming it through the man's right eye. The guard would have screamed, but it came out more of a gargle due to the bloody hole in his throat. The man fell to his back, clutching at his eye. Lawson reached down, turned him on his stomach, and broke his neck with a twist of his head. The snap echoed in the cellar. Lawson searched the man's clothes, and found what he was looking for, a knife. He let the man hold on to the corkscrew for him but took his gun. A Glock. But the gun would be a last resort now that he had a knife. Silent kills would be imperative as long as he could make them happen. It was his only shot at getting to Lexi.

42

So far, the way in had proved fruitful. He had acquired twice as many weapons as he had when he entered. He figured that gave him at least double the chance he had before of making it upstairs. Maybe two floors. He didn't know exactly where the gathering of terrible human beings would be.

"Kenny?" a man called from just outside the entrance to the cellar.

Lawson slid onto his knees down behind a few barrels that lay stacked horizontally on top of each other. He heard the door open, and just a couple of seconds later . . .

"Kenny! What the—"

The footsteps were fast and easier to hear as the man ran toward his fallen colleague. Lawson pressed the button on the switchblade, and before the blade could even fully eject, it was on its way toward the oncoming man. It sank in about midthigh, and the force of the puncture spun the running man around, and with a scream of pain he landed on his back. He scrambled for his gun, but it was too late. Lawson was already on top of him, fully mounted. Lawson reached back and pulled the blade from the man's thigh, and as he applied downward pressure on the man's throat with his left forearm, he held the tip of it just centimeters above the man's left eye.

"Your friend is dead," Lawson said, his tone even, cold. The man's eyes were wide with fear. He had not expected his trip to the cellar to end up there. "You'll be the same way if you hesitate to tell me how to get to De Luca."

Lawson let up on the man's neck just enough to allow him to speak. The man's face was red from the pressure. The man looked familiar, but Lawson couldn't place him.

"I . . . I can't do that."

Lawson responded by turning the knife downward in his hand, then jamming the blade in between two of the man's ribs, pulling it out immediately, and putting it right back above the man's eye. Lawson choked off the man's scream by once again pressing down on his throat with his forearm.

"You think this is a game? You tell me how to get to De Luca and all the pitfalls in between, or the next time I stab you, it will be the last. I'd tell you to ask your buddy over there"—Lawson nodded toward the dead guard on the floor several feet away—"but he's busy walking toward the light."

Lawson let up once again on the man's neck. The man gasped for air, but he knew better than to scream. After a couple moans of pain, he managed words.

"There's an elevator on the far wall." His eyes glanced over Lawson's shoulder. Lawson followed the man's eyes to the gold elevator doors.

"Where does it lead?"

"Second floor. It opens up right into his office."

"And?" Lawson prodded.

"And there are bookshelves, several rows of them. He

wants people to think he's smart. Then there's a sitting area, then his desk. It's a big room. Like a miniature library."

"Where's the other entrance to the office?"

"A door to the upstairs hallway is on the same wall as the elevator. On the far right side if you're facing the wall. There will be two men guarding the door in the hallway. One man as soon as the elevator opens. You're a dead man as soon as you get up there."

The man was doing his best to gain Lawson's favor. Lawson appreciated the details, but the outcome for this man was going to be the same as his friend, regardless of what he said.

Lawson rerouted. "So if I take the stairs, how many men in between?"

"Two outside the front door on the main level. Two at the back door." Lawson had already seen those two from the pool house. "And like I said, two guarding the office door upstairs."

"That's it?"

"That's it, I swear. There are more people in the office with De Luca, but I don't know who they are. A woman and a man I've never seen before. And some other guy that's only been around a couple of times."

"Who is he?"

"I don't know. The guys think he works for the government somehow. He just has that look."

That didn't mean anything to Lawson, but he could only pray that he could get lucky enough to find Adam Billings in that office too. He knew that wouldn't be the case. The director of the FBI wouldn't take the chance to be seen here. It was just wishful thinking.

"Anything else?"

The man glanced at the knife, then back to Lawson. "Look, man. I know who you are. I was in High Desert State Prison last year before I came to work for De Luca. You're a badass. But . . ."

The man was hesitant.

"But what?" Lawson said.

"But they are waiting for you. They know you're coming, and they have your daughter. A man just came in with her a few minutes ago. He said he shot and killed you, but De Luca said to remain on high alert. Nobody really knows the guy with your daughter, so it was hard to believe him. Especially those of us who know of you. Look, the only reason I know it's your daughter is because I was at the Pink Kitten when her stepdad brought her in. That's the guy that's with the woman upstairs."

Lawson's muscles tensed hearing that his daughter was there. With them. Scared to death and thinking that he was dead, and believing there was no way she was going to be saved. He knew she was there, but hearing it jolted an anger so deep, so profound, it literally burned. The man began to wince beneath him because Lawson had unknowingly been applying pressure with his forearm.

"If I don't save her, they are going to kill her," Lawson said, referring to Lexi. "Are you okay working for a man capable of that?"

Strained, the man said, "Come on, man. We are all capable of crazy things under the wrong circumstances."

This man just took up for De Luca. He rationalized the fact that killing his innocent little girl could be okay under certain circumstances.

The guard added for good measure, "You know I'm right. I saw you in prison, man. You were an animal."

Lawson slid the knife into the man's throat. "Maybe I still am."

He took the knife with him as he stood. The man bled out on the ground below him. "Any man who stands between me and my daughter is going to end up just like you. I don't care what the circumstances are."

Lawson said this more to himself than to the dying man on the floor. He didn't need a justification to kill a man who helped keep his daughter captive. Or maybe he did, and that's why he felt compelled to say it. Either way, he knew that what he said was true. He would gladly kill them all. And if there was truth to what this man said, that Lawson was in fact an animal when he was locked inside that prison, he prayed to God that that animal was still in there. Because this was as good a time as any for a killer instinct to rise to the surface.

Lawson took the guard's gun as he took his last breath.

Two guns, one knife, and ten years' worth of rage. If any man alive was going to keep Lawson from saving his daughter, it was going to take one hell of a man.

43

LAWSON KEPT ONE PISTOL IN HIS HAND AS HE OPENED THE door to leave the cellar. As he ascended the stairs, he tried to check his breathing, but the adrenaline flowed through his veins like a river. The stairway to the cellar was concealed, a door at the top, leading to what Lawson imagined would be somewhere near the center of the house. He turned the knob, a slow and fluid motion, and pushed the door ajar. It opened to the kitchen, and through the small slit it looked to be empty.

Lawson stepped out into what a real estate agent would call a chef's kitchen. Lauren had dabbled in real estate back in Kentucky, and he heard a few of these sell words thrown around. In this case, it basically meant a kitchen with all the high-end bells and whistles. And as he looked over the white marble countertops, when he saw the Sub-Zero refrigerator, he got an idea.

He walked over to the window above the sink that looked out to the back. The back door wasn't visible from there, so he couldn't see if the guards had retaken their post. He would worry about them later. He went to the fridge, grabbed a wheel of cheese and a handful of grapes. He placed them on the wooden-block cutting board. Then he took a knife from the carousel holder, a bottle of wine from the miniature counter rack, a glass hanging from under the cabinet, the white towel from the oven door, and voilà, he had a miniature charcuterie platter. He carried the cutting board like a waiter in his left hand while keeping the Glock in his right. He glanced around the kitchen entrance into the hallway. The coast was clear, so he moved forward to the front door. Once certain he was alone in the foyer, he placed the cutting board on a nearby table and swapped the gun for the switchblade he had confiscated in the cellar.

With the blade extended, he pulled on the massive oak front door as smoothly as he could. As the large door moved inward, he could see the left shoulder of the guard posted on the left side of the door. The guard didn't move as the large door swept inward, and Lawson hoped guard number two on the other side was just as clueless.

Once the door was opened just enough for him to slide through, he moved forward. He readied the knife with the blade facing down in his right hand. He brought it up to his chest, and the moment the guard's neck came into view, he stabbed right, sinking it into the man's jugular vein, and immediately pulled out, turned his fist palm up, and stabbed blindly to the left, but all he hit was the other side of the front door. The blade carved into the wood, and as Lawson stepped out to see what he had missed, there was no guard to be found.

"Damn that feels much better," a man said, walking around the house on Lawson's left. He was dressed in a black suit like the rest of the guards, zipping up his fly. His face

243

registered Lawson, then his comrade bleeding out below Lawson's feet. He reached for his gun that was tucked in his hip holster. Lawson covered the ten feet between them in three quick steps and tackled the guard out onto the plush lawn, driving him down into the ground with his shoulder. Lawson heard the air get knocked out of the guard when Lawson's big body landed full weight on top of him, but this man was no stranger to a fight. Lawson could tell that instantly when the man rolled and his back hit the ground, flipping Lawson forward a few feet away. Both men rose to their feet at the same time, both about the same height and build.

The two of them rushed at each other, the guard reaching back for a powerful right hand, Lawson leading with a quick left jab that got there first. It snapped the guard's head back, and Lawson twisted his hips around to the left, delivering a leg kick to the man's calf muscle. His leg buckled beneath him, he staggered back, but before he could recover, like a pit bull Lawson was on him. A left hook to the man's jaw that stood him up straight, a right cross that toppled him over like a bowling pin. Lawson walked over to the front door, pulled the knife from the oak door, walked back over to the guard, and made certain he couldn't come back to haunt him.

Lawson wiped the blood on the blade of his knife against the stiff grass in an attempt to clean it. He then removed the guard's earpiece, placed it in his ear, took the sunglasses from his lapel pocket, and slid them over his eyes. Lastly, he removed the man's black suit jacket, put it on, and walked back inside the house like he was a regular there.

He double-checked that he still had both pistols. He took one of them out and draped the white kitchen towel over it. He then picked up the cheese platter with his left hand, supporting it underneath with the concealed pistol, and made his way up the long, winding staircase.

In his ear, he heard one of the other guards in the house ask if everything was clear, that he had heard some commotion at the front door. Lawson pressed the small button on the earpiece and gave a one-word answer. "Clear."

The guard spoke again. "No sign of Lawson Raines? Or the police? There are still lights flashing in the neighborhood behind us. I know that guy said Raines is dead, but boss said to stay alert."

There was the second confirmation. Bobby had in fact brought Lexi to De Luca. The guard in the cellar had been right, Bobby had told him that he shot and killed Lawson. Maybe that was why their guard had been down and Lawson was able to move through them a little more easily than expected. Or maybe that was why Nero De Luca was so worried about his organization, because his men were quite a bit less than spectacular.

"No sign." Again, Lawson kept it short.

Lawson reached the top of the stairs and paused before he made his right turn in the direction he was told two guards would be waiting at the door to De Luca's office.

"What the hell crawled up your ass, Williams?" the man said in his ear.

Lawson didn't answer. When he stepped into the hallway, in front of him were two men guarding a door, just like he was told. One of the men had his hand to his ear, probably the man he was hearing in the earpiece. Both men startled when they noticed Lawson walking toward them.

"Damn, Williams, you scared the hell out of me. I didn't know boss called for a snack." The guard was eyeing Lawson's cheese platter.

Lawson continued to walk toward them with confidence. He knew they would recognize he wasn't who they thought he was at any second. He hoped he could be at arm's length first.

"Hey, you're not—" Both men reached for their guns.

So much for another silent kill. The party was about to start, and it was going to be a loud one. He sure could have used that silenced SIG that Cassie had brought him right about now. Instead, when he squeezed the trigger on the Glock four times in quick succession, the bangs in that hallway sounded like the grand finale at a fireworks show. And the two men on the wrong end of the bullets fell like the sparks of those fireworks as they rain down the dark sky. Lawson heard a different man's voice in his ear, frantically shouting to know what was going on. He dropped the cutting board just before he put another bullet in each man in the hallway.

Lawson looked up at the wall above him. The camera fixed to the wall moved and focused on him. He removed his sunglasses and stared into the lens. As he removed the suit jacket he'd borrowed from the outside guard, his stomach turned when he heard De Luca's voice in his earpiece.

"Back from the dead, I see. Your partner's husband must not be as good a shot as he thinks he is."

Lawson didn't speak, he just continued to glare into the camera.

"Just how exactly do you think this is going to end, Mr. Raines?"

Lawson broke his silence. "You're going to give me my daughter."

"And if I don't?" De Luca's voice was full of arrogance.

Lawson involuntarily clenched his fists as he answered. "You're a dead man."

"It hardly seems like you're in the position to be making threats. She's such a beautiful young lady. So much life ahead of her."

Lawson's chest was heaving. Sweat began to roll down the small of his back. His insides were burning white hot at the sound of De Luca's taunts. After letting De Luca's words hang for a moment, Lawson decided to cut through the bullshit. "You let her go, I let you live, and I walk away. Any other scenario, and I don't quit coming until you're six feet under."

"You've got no leverage, Raines. You have no proof to trade for your daughter's life. You have nothing to offer me."

"And you have nothing to gain by killing her. Even if you did survive me, the police would put you away forever for murdering a twelve-year-old girl."

De Luca laughed. "As you are fully aware, Lawson . . . I own the police. This ends how I want it to end."

Lawson's heart nearly stopped when he heard Lexi's voice in a panic. "Lawson, just run! He'll kill you if you don't!"

Then De Luca. "Shut her up."

Then Lexi screamed so loud he could hear it through the office door.

The negotiations were over.

44

Hearing Lexi scream rebooted Lawson's processor. Consequences dropped from his conscience, and he turned, opened the door, shot three times at the back of the office to give himself cover, then dove behind the first row of book-shelves.

Gunfire came in return, but Lawson had seen what he needed to see. There were two men dressed as security behind De Luca's desk. Two other men stood beside Lexi and her aunt Erin, one of which was Erin's husband, Dan. The other man was too far away to place. And of course, there was De Luca.

Pages from books blown to bits by the security guards' bullets were showering all around Lawson as he sat with his back leaning against the book shelves. In between the shots being fired he could hear Lexi screaming for him. He could hear Erin shouting in fear as well. As soon as one of the men's guns clicked empty, they would reload and keep shooting. One gun was an automatic, spraying bullets by the dozen, and one was a pistol. Lawson was pinned down.

Nowhere to go. But he still had the advantage. He was sheltered, the guards firing on him had no cover. He just needed to find a small window to get some shots off of his own, but the bullets were still steadily coming his way.

He looked down as he pulled out the pistol with the fresh magazine. It was already locked and loaded. He closed his eyes for a moment as the chorus of gunshots blasting through books and wooden shelving filled the air entirely. He took a deep breath when he heard Lexi scream again, and to his surprise Lauren's face appeared. She wasn't smiling, she wasn't speaking; instead she just gave a solemn nod. Lawson wasn't a man who ever contemplated the afterlife. He'd always felt it was a waste of time pondering something that no one had ever seen. But what he felt when he saw Lauren nod to him in his mind's eye was something more than just a daydream. And even though he knew it wasn't really her, and she wasn't really there, he felt a calm come over him.

A cold and knowing calm.

Knowing, because he was doing all that he could do to save his daughter. How she got there, how he got there, and all that happened to put them in that horrible position, none of it mattered. Cold, because it didn't matter what he had to do, he just had to save her. He was willing to die right there in that room if it would set Lexi free of all the terrible things these men had brought into her life. She may never be able to live a normal life due to the scars of these horrific moments, but with God as his witness, Lawson was going to make sure she at least had the chance.

Lawson rose to his feet. Behind him he heard one of the guns click, an empty magazine, and the automatic gunfire stopped. He took three steps toward the aisle that separated the rows of book shelves, turned the corner, and the entire office came into view. Forty feet away, he could see his first three bullets hit the chest area of a man swapping out a magazine in his large gun. Lawson had found him in his sights immediately when he turned the corner, because when he rushed into the office a moment ago, he had marked one of the guards as standing directly below the six on the large clock hanging from the back wall.

Lawson moved his pistol two inches to the right, and as he squeezed the trigger, he felt two painful thumps hit his chest and stomach, nearly taking his breath away. The bullets hitting his vest stopped him dead in his tracks. Dazed, he watched the second guard drop to the ground. Lawson's bullets had hit their mark. With the room finally free of gunfire, Lexi screaming "Lawson! No!" echoed in the large open office. Lawson took a second to peek down his shirt, and though the pain was severe, the bulletproof vest had done its job. He looked up to tell Lexi he was okay, when he felt what seemed like a Mack truck blindside him, literally knocking him off his feet. He slammed into the bookshelf two feet behind him, the top of his neck and back of his head taking most of the impact. He had forgotten about the man guarding the elevator.

Lawson barely had time to look up before being yanked up by the shoulders of his bulletproof vest, and the next thing he knew, he was flying through the air and then crashing into the coffee table in front of the couches. His back smashed through the wood table, and he landed sitting upright on the floor, propped against the oversized chair. His back was turned to De Luca and Lexi, but he could hear De Luca laughing. And he could now see what was strong enough to throw him around like a rag doll.

Vincent Ricci.

De Luca's number one enforcer. More of a gorilla than a man. He began stalking toward Lawson. Lawson tried to move, but his body was temporarily out of commission.

"Told you I would see you soon, Raines." He tossed a couch aside and kept walking toward Lawson. "And I told you you'd be getting yours, and here it is. Much better to embarrass you in front of your daughter than a bunch of prison inmates anyway."

De Luca must have pulled some strings to get him out of jail. The longer Lawson had been out of prison, the more it seemed laws didn't apply to anyone anymore. Especially a lifelong criminal with money like De Luca. Lawson wanted to say something to Vince, but he still hadn't gotten his wind back that had just been knocked out of him.

"Leave him alone!" Lexi screamed.

Vince once again grabbed Lawson by the vest and stood him up. "Cute kid. Too bad this is how she will remember her daddy." He punched Lawson in the gut so hard that it felt like Vince's knuckles scraped against his spine. "As a sorry son of bitch who couldn't do a damn thing to save her."

De Luca spoke up. "Stop talking and end this thing, Vince."

Lexi screamed again. "No! Leave him alone!"

Lawson turned to look at his beautiful daughter. Her face a shade of red that only fear and hurt could turn a person. The tears running down her cheeks glistened in the overhead lights. Lawson tried to take a breath, but it still wasn't coming.

"Let go of him!" Lexi screamed again.

This time, Dan stepped around Erin, and Lawson caught a glimpse of what Lexi's childhood with that man was like.

"I said shut your mouth, Lexi!" Dan screamed. Then he slapped her.

When Lawson saw the man who murdered his wife put his hands on Lexi, something broke in him. It was almost as if he could hear it click. As Lexi grabbed at her face and sobbed in pain, Lawson turned his head and locked eyes with Vince. Vince must have seen it too because his chiseled jaw went slack and he pulled back his fist, almost, it seemed, out of fear. When he brought his fist forward, Lawson simply lowered his head, and when Vince's fist slammed into the top of Lawson's skull, everyone in the room could hear his hand break. As Vince took two steps back and shook his arm in pain, that breath finally came to Lawson. And when he heard Lexi shout the words "Get him, Daddy!" enough adrenaline flooded his system to fuel three men.

"Kill him, Vince! Now!" De Luca shouted from behind his desk.

However, for the first time since Lawson had known Vince, he saw in his eyes that he wasn't sure he could make it happen. Lawson stepped forward. The monster that had come to life in prison was still there inside him. Stronger than ever. Because now, this wasn't only about his survival, it was about the survival of his daughter as well.

Lawson jabbed a lightning left hand to Vince's throat, striking his Adam's apple. Vince's hands shot up to cover his throat, and Lawson delivered a right hand to his forehead, thrown so hard that the 250-pound man backpedaled five steps from the force. He caught himself on the arm of a chair and stood himself up straight. But Lawson was already on his way in. He rushed forward, lowered his head, wrapped both arms around Vince's waist, drove him backward, pushed against the man's barrel chest as he moved his right foot behind Vince's left leg, and tripped him. Lawson landed on top of Vince on the floor and immediately passed over his legs into a full mount.

"Shoot him, Kevin!" De Luca shouted. "Do your job!"

Lawson heard De Luca, but it didn't register. All he saw was red. Vince reached both arms up to try to block, but it didn't matter. Lawson drove his forearm down so hard that it went right through Vince's muscular arms, and his elbow glanced off the top of Vince's head. Vince's arms went limp, he was unconscious. Lawson raised back up and dropped the same elbow, but this time it landed flush to Vince's forehead.

De Luca was incensed. "I said shoot him! Do it now!"

After one more elbow, Vince was dead.

Lawson stood, hovered over him for a moment, then turned to find the man in the room whom he hadn't first recognized holding a gun on him. Beside him, De Luca was incredulous. "I told you to shoot him, Watson, what are you waiting for?"

The FBI hit man Lawson had let live early that morning in his hotel room at the Flamingo had Lawson dead to rights. His moment of weakness was going to get him killed and ruin the rest of his daughter's life in the process.

45

As Lawson stared helplessly down the barrel of Watson's gun, it occurred to him that his initial instinct about FBI Director Adam Billings had been correct. He wasn't the type of man to collude with the mob. De Luca had bought Kevin Watson and had clearly brought him in to take Lawson out if his plan of getting Lawson to work for him backfired like it did. Director Billings didn't send Watson in. Cassie had been mistaken. Her initial speech back at the motel was probably true. Billings probably wanted Lawson back with the FBI so he could go after De Luca again, the legal way, and bring him down once and for all.

That revelation only brought on more questions. If Director Billings hadn't been leaking information to the De Lucas about how close Cassie and Lawson were to taking them down ten years ago, then how did they know to come after Lawson to stop it from happening? And why was it Cassie's husband, Bobby, and Dan who came out to the boat that morning?

Lawson knew that he would never get those answers, so

none of it mattered now. But the mind runs independently of its host sometimes, and you never know what you'll think about in the last moments of your life. Lawson was a detective through and through, so it wasn't surprising that in his final moments his mind was full of questions.

"Shoot him!" De Luca screamed.

Dan turned toward Watson and raised both arms, palms up in frustration. "What the hell are you waiting for, man? Shoot the big bastard. Or give me the gun so I can!"

Lawson knew he was a dead man, but he didn't want to go without at least telling his wife's killer that he knew. He glanced over at Lexi, and to his surprise she was looking at him. Not with fear in her eyes the way he had expected. Instead, she was tapping her index finger on the left pocket of her jeans and looking at him wide eyed as if she was trying to tell him something.

The recorder.

Lawson slid his hand in his pocket.

"Hold it right there," Watson shouted. "Take your hand from your pocket slowly, or I will shoot you right now."

"Give me your gun right now, Watson," De Luca said. "I'll shoot him myself!"

Watson glanced at De Luca. "I'm not going to kill him in front of his daughter."

Lawson slowly lifted his hand out of his pocket then raised both hands about shoulder high.

"Just tell me one thing before you have me killed, Nero. You at least owe me that much."

De Luca scowled. "I don't owe you anything, Raines."

Lawson asked anyway. "How did you know Cassie and I were about to take you and your father down?"

Dan stepped forward. "I'd be happy to tell you that,

Lawson." Dan had a knowing smirk on his face. He glanced at De Luca, and when De Luca didn't stop him, Dan continued. "I used to be a big-time poker player here in Vegas. One of the best. But I only played where the real money was, not these big flashy television tournaments. One night I'm at a table with this guy named Bobby. I could tell he was a small-timer, but he was on a good run that night. After I took him down in a heads-up cash game, I took him out for some drinks. He was a lightweight, couldn't stop talking about his girlfriend and how she was about to take down some big crime boss named Tony De Luca. Then I became interested. At first, I thought he was just some drunk, spouting off about things he didn't really know about. Then he mentions your name, Lawson."

Dan smiled at him. He was loving this moment, Lawson could tell. Lawson didn't react.

"I remembered Erin here saying something about you being in the FBI in Vegas. She was always wanting to go see Lauren, but I couldn't let her be hanging out with some Fed's wife. I don't care if it was her own sister."

Erin began to cry. Lexi tried to console her by rubbing her shoulder.

"Give it a rest, Erin," Dan told her.

"Finish the story, Dan," De Luca said. "I want to see the look on Lawson's face."

"Right, anyway. So when I heard your name, Lawson, I knew the guy was telling the truth about the FBI, and how you and your partner were about to take down De Luca."

Lawson finally spoke. "So, for a little money, you killed your wife's sister?"

Erin stood from the chair she was sitting in. A look of shock hung on her face. "You did what?" she said to Dan.

"Money? No, no. This wasn't about money. Not for me. For Bobby maybe, but not me. No, I owed Tony De Luca everything. About two years before all of this, I was completely broke and owed a lot of money to a lot of bad people. Tony De Luca bought my debt and let me have time to pay him back. I owed the man my life."

Lawson couldn't believe the series of events that had led to all of this tragedy.

To the murder of his wife.

"So anyway," Dan continued, "we did a little investigating of our own and found out that you were the lead in the investigation of the De Lucas. Nero here asked me to take care of it for Tony, so I did. As you can probably guess, it was supposed to be you. But your pretty wife got in the middle of it. Good thing De Luca here had the chief of police and the district attorney in his pocket."

De Luca laughed. "I knew it would come in handy. But even I didn't know they would be able to pin all of that on you. Money and power make up for a lot of sins, Lawson."

Dan spoke again. "I wish it would have been you I killed on that boat, Lawson. I really do. But watching the way everyone worked together to make sure you took the fall was quite a sight to see. That's why I made friends with the De Lucas when I did. You never want to be on the bad side of powerful men like them. You should have thought of that instead of trying to take them down. So, really, it's your fault your wife is dead."

Lawson made a move for Dan. He couldn't listen to another word.

"Hold it, Lawson." Watson stepped closer to Dan and made sure Lawson could see he still had the gun on him.

"I'll never forget the way she looked in that yellow biki-ni." Dan whistled and licked his lips.

A rush of anger flooded over every inch of Lawson's body.

Then something happened that none of them saw coming, not Nero De Luca, not Dan, and especially not Lawson.

Watson looked over at De Luca. "So it's true? Lawson didn't really kill his wife?"

De Luca gave a disgusted look. "Who the hell cares, I'm not the FBI. I'm not paying you to give a damn about who did what."

Now Watson looked disgusted. "Who cares? I almost shot an innocent man. And it almost got *me* killed. I would be dead if Lawson hadn't spared me. You said the governor only pardoned him because Lawson was doing him favors. You assured me that he was a murderer and that he was coming to kill you because of an old grudge. I would have never—"

"Who is this guy you hired, De Luca? A priest?" Dan butted in.

Watson turned the gun on Dan and pulled the trigger without hesitation. Dan's smirk blew against the far wall, along with the rest of his head.

Lexi and Erin fell to the floor in a defensive position as they screamed and sobbed in fear.

"What the hell are you doing?" De Luca shouted as he backed up against the wall behind him.

"Lawson could have killed me this morning," Watson replied.

De Luca said, "What are you talking about? You said you never found him!"

Watson disregarded De Luca. "But instead, he let

me live."

"And I paid you to kill him. So kill him, you son of a bitch!" De Luca pleaded. "Lawson doesn't deserve to breathe the same air that we do."

Lawson began to walk toward De Luca.

"What are you doing? Shoot him!" De Luca shouted.

Watson took a step back and tucked his pistol down in his shoulder holster.

"SHOOT HIM!" De Luca pleaded one last time. His face finally held true fear, instead of that smug "I own the world" smirk. This time, his words didn't come out forceful, they were more of a frightened yelp.

It fell on deaf ears.

Lawson walked right by Watson. Watson didn't try to stop him.

De Luca turned to Lawson who was coming at him fast. "You touch me and so help me God I will make sure that you and your daughter will end up just like your wife!"

Lawson held the switchblade in hand, the blade already out of its sheath. He took one last step forward, and with the arc of an uppercut Lawson swung the knife up as hard as he could, jamming it all the way through Nero De Luca's throat. He stared into De Luca's dying eyes as he held the knife in place. He wanted to watch him go. He wanted to watch the man responsible for a lifetime of pain finally get what was coming to him. Lawson could only hope that whatever awaited De Luca on the other side was even worse than his final moments there on earth.

Lawson searched his eyes, shook him, making sure De Luca could still hear him.

"There's a special place in hell for you, De Luca. Be sure to say hello to your father for me."

46

THE ENTIRE NEXT DAY WAS A TOTAL NIGHTMARE FOR ALL parties involved. The police showed up at De Luca's mansion not long after Lawson ended Nero De Luca's miserable life. Lawson had a mind to run before they arrived, but he honestly didn't have the heart. He did, however, tell Kevin Watson about the secret escape route through the cellar. They all decided together that no one would ever say a word about seeing the FBI hit man there. Though his voice was on the tape, Lawson would just say he didn't know who the man was. Letting Watson live after torturing him in that hotel room ended up being one of the most fortuitous decisions that Lawson ever made. And like most of the good decisions in his life, he never would have made it without Lauren. Her voice acting as his conscience had saved not only his life but most certainly Lexi's and Erin's as well.

Even though Lawson was able to produce the recording of Dan confessing to everything, he and Cassie still had to spend the night in jail. Until the police were able to put all of the day's murderous events together, they couldn't let them go. For Lawson, it was a familiar feeling being locked in that cage. He imagined it was a much harder night for Cassie, seeing as how she had never been on the inside of those bars. Lexi and Erin were held at a nearby hotel, guards at the door but the location undisclosed.

The hardest part about the night in jail for Lawson wasn't the fact that he was behind bars; it was because he wasn't sure where things stood with his daughter. Twenty-four hours ago she wasn't sure if he had murdered her mother or not. And while Lawson was confident in the fact that she now believed he wasn't responsible for Lauren's death, he still didn't know where that left them. They had shared some tender moments in the car. She had called him "Daddy" when things were getting crazy in De Luca's office. But that didn't mean she wanted to be around him. All things considered, they were strangers. Lawson of course didn't feel that way. You could spend a lifetime away from your child and there would still be that overwhelming bond you feel toward them. Lawson could only pray that Lexi felt that same pull.

The recorder ended up being a lifesaver. Once again, something of Lauren's had helped save Lawson and bring her killers to justice. The entire night, all Lawson could think about was hearing his daughter sing. Lexi and Lauren were so similar that he figured Lexi probably sounded just like her mother, who, when she would sing to Lawson, whether it was while they were reading on the couch or singing drunk karaoke, always sounded like an angel to him.

Lawson still managed to get all of his push-ups, sit-ups, and squats done in his cell that morning. But they wouldn't let him go for his ritual five-mile run. No matter how much he begged. And at five o'clock the next evening, after hours of nonstop interrogation, and corroboration from Cassie,

Lawson once again was walked out of jail, a free man. It felt much different this time, however. This time, the sun *did* feel different on the freedom side, as he'd heard many men say. Maybe because this time he actually was a free man. No more questions hanging over him. No more incessant pouring over who did what and who was working together. By the time Lawson walked out of that prison, the news outlets across the country were in a frenzy about all the people tied to this horrible event. Evelyn Delaney's murder was tied to Nero De Luca, the chief of police was brought in for questioning, as the new DA was building the evidence against him. Cassie's ex-husband Bobby was wrangled by TSA at McCarran Airport, just before he made his plane bound for Mexico.

There were thousands of questions about Johnny De Luca, Serge Sokolov, Kiara Sokolov, and everyone in between. All were answered satisfactorily enough to let Lawson and Cassie go. The other thing that was different about this walk to freedom was that this time Cassie was there waiting for him. And this time when she ran and threw her arms around him, Lawson welcomed the embrace.

Cassie pulled back. "You've come a long way in the last two days. I'm proud of you, Lawson."

"It's been a long two days."

"How's your shoulder?"

Lawson gave it a quick rub. "It's fine. Bullet went straight through. They patched me up late last night."

"Well, you look like hell, did you sleep at all?"

"Thanks, Cass, you always were a gentle nurturer."

Cassie laughed and ushered Lawson toward her car.

Lawson got in the passenger seat. "And no, I didn't sleep much."

"Me either. Whatever could have kept you awake?" Cassie joked.

"Yeah, no idea. So, where we headed?"

"I have a little surprise for you."

"I've had enough surprises for one lifetime. Spare me the agony."

Cassie's smile was wide. "Relax. You'll like this one."

Cassie turned onto the Strip. The police department where they had been detained wasn't far.

Lawson winced when he saw the casinos. "I'm really not in the mood to gamble."

"Just relax, would you? Maybe talk to your old friend a little about something *other* than murder?"

Lawson shifted in his seat. "I'm a little out of practice in small talk."

"Okay, I'll give you that. I'll start. So, what now? Now that you don't have to focus on the one thing that's dominated your mind for ten years, any idea what you're gonna do?"

"So much for small talk. Go big or go home, I guess."

Cassie laughed and said sarcastically, "I want to get to know the *real* Lawson Raines."

Lawson hesitated, but after the war that he and Cassie had just been through, he felt closer to her than ever. "That's actually what kept me up most of the night."

"Do tell."

"Just all that happened. How I lost so much time because of injustice. And how we almost didn't get justice at all. I could have spent the rest of my life behind bars."

Cassie nodded. "Yeah, if it wasn't for Lexi giving you that old tape recorder, both of us would still be in jail. And there for a long, long time. So, what of it?"

"That must happen a lot."

Cassie shook her head. "I really don't think it does. Your situation was pretty out of the ordinary."

"I don't mean something that fantastical. I'm talking about injustice in general. It happens every day where people are framed and wrongfully accused. Their lives ruined. Not as lucky as me to get the chance to make it right."

"Okay. Sure. I'm sure it does happen. I don't know about a lot."

"Maybe I can make it happen a little less."

Cassie was quiet for a moment. "I don't get it. You mean go back to work for the FBI?"

Lawson shook his head. "Too many rules."

"I'm not following."

"We worked for the FBI. Look where that got us."

"So you're saying you want to be Batman? And POW! BAM! your way through crime? I don't think you can afford a Batmobile or fit into that costume he wears."

"Forget it," Lawson said.

"Come on, Lawson. Out here we have a sense of humor. I'm just messing with you."

Lawson didn't say anything.

"Seriously, what are you saying? Private investigator? What?"

Lawson gave Cassie a long look. She returned it with an overdone smile and a bat of the eyes.

"I haven't thought that far ahead. I just don't want people like De Luca getting away with what he did for so long. Just because they have money and influence. It's disgusting. I can fix that, if I know about it."

"Very noble of you, Mr. Raines. But someone has beat you to it, it's called the FBI."

Lawson gave her a look.

"Right. Well, we can pick this up later. We're here."

Cassie had turned off the Strip about half a mile back, and now she pulled the car into the Hyatt across the street from the Hard Rock Casino Hotel. Lawson had no idea what they were doing there.

As they got out of the car in front of the Hyatt Place Hotel, Cassie stopped Lawson.

"Speaking of the FBI, I forgot to tell you, as soon as they let me out, I got a call from Director Billings."

"Oh yeah?" Lawson said.

"Yeah. He said he'd been briefed and that he was proud of both of us for staying with it all the way until the end. Even though all the forces were against us."

"Forces?"

"His words, not mine. Anyway. You have a job waiting for you if you want it. Anywhere in the country."

"I'm flattered," Lawson said sarcastically.

"See," Cassie pointed. "I knew that sense of humor was in there somewhere."

Lawson turned toward the Hyatt's entrance. "So, what the hell are we doing here anyway?"

Just as soon as the words left his mouth, the glass revolving door began to spin, and after a moment it spit out a golden-haired girl, about twelve years old, wearing a pink T-shirt and jeans and a really big smile. Her hair bounced as she ran toward Lawson, arms open wide. She skipped the last couple of strides and jumped into him. Lawson let her hug him. For some reason he was slow to react.

Lexi leaned back, "This is the part where you hug me back."

"Sorry." Lawson knew he still had a long way to go at this fatherly affection thing. He bent down and gave her a hug.

Lexi leaned back from his arms and patted on his chest to let her go. "I've made a decision."

Her aunt Erin and Cassie walked up behind her.

"A decision? About what?" Lawson said, a hint of trepidation in his voice.

"The way I see it, we have a lot of catching up to do."

Lawson smiled. Though his heart would forever be hardened by what he had been through, she was certainly always going to have a soft spot there of her very own. "Can't say I disagree."

"And Aunt Erin was telling me that Mommy always used to say that the best way to get to know someone—"

"Is to go on a road trip."

Lawson said the line along with Lexi. He had heard Lauren say that very same thing a thousand times.

Lexi's jaw dropped. "How'd you know I was going to say that?"

"I heard your mom say it a few times over the years."

"Cool." Lexi was loving it. "I figure that's what we'll do. All of us."

Lawson smirked. "Even Cassie?"

"Ha-ha, Lawson. You are a riot," Cassie said.

"You wanted sense of humor," Lawson told her.

Lexi smiled. "Yeah, she already cleared it with her boss, she's going."

Lawson and Cassie shared a glance. Lawson said, "Is that so?"

"Yeah, it will be so much fun," Lexi said. "And we're gonna leave right now. Okay?"

Lawson wasn't thrilled about having to share a car with three women. How would he know what to say? He hadn't been around women in a casual way for a really long time. But all he cared about was spending some long-overdue time with his daughter. He would find a way to talk, or he would just listen. "Okay. But where are we going?"

"A lot of places along the way, but we'll end up in Lexington, Kentucky."

"And what is in Lexington besides your home?"

"Mom."

Lawson's expression shifted from joy to sadness. Lexi saw it, and her smile turned into a frown as well.

Lexi dropped her head. "We don't have to. I just thought you'd want to visit her. Since you haven't seen her in such a long time."

Lawson bit back the emotion. For him the wounds were all still so fresh. He had never let them heal over. The questions that always surrounded her death had always left everything so raw. Lawson bent down to where he and Lexi were at eye level, gently tilted her chin up with his index finger, and gave her the best smile he could manage.

"I think it's a great idea."

Lexi's face lit up. "Really! You mean it!"

"I mean it."

Lexi turned and wrapped her arms around Cassie and Erin. "He wants to go!"

"I just need to stop somewhere and get a few things," Lawson said.

Lexi wheeled around after bending down to pick something up. It was a black duffel bag, and she handed it to him with a proud smile on her face. "No need, Lawson. Me and Erin went and picked up everything you'll need. Cassie helped us with the sizes."

Cassie said, "And my bag is already packed. I thought a road trip was a great idea. I'll spot you some cash until you can pay me back."

It hadn't even occurred to Lawson that he had nothing until that moment. Not a piece of clothing, a house, a car, or even a dollar to his name. But Cassie mentioning cash jogged something in Lawson's brain.

"Then we're going. But I have one stop I need to make before we leave town."

Lexi said, "Okay, but let's make it quick."

The four of them piled into Cassie's Nissan and headed out onto Las Vegas Boulevard. Lawson directed them, keeping the final destination to himself.

48

CASSIE LOOKED OVER AT LAWSON LIKE HE HAD LOST HIS mind. "The Pink Kitten?"

Erin said from the backseat, "Is this some sort of joke?"

Lawson got out of the car and leaned back in the open window. "You all coming or not?"

Lawson turned and looked at the strip club. There was police tape everywhere and a couple of unmarked cars out front. Lawson figured they were the detectives combing through the crime scene, trying to piece everything together.

Everyone got out of the car. Cassie said, "Well, seeing as how you can't get in here without my badge, I guess I'm coming with you, at least.

"Yeah, we're not going in there," Erin said.

"Speak for yourself, Aunt Erin. I'm going in with Lawson."

Lawson said, "Pop the trunk."

Cassie hit the button on the car's remote and the trunk popped open. The look on her face was one of curiosity and worry.

"What?" Lawson shrugged.

"I don't like anything about this," Cassie said.

Lawson went around back, opened up the duffel bag that Lexi had packed for him, and emptied it into the trunk.

"Now I like it even less."

"You'll love it. Now be quiet and dump your bag out too," Lawson told Cassie.

Cassie put her hands on her hips. "I'm not dumping out my bag, and I'm not taking it inside for whatever weird thing you've got going on here."

"Cass . . . you're going to want the empty bag."

"The detectives aren't going to let us take these bags in there."

"You're the FBI, they'll let you do whatever you want."

Cassie rolled her eyes and dumped out her carry-on suitcase. "This better be good."

Lawson assured her, "It's going to be better than that."

A man in a suit walked out from the entrance of the Pink Kitten. "You guys can't be here. Crime scene."

Cassie, empty suitcase in hand, walked around the car with her FBI credentials extended. "FBI. There is a possible matter of national security inside. We need to go in right now."

"National security? I'll need to check with my superiors before—"

"And possibly blow up this entire block? You sure about that?"

The man was stunned. "What—blow up? There's nothing . . . that little girl for sure isn't going in there then." He pointed at Lexi.

"This is the *young lady* that was held hostage in here last night. She is the only one who knows where the bombs are."

"Bombs? I—"

Cassie pushed past him. "Come on, guys, we have to hurry."

The four of them walked inside the Pink Kitten.

"Nice job, Cassie, good touch with the bomb thing." Lexi gave Cassie a high five.

Cassie glared over at Lawson. "This *really* better be good."

Lawson said, "I told you, better than good."

Lawson led the three of them toward the door to the back, up the stairs, and down the hallway to De Luca's office where Lexi was being held the night before. He was relieved to see that the bodies had already been carted off, he didn't want Lexi's nightmares to be even worse than they surely already would be. They walked around the bullet-hole–filled desk, which was still standing on its side, and into De Luca's office. Lawson set his empty duffel bag on one of the three chairs in the room.

"Okay." Cassie was skeptical. "What now, P.T. Barnum? We're waiting for the show."

Lawson started to drag one of the other chairs behind him. He motioned for the three of them to step back, and he walked over to the back wall. He started on the far right side of the wall, knocking and listening.

"Are you about to hang a picture?" Erin joked.

Lawson paid her no attention and continued to knock on the wall, moving left with each knock. All of the knocks continued to sound hollow until he got to the center of the wall, right under an oversized portrait of a hundred-dollar bill.

"I should have known," Lawson said.

He proceeded to take the large canvas painting off the wall, then picked up the chair.

"Have you lost your mind?" Cassie said.

Lawson had no idea if the rumors were true, but Nero and Tony De Luca had taken a lot from him, so he figured it was worth looking into at least. He had nothing to lose and everything to gain. He pulled the chair behind him, then twisted forward, slamming it into the wall. It made a small hole, but so far nothing was gained.

"I want to help!" Lexi ran forward and kicked at the hole, making it a little bigger.

Lawson put the chair aside and kicked with her. After a moment, all four of them were kicking the wall, the three ladies laughing as they did so. Finally, the hole was big enough to where something black could be seen behind it.

The rumors had been true.

Lawson motioned for everyone to take a step back. He grabbed the broken drywall with both hands and began to tear it away. Before long, they could see that an entire area of about six feet wide and eight feet high was filled with large black plastic-bag–covered squares stacked on top of each other. Floor to ceiling.

The three of them eyed the squares, but only Cassie spoke. "What the hell is that, and how did you know it was there?"

Lawson reached in and took one of the bag-covered squares from the top of the pile. "When you keep someone from taking a beating—or worse— from living through a horrible moment in the showers while you're in prison, they tend to want to tell you things they probably shouldn't."

Lawson set the square in the empty chair. "Things that no one is supposed to know."

Lawson took the switchblade from his pocket, the same one that had been inside Nero De Luca's neck not too long ago. He thought it fitting to be opening this bag with that knife, so he was glad that he had pressed the detectives so hard to let him take it with him. They didn't want to, but after all he'd been through, they slid it to him under the table. He sank the blade in the bag, cut a slit along the top of it, and reached in.

Lexi was anxious to see what was inside. "We're on pins and needles here, Lawson. Are you going to blow us up like Cassie said?"

"I was hoping to blow your minds," he said as he pulled a large stack of cash wrapped in cellophane from the inside of the black plastic.

"Oh. My. Gosh. Is that money?" Lexi's mouth gaped wide in surprise. Cassie and Erin shared a similar expression.

"Everything all right in there?" the detective shouted from the stairs.

Cassie smiled. "No! We found the bombs! Evacuate the building!"

Cassie, Erin, and Lexi all laughed, and then each one of them began pulling money from the wall and filling the two suitcases they'd brought in with them. Lexi started stuffing stacks of cash down her jeans, and Cassie laughed with her as she stuffed them down her pants. They filled the bags as high as they would go and still zip closed. All of them except for Lawson weighed substantially more than when they walked in, square molds showing through every part of their wardrobes. They were having fun with it. Lawson thought it was silly, so he just let his bag hold the money.

When they got to the front entrance, the two detectives were taking cover behind their cars.

"Stay down!" Cassie shouted. "We've got the bombs, but we have to get them out safely. Whatever you do, keep your heads down!"

This even brought a smile to Lawson's face, and the four of them laughed as they ran to Cassie's car, threw the bags full of money in the trunk, and fell into the car themselves. Lawson got behind the wheel and threw the car in gear, speeding out onto the road, gas pedal to the floor. The detectives acquiesced to the FBI agent and did not give chase. Lawson was sure that Cassie was going to hear about it once they found the rest of the money in the wall, but at that point he didn't really care. They had enough money to last them a while. Lawson hoped it would be long enough to figure out what was next for him.

A couple of hours later, the sun began to fade behind them as they traveled northeast on I-15. Lexi wanted to take the route through Colorado so she could see the Rocky Mountains. Lawson was happy to oblige, especially since it had been the shortest route anyway. They filled up the gas tank, filled up on McDonald's, and pulled back out on the interstate. The McDonald's double cheeseburger was a transcendent experience for Lawson after years of horrible prison food. Lexi was riding shotgun, in full control over the radio. All the songs sounded like a foreign language to Lawson, except when Lexi began to sing along. He had been right, she sounded just like Lauren. He wanted to bottle up these moments and save them forever. He didn't know what was to come of his life next, but Lawson knew he wanted to cherish this time with his daughter.

Behind him, Cassie and Erin were bobbing their heads along to the beat. The music wasn't his taste, but at least it kept him from having to talk. Twenty-four hours ago he would never have imagined he would be in such a good spot. And if the last ten years had taught him anything, it was never to take any of the good spots, no matter how small, for granted.

Lexi reached for the volume and turned it down. Then she turned in her seat to face Lawson.

"Dad, can you tell me a happy story about Mom?"

Dad.

He glanced in the rearview, and he could tell by the smile on Cassie's face that she had heard it too.

He looked over into Lexi's ocean-blue eyes. Though avoiding conversation had been his goal on this road trip because he didn't think he would know the right things to say, Lauren was the one subject he could talk about for hours. And as they drove along the interstate, driving away from the madness of the past and into the great unknown of the future, that's exactly what he did.

SHOOTING STAR

Lawson Raines Book 2

Ready for more Lawson Raines?

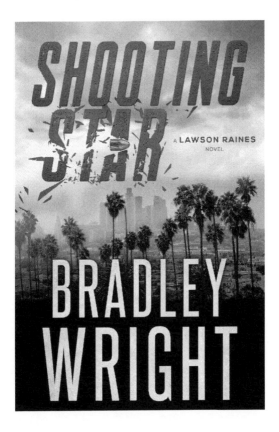

AVAILABLE AT AMAZON NOW!

ACKNOWLEDGMENTS

First and foremost, I want to thank you, the reader. I love what I do, and no matter how many people help me along the way, none of it would be possible if you weren't turning the pages.

To my family and friends. Every creative person is neurotic as hell about their creations, and I just want to thank you for always helping to keep my head on straight. And for indulging all of my ridiculous ideas.

To my editor, Deb Hall. Thank you for continuing to turn my poorly constructed sentences into a readable story. You are great at what you do, and my work is better for it.

To my advanced reader team. You are my megaphone in helping spread the word about each new novel I release. You all have become friends, and I thank you for catching those last few sneaky typos, and always letting me know when something isn't good enough. Lawson Raines appreciates you, and so do I.

And finally, to the man who distilled that first beautiful

batch of Kentucky Straight Bourbon Whiskey. Speaking for those of us who imbibe, your work fuels many of the celebrations that make lasting memories in our lives. Your legend will forever live on in our hearts, and in our failing livers. Cheers to you.

ABOUT THE AUTHOR

Bradley Wright is an emerging author of action-thrillers.
When the Man Comes Around is his fifth novel. Bradley
lives with his family in Lexington, Kentucky. He has always
been a fan of great stories, whether it be a song, a movie, a
novel, or a binge-worthy television series. Bradley loves
interacting with readers on Facebook, Twitter, and via email.

Join the online family:
www.bradleywrightauthor.com
info@bradleywrightauthor.com